David Paton was born in Yorkshire but now lives in Edinburgh. In 2008 (as David Paton-Williams) he published *Katterfelto: Prince of Puff,* the biography of a Georgian conjuror, quack and showman. *The Hand of Truth* is his first novel. He is married with two adult sons and is as an Anglican priest.

THE HAND
OF TRUTH

DAVID PATON

The Book Guild Ltd

First published in Great Britain in 2019 by
The Book Guild Ltd
9 Priory Business Park
Wistow Road, Kibworth
Leicestershire, LE8 0RX
Freephone: 0800 999 2982
www.bookguild.co.uk
Email: info@bookguild.co.uk
Twitter: @bookguild

Typeset in Adobe Garamond Pro

Printed and bound in Great Britain by CPI Group (UK) Ltd, Croydon, CR0 4YY

ISBN 978 1912575 787

British Library Cataloguing in Publication Data.
A catalogue record for this book is available from the British Library.

Map created with thanks to Cat Outram

To Brendan for planting the seed
and Jenny for helping it grow.

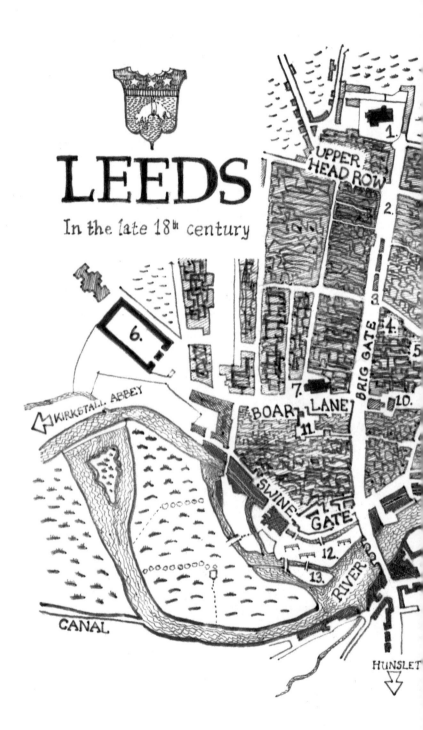

LEEDS

In the late 18th century

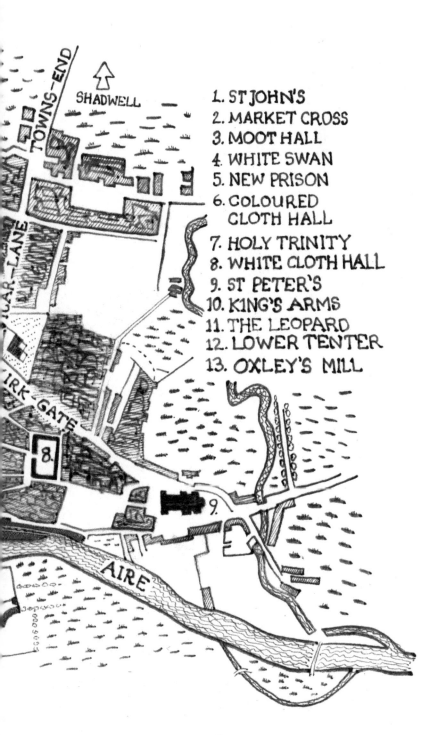

SHADWELL

TOWNS-END

_UAR-LANE

IRK-GATE

8.

9.

AIRE

1. ST JOHN'S
2. MARKET CROSS
3. MOOT HALL
4. WHITE SWAN
5. NEW PRISON
6. COLOURED CLOTH HALL
7. HOLY TRINITY
8. WHITE CLOTH HALL
9. ST PETER'S
10. KING'S ARMS
11. THE LEOPARD
12. LOWER TENTER
13. OXLEY'S MILL

PROLOGUE

Walter Watson had a nose for treason. He had smelled it only once before but, like the reek of death, once was enough. It was never forgotten.

'So he was asking after a Frenchie.' He sipped at his coffee.

The Dutchman gave the smallest grunt.

'Thank you, Pieter. I'll take it from here.'

A small bag of coins passed across the table. Shrugging, the Dutchman swept it into his pocket in one smooth action.

'At your service, as always.' The man rose, nodded and made his way towards the door.

Watson rolled a pinch of tobacco slowly between his fingers, scanning the coffee house clientele: the two Germans dicing as usual, despite last night's transfer of Lady Beatrix's favours from one to the other; the radical Patriots in a heated debate about the future of the Republic, oblivious to Prince William's agent among them; and Van Thieu, the grossly overweight financier, squeezing a boil on the back of his neck, who was about to discover that he was a bankrupt.

These days Watson preferred to pay others for his information.

He placed the little ball in his mouth and began to chew.

An Englishman…

He watched a small beetle as it made its way around his tobacco pouch. Placing his thumb on the beetle's back, he pinned it gently to the table.

This would require more than hireling spies.

He twisted his thumb down hard against the rough wood.

Watson looked out across the canal and into the study of Monsieur Jean de la Croix. At his desk, the merchant shuffled his papers and glanced once again at the wall-clock.

What people did in front of a pane of glass had long since ceased to surprise Watson: the politically sensitive business deals; the secret diplomacy; the domestic violence; the extra-marital liaisons – all within range of a simple spyglass.

His was a thing of beauty: the bone intricately carved with Diana and her bathing nymphs, the grinding of the lenses unsurpassed. It was his badge of office, won from Major Campbell on the very evening the old warhorse had enlisted him.

A sudden blaze of orange dazzled him and he jerked the glass away. The setting sun, on the house's twelve great windows, transformed the building into one enormous conflagration. And the man he had been waiting three hours for sauntered up the street.

Watson cursed: was he, at the crucial moment, to be foiled by glare?

He trained his glass on the man. A Yorkshireman, so Pieter had said, going by the name of Micklethwaite, though he put little store by that. Average height, medium build, well dressed, in the English style – nothing too ostentatious, nothing apparently worthy of note. But then conspirators blended into the background. It went with the territory.

The man arrived at the house and with no undue haste was received inside.

The panes continued to burn and he tapped the spyglass on the sill in irritation.

A shadow of cloud flowed up the street. The spyglass froze, two inches above the sill. The watery grey seeped up the side of the house opposite.

And in the study window, framed by a still-fiery creeper, Monsieur de la Croix pressed down with his seal – once, twice. The letters passed across the desk to the Englishman and a handshake – a little guarded to Watson's eye – concluded the proceedings.

Watson exhaled with a grunt. The smell was getting stronger.

Watson knew about luck. He had made a special study of it. Whether at the gaming tables or in the coincidences of life there was a pattern. Like the sand of an hourglass, luck would flow in one direction until an invisible hand upended the glass and it ran the other way. The trick was to spot the moment and then join the game – or leave it. He was well known for his sense of timing.

Luck was with him tonight. He knew it from the moment the cloud had doused the setting sun and trusted to it as he tracked Micklethwaite through the port's darkening streets. Turning a corner, the avenue ahead was empty but for a boisterous group of sailors – two fishing a third out of the canal; the remainder jeering. Three taverns lined the water. He chose the second and, shrugging off a gaggle of whores, pushed his way to the bar: Micklethwaite was at the fireside savouring a wine. Next, at the entrance to the Ganzemarkt, a cart pulled across him, blocking the alley. He berated the driver as the man and his boy unloaded their barrels. Flustered, the young lad missed his grip and dozens of twitching herring slid, like silver rain, to the dark cobbles. Watson kicked them angrily away. The cart moved off. He turned, instinctively, into a narrow side-passage but it was blocked again – by his quarry conducting a vigorous transaction with a woman of the quarter. And now, approaching the harbour, he cut a corner and began to close on the Englishman from the opposite direction. The near-full moon, playing on the gently stirring water, showed that luck was still with him: they had the wharf to themselves.

Watson's ebony stick rapped out a steady pace along the cobbles; the bulbous, lead-filled knob comfortable under his palm. It was not the only weapon he was carrying but he liked its style – and the damage it delivered at close quarters.

He touched the rim of his hat as he passed the man. Then he turned and swung. The shillelagh's heavy knob struck the back of the man's head and he dropped to the ground like a stone. Watson dragged the body behind a pile of potato crates, rolled the man over and crouched down beside him.

Still breathing.

Watson raised his eyebrows: he must have caught the skull a glancing blow. No matter. The *coup de grâce* would be a mere formality.

Unbuttoning the man's jacket, he reached inside and withdrew the letters. He noted the names of the recipients before breaking the seal on the first and reading it quickly. It was carefully worded but, knowing de la Croix, what was unsaid in its few lines was blatant.

He glanced at the still prone Englishman before reading the second, virtually identical, letter. His instincts had been right. He found that they usually were. Now only one task remained.

He reached for his stick, turned back to the body and, for the second time in his life, looked on the face of a traitor.

Then the traitor's eyes opened.

A flash of steel.

Watson heard the blade grate against his ribcage. Coughing, blood spurted from his mouth. The knife twisted, then withdrew. Watson staggered and toppled into the canal.

The hand had turned the glass and it was high time to leave the game, but somehow – incredibly – he had missed the moment.

The look of disbelief was still on his face as the dark waters closed over it.

1

Leeds, January 1780

Blood flowed down the heifer's neck, shining for a moment in the early morning light before joining the fetid contents of the gutter. A flailing hoof cracked on the butcher's shin. He swore and drove the knife deeper. The beast's frantic bellows mingled with the shouts of poultry traders gathered around the market cross and the curses of clothiers, woven rolls perched on heads, pushing through the throng towards the Cloth Halls. And above the ruckus, one voice fought to be heard.

'The absolute annihilation of quackery! We need nothing less!'

Taller than most and peculiarly thin, the man wore a faded frock coat and tricorn hat. His brass-headed cane beat in emphasis upon the worn, stone step of the cross.

'... We are beset by a plague of impostors. They masquerade as respectable physicians but are worse than a band of robbers. Far worse, for they empty your purse and then steal your very lives...'

'Bugger off or I'll steal yours!' snarled a trader.

The man's harangues were a familiar irritant to buyer and seller alike. Only one person, standing on the edge of the crowd, was concentrating. In his early twenties, he was respectably dressed but for the tangled creases covering his damp, mud-stained coat. Brown curls stood out in all directions and dark rings sagged under strikingly deep brown eyes. He looked as if he'd spent the night under a hedge.

'… They are nothing less than a race of destroyers. I say it again: a race of destroyers! They flaunt their nostrums and tell you nothing of their deadly poison. But do you care?'

'Not if they can cure the clap,' shouted one wag, drawing laughter.

'I know you, Tom Theakston. Don't think you can go making fun and expect me to come out for you in the middle of the night.'

A woman's voice: 'You can come out for me any time, Doc!'

More laughter.

He soldiered on. 'The truth is that you do not care. No wonder these pernicious quacks make off with the wealth of our nation. No wonder they send myriads of Britons to an untimely grave. Would that you had the wisdom to reject their wares and that our Corporation would act. Then you will be safe in your beds and these vermin will be driven from our town!'

There was a soft, crunching sound and the doctor swung fiercely around. A broken egg dripped from his coat. Another narrowly missed his shoulder and burst against the stone cross. As the crowd jeered, he stepped down and stalked away.

The listener watched him go with a modicum of sympathy. He, too, knew about fighting to be heard and being baited to the edge of rage and beyond. Even so, this was a zealot he would need to be wary of.

'Who was that?' he asked no one in particular.

'That's our dear Doctor Barnard.'

He turned to see a lady, some ten years his senior. Blond ringlets fell to her shoulders from under the hood of a grey cloak.

'You do have to admire his perseverance.' She shook her head. 'He'll be back again next week.'

'May I be so bold?' The young man gave one of his more flamboyant bows. 'Doctor Charles Rossi – recently arrived from York. Charlie to my friends,' he added with the hint of a wink.

She took in his dishevelled appearance with an amused smile.

'Well, sir, doubtless there is room to spare for another physician in our town but, as you see, the ones we already have may resent the competition.'

'I dare say,' he replied grimly, 'but there are new ways of healing now – ways which him and his ilk will have to accept. They can't have it all to themselves, whether they like it or not.'

'So you propose to challenge our medical establishment.' Her smile grew wider. 'Well then, sir, let me not delay you any further.'

The encounter did nothing to improve his mood. It had begun the previous evening when a dark, swollen mass of water – a river bursting its banks – had forced his coach to quit the turnpike from York. Time and again, the horses had slowed almost to a standstill as the rough lanes were rutted thigh deep by the sudden traffic. With the guard's invective ringing in their ears, the sodden passengers were repeatedly forced to push the coach out of the quagmire. Reaching Leeds four hours late, Charlie Rossi had trudged through the deluge in search of a bed. At the King's Arms, a modestly-appointed tavern on the main thoroughfare, he had spent a tortuously long night, buzzing with anticipation. Then, an hour before dawn, just as he was nodding, the hubbub from the taproom below, where many a fast was being broken ahead of market day, had driven him out into the crisp air.

His day did not get any better. Leaving behind the raucous market place, he turned into a narrow side street but, rounding a corner, the walls of the houses began to close in over him, their roofs almost touching in places. An endless clatter of shuttles assailed him from large first-floor windows. Their panes hungrily consumed the thin light, leaving scant pickings for the grey-faced women who sat spinning and carding in doorways, or the bare-footed children playing hopscotch over stinking pools.

'Do you know where I might find rooms for hire?'

'I've got a lovely little one down below that's nice and warm, but she don't come cheap!' The woman's cackle pursued him round the corner.

The alley divided. He chose the wider of the openings. Every few yards, every few doorsteps, another ginnel crossed his path, as if some invisible hand was weaving the town together in front of him – laying down the warp and weft on which these people lived out their lives. He took a left, then a right. The airless maze continued. He needed out.

He turned again, lured towards a pool of light, but it was no more than a small yard. Three rows of wooden tenter frames, covered in tightly stretched cloth, fought each other, like so many hungry saplings, for scraps of sun and air. He paused, dragging chilly sweat from his forehead through his tangled hair. Pushing between the frames, he ran his fingers across the damp wool. On this, countless lives depended; on this, fortunes were being made.

He pressed on past a group of workmen, forcing yet more houses into another yard, no bigger than the last. And then, turning a corner, he stepped out into a broad thoroughfare. Tall, elegant homes, with glinting roofs, dotted it like a string of pearls. Each was surrounded by a well-kept garden and behind, to the south, orchards stretched away towards the river, where vestiges of a thin mist still clung. As he walked, he could feel the tension begin to seep away. More than anything, he thought, wealth buys you space.

Towards the edge of town, the houses and gardens stopped abruptly where a vast, rectangular building straddled the road. Over a central archway, shining letters proclaimed: "Coloured Cloth Hall". Two iron gates barred the entrance to an immense, silent courtyard. He grasped the cold metal bars in both hands and sucked the air deep into his lungs. He held it there until it hurt.

And the air smelt of wool and of power.

The next morning, well rested and spruced up, Charlie Rossi stepped out of the King's Arms onto Briggate. The grassy slopes on either side, which the day before had been hidden under a confusion of livestock, stalls, and auctioneers' rostrums now gave the street a broad, open feel. And more room for the biting wind.

He pulled his cravat a fraction higher and set off, up the gentle incline, past the bow-windowed shops and apparently endless taverns. At the top of the street, his way was all but blocked by the Moot Hall, fronted by carved pillars and a pair of arches, and topped by a large clock. To one side of the entrance steps, an elderly man was held in the tender embrace of the town's pillory, his face smeared with something green and rank. Charlie took a half-eaten apple from his pocket – the remains of a hasty breakfast. The man screwed up his face and turned his head away as best he could but Charlie pressed the fruit gently to his lips. The man sucked hard on its colouring juices and bit as deep as his rotting teeth would allow.

'God bless you, young fella. You're a rare one.'

Charlie shrugged and hurried on through the narrow Shambles at the side of the Moot Hall, picking his way past the dried animal blood and excrement from the previous day's slaughter. Beyond the now deserted market cross, the churchyard of St John's opened up to his left and he watched the congregation making its escape from the south porch. Leading the charge was a couple: a short, portly gentleman with leathery, weather-beaten skin and, on his arm, a considerably younger and taller woman. Blond ringlets flowed from under a cream bonnet.

As they drew closer, she acknowledged Charlie's bow. 'Oh, good morning, Doctor…?'

'Good morning, madam… sir. Doctor Charles Rossi, at your service.'

He flashed a charming smile but, with a snort, the man strode away down the street.

The lady shook her head. 'I do apologise for my husband. He is not really as unchristian as his rudeness might suggest, although I own that his views on religion allow little room for his fellow man.'

So: wife not daughter. Never mind.

'If I may,' she continued, 'I am Sarah Armstrong and my husband is Josiah. His is a name which you may encounter again, for he has made it his business to become one of the more successful of our famous cloth merchants. However, I fear that you are unlikely to recruit him to your practice. His views on physicians, surgeons and apothecaries are not for polite society.'

He grimaced. 'That may be of little consequence unless I can find rooms.'

'What is it you require?'

'Just a pair. One sufficient for my lectures; the other needs only the space for private consultations and treatments.'

'Lectures?'

'Indeed, madam – on the wonders of electricity and its restorative powers.'

'Ah, the electrostatic machine.'

He was taken aback.

Mrs Armstrong laughed. 'We do not all live in the Dark Ages, Mr Rossi. Such things have been seen in these parts before you arrived. Joseph – Reverend Priestley that is – was among us for several years. Despite his dissenting views, he was one of the few clerics my husband could ever tolerate. He gave us several private demonstrations of his machine, although he had little time for some of its more enthusiastic advocates.'

Charlie frowned but she smiled disarmingly. 'But who knows? Perhaps, after all, another "Joseph" might not be wholly unwelcome.' She chuckled. 'You must forgive me, for I delay you once again. I wish you good fortune… Doctor.'

However, fortune continued to elude him as he roamed the town centre, so in the afternoon he headed for the outskirts. To the west, beyond the Coloured Cloth Hall, he discovered a newly built infirmary. He stopped to take in the dark walls and small windows looming over him.

What screams and silences were confined within? He shuddered.

'You'd be better off at the old wells.' An elderly lady sitting on the pavement took a swig from her bottle.

'Wells?'

'Aye,' she coughed, 'we still hold by them: St Peter's for your joints, Canker Well for tumours, the Eyebright for sore eyes. You name it, we've got it.'

'What about this place?'

'Pah!' she spat. 'That's nowt but a gateway to death for them as can't afford a quack. You want to stay out of there young fellow.'

'Aye, but it's still more competition,' he muttered as he moved away.

To the east, smoke belched from a brickworks, and he stopped to admire a team of dray horses. They had a strikingly reddish hue but, when he stroked one of them, his hand came away the same colour. A pair of red-dusted labourers strode out of the works with hods of bricks over their shoulders. As the pile on the cart grew, he pictured yet another yard in the town crammed full of houses. He shook his head: then they would start on the fields.

He crossed over the river to the south and wandered among another patchwork of houses and cloth-laden tenter frames; the land here also pockmarked by a mass of winches and slag piles.

A woman hauled on a rope and a large bucket of coal emerged from the bell pit under her feet.

He nodded to her. 'I used to catch a ride on one of those when I was a kid.'

'Not round here you wouldn't – you'd catch a belt on your backside.'

'Aye, but that was Northumberland.'

'Never mind, you'll get over it.'

He grinned and left her to it.

A pair of wooden rails crossed his path – a waggonway. He had heard of them but not seen one before. A young lad walked past, leading a horse and wagon towards the wharves on the Aire. Charlie peered in and whistled: it looked like a dozen tons of coal and just a single horse. Bigger and faster, that was the way now – everywhere.

He walked further along the road to Hunslet but even this far out his enquiries fell on stony ground. So, with the afternoon sun caressing the roof tops, he crossed back over the town's bridge and paused to peer over the edge. Down below, chains of stevedores were loading bale upon bale of cloth onto tightly packed barges, moored beside tall new warehouses. Just one more sign that Leeds was expanding and exuding prosperity – for some. He spat into the turbulent waters.

Was it going to refuse him a share of its wealth?

In a high-sided settle, in a corner of the taproom, Charlie nursed his pot of ale.

'I see you're not in the mood for company.' Sam Tinker, the landlord, perched himself on the bench opposite, ignoring his own insight.

With muscles that hefted barrels for a living; a stomach lovingly nurtured on his own ale and his wife, Beth's cooking; and an open face with broad forehead and wide chin, Sam had all the solidity that befitted his profession.

'What about this machine of yours, Charlie? You heal people with it you say. How does that work, then?'

'Well, the key to it all is the human body…'

With his job as landlord done, Sam allowed himself a satisfied grin. He took a long draught of ale. Then, as he listened, "Leyden jars", "prime conductors" and "electrometers" began to whirl in his imagination.

An hour later, the men's laughter was interrupted when a young boy hurtled through the door and skidded to a halt on the damp sawdust. A note was thrust under Charlie's nose. He took it and placed a few coppers in the grubby hand. The urchin disappeared as quickly as he had arrived.

He read, his brow furrowing.

'What's up?' probed Sam.

'A proposal, it would seem, from Josiah Armstrong. The man wouldn't give me the time of day this morning. Though, his wife was sweet enough,' he added with a smirk.

'Now her,' said Sam, 'you need to watch.'

At first light the next day, dressed in his best frock coat and britches, and with his hair in some semblance of order, Charlie arrived in front of a milliner's shop in Vicar Lane. Between it and the neighbouring bakery, a door led to a narrow staircase, which he climbed to find a sizeable, well-lit room; empty but for a large table and a couple of benches either side of the fireplace. Through a door at the rear came Josiah Armstrong. The merchant's greeting was no more than a grunt.

'For a reason which I fail to comprehend, my wife seems to think that we should take pity on you. Although I prefer to reserve my pity for those who merit it, I do value the happiness of my wife. From the previous tenant I received a sum of two guineas a week and to satisfy my wife's *charitable* concerns I am prepared to extend the same arrangement to you.'

Charlie's lips pouted involuntarily. This was surely more than the property was worth and it was going to stretch him to the limit.

'May I?' he asked. Not waiting for an answer, he moved past Armstrong to examine the smaller room beyond. It was barely adequate but he was out of options. He returned and offered the merchant his hand.

'I accept.'

Ignoring the gesture, Armstrong held out his own palm for the rent and then walked to the door. 'Further payments are due Tuesdays at my home: Red Hall on Upper Head Row.'

And with that, he was off down the stairs, leaving Charlie to ponder his new practice – and his strange benefactors.

In the office of the *Leeds Mercury*, a plump grey-faced clerk was sitting, cowed behind his desk. A slender young woman had her face only inches from the clerk's, from where her words assailed him.

'Well, if that really is the best you can manage, don't let me keep you from your duties!'

Swivelling on the spot, she pushed past Charlie and slammed the door behind her. He was left with the impression of dark eyes, black hair and a face of thunder. After an awkward silence, the clerk glanced at him and raised his eyebrows as if to say 'Some people'. He took this as an invitation to begin business.

'Good morning. I wish to place an advertisement in your next edition.'

'Indeed, sir.' The tone was one of threadbare patience. 'But, as I was trying to explain to the young lady' – the man looked to the door – 'we are shortly going to press. We might be able to squeeze a few lines on the inside but, for the front page, if you were able to wait until next week…'

Sharing the woman's irritation, he bit his tongue, mentally tore up his favourite testimonial and began to dictate a new advert.

With his apparatus transferred from the King's Arms on the back of Sam's wagon, and with his helpful but highly inquisitive new friend dispatched to locate the required seating, most of the arrangements, although not exactly ideal, were now in place. As he stepped out into Vicar Lane, he indulged a fantasy of full benches and a practice that turned the tables on the likes of Doctor Barnard. However, turning into Briggate his eyes were drawn to a freshly posted handbill by the door of another inn:

BELTESHAZZAR
Professor of Natural Experimental Philosophy
and other Occult Sciences,
who has instructed, amazed and entertained
the Royal Families of Europe,
will now in this town deliver an evening of Marvels –

Electrical, Magnetical, Mechanical, Chemical and Optical.
Such are the astonishing accomplishments
of this divine philosopher that in a less enlightened age
he would surely have been called SUPERNATURAL.
He will also demonstrate the most accomplished
Sleights of Hand as performed by the conjurors of Europe
and will disclose the thoughts of those present
in a way most MIRACULOUS.
The marvellous BELTESHAZZAR also sells
a tincture for the remedy of many nervous complaints
and, at the touch of his marvellous hands, all pains disappear.
Seekers of Enlightenment should attend each evening this week
at the Long Room of the White Swan.

He swore under his breath. It was bad enough having Barnard
waging a vindictive little war without this penny conjuror seducing
people with his quackery – another squeeze on an already over-tight
purse.

Why the hell hadn't he stayed in York?

2

In the yard behind the White Swan, a maid was hanging out a bulging basket of laundry. The warder of the adjacent prison skirted round her, carrying a tray of tankards back to quench the thirst of his inmates. In the corner, a small man was unloading crates from a large covered wagon. Beside it, a woman in her early twenties, with black, slightly wild hair, stroked one of the horses and studied him as he worked.

He wasn't the man he had been. His face was paler, his back more stooped and his movements slower. She could see that the long weeks of sickness in the autumn had taken their toll. Gone were the days when her father had performed before Louis XV and his courtiers; feted as one of the most famous conjurors in France. Had it been true? It hardly mattered now. Anyway she didn't have the heart to deny him his illusions. These days it was all half-empty benches and too many nights sleeping under the wagon. Pottering around the yard he was barely recognisable as "the great Belteshazzar". True, he could still harness the energy of a performance to transform himself but the magic drifted away as quickly as the audiences, draining him that little bit more each time.

He had been so different at their first meeting. She could still remember his dark, shining eyes and strange accent, beguiling her with tales of wonders and illusions, courts and kings, travels and adventures. Wary and unsure of what to believe, she had looked at the matron, who smiled one of her few smiles, nodded and said that, yes, this was her father and that he had come back for her.

Growing up in the foundling home, the other children only ever spoke of their mothers – the angelic creatures who would some day return to claim them. Fathers were never mentioned – except once. She had asked the matron about the ring that had been hanging round her neck for as long as she could remember.

'That thing?' replied Mrs Weller with a sneer. 'It's just your token in case your Froggy father ever comes to claim you. You'll not be needing it, though – not with this war.'

She took the hint and dismissed any thought of fathers or freedom. She accepted the daily hardship, the fights, the cruelty. It was her reality and she never allowed herself to dream that it might be any different. That was the road to pain and despair. A life in service was the best she could expect – far more likely a brothel. But then, at the age of seven, everything changed.

'You're wanted in matron's room,' the cook growled, slopping out the greasy soup.

She didn't hurry to eat it, meagre though it was.

'Matron! Now!' shouted the cook across the crowded hall.

She opened Mrs Weller's door with an air of resignation. She couldn't remember what she had done but it didn't matter – the tawse would be waiting for her all the same. But there was no strap, just a short, thin, dark-haired man standing next to the tall, buxom matron, who was wearing her very best face. The man smiled anxiously at her.

'*Bonjour*, Isabelle.'

In one moment, her past became mysterious and her future uncertain but, above all, they were different. She was different.

Over the next few weeks, as she took the first faltering steps towards trust, she found the confidence to ask the question that had been haunting her since their first meeting. Slowly, and as sensitively as he could, her father had explained.

And then the anger had begun.

***

Doctor Barnard beat upon the door with his cane. The wood was only spared a second assault by the swift attention of the doorman, who informed him that, no, Mr Crompton was not at home, being still at the Cloth Halls, and that, yes, he was welcome to await his return.

Upstairs in the drawing room, Barnard sat crunching his newspaper in his hand. He began to pound the cane into the richly patterned, Turkish rug. The clock on the mantelpiece struck nine.

'Damn the man!' he exclaimed, rising from his seat.

The door opened and in walked the tall, commanding figure of Robert Crompton, cloth merchant and Treasurer of the Leeds Corporation.

'Ah, Henry. How good to see you.' He waved Barnard back into his chair. 'To what do I owe this pleasure at such an early hour? Do take some refreshment, some tea perhaps or some wine – very fine it is too.'

'Thank you, but no.'

'Oh, I forget, you abstain from all things that may affect the blood. Doubtless very wise, dear Henry, and you set us the finest of examples. However, I fear that such a regime is far beyond the reach of the common man.'

Barnard doubted that Crompton had ever thought of himself as a common man.

The merchant moved to the dresser where a decanter of wine stood ready. He poured an ample glass and stood savouring it, while his physician shifted restlessly.

'The thing is,' Barnard burst out, 'the paper this morning. Have you seen it?'

'I confess, I have not had the leisure.'

Barnard unfolded the crumpled pages and read, his words shot through with disdain: 'Doctor Rossi M.D., Electrical Physician' – he snorted – 'announces to the Ladies and Gentlemen of Leeds, that his medico-electrical apparatus treats all manner of palsies, pains, eruptions, swellings and nervous complaints. From tonight, he lectures on the wonderful properties of electricity, and his enlightened and speedy techniques are effective in the removal of ailments that have been, until now, beyond the powers of the Gentlemen of the Faculty.'

'How diverting!' chuckled Crompton, taking a chair opposite Barnard.

'Diverting! He is nothing but a puffed-up quack,' snarled the doctor. 'He assumes medical qualifications to which he surely has no right and proposes a treatment which most certainly has no benefits. More than that, I understand it to be harmful, even fatal on occasions. It is a scandal that he be allowed to practice his quackery in our borough – a scandal!' Barnard paused for breath before ploughing on. 'To add insult to injury we are also playing host to a vagabond, delighting in the title of "the marvellous Belteshazzar", who offers to defraud the good people of Leeds with pills, potions and "healing hands". The man is a charlatan and a rogue who, if left unchecked, will bring our residents to an early death. Surely, now is the moment to nip this evil in the bud. I look to you, Robert, to bring it to the attention of our Corporation.'

Crompton steepled his fingers and looked thoughtfully into Barnard's eyes. He sighed. 'We have been through all this before, Henry. The Corporation has rejected your pleas in the past. What precisely are you asking of it this time?'

Barnard leaned forward in his chair. 'Other boroughs may have indulged these peddlers of trash but let us set an example. We must outlaw them or, at the very least, require of them a licence.

15

Then their claims can be weighed by experienced and reputable practitioners before they are set free to prey on our citizens.'

'But the Corporation has already made it plain that it does not think it fit to restrict trade in this area of our life.'

'Trade!' Barnard could contain himself no longer. 'It is not trade but the lives of our people. The sole reason for our Charter was to restrict trade and to protect our clothiers. You are not slow to take action to defend your own wealth, oh no. But, when it comes to the health of our citizens, you let fraudsters and fakers act with impunity.'

'Doctor Barnard, you go too far. Insults will not serve your cause.'

'Before long, people will die and where will our fine manners have got us then? To whom can our people turn when we are beset not only by medical quacks but also political ones? Well I, for one, am not prepared to stand by and do nothing. And if we do not have aldermen who act for the good of the town then we shall have to find others who will.'

Barnard rose from the chair. It galled him even further to see that Crompton was smiling.

'May I remind you, Doctor, that we are appointed for life.'

'Well, we shall see about that!'

Barnard hurled the newspaper to the floor and stormed down the stairs.

Crompton remained seated. He had rather enjoyed that. The man was sincere but an utter fool. He picked up the paper, found the advertisement and began to read. He laughed to himself. Yes, this should be very entertaining and he would invite some of his friends. That would infuriate Barnard even more.

***

'Ladies and gentlemen, in the name of enlightenment and well-being, I welcome you.'

The candlelit room was tolerably full for a first night but what gratified Charlie more was the number of the well-to-do on the front benches. They made up for all the penny-pinchers squeezing onto the "servants' benches" at the back. Among these sat a fidgeting Sam Tinker.

He had invited his landlord to the first lecture and, in his eagerness to see the electrical machine in operation, Sam had accepted without a moment's thought. However, he soon discovered there was a catch. Experience had taught Charlie that, on first nights, if people didn't hold back then you got the idiot volunteer who wanted to impress his friends. Sam would provide a most suitable alternative. Now, as Sam shifted nervously in his seat, Charlie could imagine the questions buzzing in his head: what happened when you were electrified; was it painful; would he make a fool of himself? Well, he would find out soon enough.

'We live in an age of great wonders,' he proclaimed, as the noise in the room began to subside. 'Not the least of these is the mysterious fluid we call electricity. Since we left the Garden of Eden, mankind has been witness to the drama of the electrical fire played out in the heavens. Many a time, mankind has cowered as it reached down to the earth and set it ablaze; many a time, people have been struck dead by this elemental force.'

With one palm on top of the other, he reached towards his audience and then whipped his hands apart. A bright flash shot between them. Cheers broke out and tickets waved. This was the simple stuff they liked.

'But now,' he continued, 'this awesome power has been tamed and its occult mysteries laid bare by the light of human reason. Now we see that the electric fluid has power not only to take life but to give it; not only to cause many of the imbalances in the human body but also to cure many of its ills. And much of this new wisdom comes to us from Mr Franklin in our troubled colonies—'

'Yankee bastards!'

'Aye, it's our boys who should be learnin' them – with canon.'

With the war in America not going well and his lecture drifting too soon into philosophical waters, the grumbling began to take hold. With a flourish, he whisked away a cloth that had been covering the table behind him.

'... And so, ladies and gentlemen, let us open our minds to the wonders of the electrostatic machine.'

Candlelight danced off sculpted glass, polished metal and waxed wood. Silence descended. Sam was looking on in wide-eyed amazement. Charlie rotated a small wooden wheel and a large jar beside it began to spin. He lowered a piece of leather against the glass.

'... And so, in this simple act, we generate the mysterious thing we call "vitreous electricity". It builds up on the surface and then passes along this thin glass tube – the prime conductor – until it comes to rest in the Leyden jar here.' He pointed to another large glass container, the lower half of which was coated in foil and a metal rod stuck out of the top. 'When we want to extract it again, we merely adjust this brass screw, which we call the electrometer, to control the quantity of electrical fluid that passes into an object or person. All this I shall now discover to you with the help of a volunteer: Mr Samuel Tinker.'

Sam's face changed from wonderment to horror as he was beckoned forward. He shuffled slowly to the front, where Charlie asked him to stand on a thick, circular tablet of wax.

'Thank you, Sam. Now all we need to do is to connect you to the Leyden jar.'

Picking up two glass conducting rods, through which passed metal wires that were attached to different parts of the jar, Charlie placed one on each of Sam's hands and immediately the audience began to laugh.

'Don't worry, Sam,' he consoled, 'it happens to everyone.'

'What does?' Sam pleaded.

'Your hair: it's standing up as straight as a hedgehog's spines.'

A shout came from the back of the room. 'Hoy, Tinker, is owt else standing on end?' The laughter rose again.

'Ladies and gentlemen, Samuel Tinker is now bearing the electrical fire in his own body. He has become nothing less than a living Leyden jar.'

He produced a filled wine glass. 'Now Sam, if you would be so kind as to stretch out your finger, these spirits will reveal your truly electrifying powers.'

Tentatively, Sam reached towards the glass, anxious at what new humiliation lay in store. But, as his finger got closer, a bright blue spark flew from it and the liquid in the wine glass burst into flame. Sam snapped his hand away and the audience took a collective intake of breath. Applause broke out as Sam stared, open-mouthed, at the flames and then at his finger.

Charlie winked at him. 'And of course, we can only imagine what effect your new powers will have on your dear lady later tonight.'

Sam grinned broadly as the audience hooted. He stepped off the wax and, with his embarrassment forgotten, was clapped back to his seat.

'That is mere showmanship,' Charlie continued, 'but our purpose tonight is the application of electricity to the well-being of humanity. Our natural philosophers have shown that within the depths of the earth lies a vast reservoir of electrical fluid. And like a world in miniature, our body contains its own store of this life-giving power. But woe betide us if it is out of balance.'

He plunged the conducting rods into a dry clay tablet, lying on the table. After a moment a rough crack broke the surface and then another. Moments later, it was lying in pieces.

'Thus, the earth fractures and great Vesuvius pours forth its fiery lava. And so it is that the same forces create those eruptions and emissions which afflict the human body.'

'They afflict my old man's every night!' sniggered a woman on the servants' benches.

'Whereas, if we electrify this wet clay…' the slab began to swell, 'we behold the cause of the rising and falling of the earth, which

19

has power to devastate whole cities. Think of the poor citizens of Lisbon.'

'Aye, he's right there.' People nodded sympathetically.

'By the same principal, blockages in the electrical fluid bring forth swellings to assail us, both within and without.'

More bawdy laughter.

'Finally, our natural philosophers have deduced that whirling pools and great waves at sea result from similar electrical disorders. In the same way, ailments afflicting our emotions, nervous constitution and digestion arise from the motions of our inner electrical fluid.'

A man by the fireplace broke wind loudly.

'And so, ladies and gentlemen, it is my pleasure, nay my duty, to inform you that with the aid of this most elegant and efficacious machine, these imbalances may now be remedied and health restored to the whole body. For six long years, Mr Eustace Fitzsimons of Newcastle suffered a terrible incapacitation of his arm, which the most skilled physicians had proved impotent to remedy. And yet, after only a month's course of electrifications, his pains were permanently relieved' – he produced an envelope from his jacket pocket – 'as his own testimonial bears witness.'

'Wrote it yourself, you quack!'

He picked up one of a cluster of small brown bottles. 'While other letters tell of the healing power of my unique, electrified physic for toothache, gout and the king's evil. Individual consultations will be available daily, at this address, and a course of treatment is on such favourable terms that will not to be repeated in this town for many a year.'

And, with that, his first lecture was over. He bowed as low as he could. He found it reduced the target area.

**

Robert Crompton weighed up the other aldermen and assistants as they took their places around the vast oak table that all but filled the meeting chamber of the old Moot Hall. On his left, the "sheep" huddled together as always: the ancient schoolmaster, Morley; Scorsby, from the new pottery; the owner of the brickworks, Harland; Firth, the recently elected colliery owner; and Whitwell and Bell – wire maker and surgeon. Around the rest of the table, the ranks of the wool cloth trade were utterly dominant. He knew it had been like this since the founding of the Corporation, a hundred and fifty years before and he was sure it would still be the same, a century and a half to come.

As the mayor, Richard Micklethwaite, called the meeting to order, Crompton noticed that George Thomson's seat was empty.

Damn it. Where had he got to?

'The first item today,' began Micklethwaite, 'is the resignation due to palsy, of our esteemed Alderman Emmet. Regrettable as this is, we must turn to the election of his successor. Assistants' – he nodded to the door – 'if you please.'

The junior members left the room and, as the door clicked to, Crompton launched his bid.

'Mr Mayor, may I propose Mr Oxley. He has shown himself to be a most faithful servant of this town. His mill produces some of our finest cloth and he is providing much valuable employment during these challenging times. I trust we will all agree that James Oxley would be a worthy addition to our number.'

The Treasurer scanned the room for signs of support. The "sheep" were nodding but their allegiance was already in the bag. He needed more, knowing that some would take any chance to thwart his ascent to the office of mayor. He looked across at Josiah Armstrong. The old stager's eyes narrowed, holding his, but he kept his peace.

Instead, it was the mayor who spoke. 'Oxley? Can you be serious, Alderman? The man has not yet served a twelve-month as an assistant. He lacks experience and his attendance at meetings has hardly been meticulous. I note that he is not even here this evening. Nor is his reputation within our community – how can I put this? – all that it might be.'

Crompton's eyes flashed. 'Mr Mayor, with all due respect, I grant that his work has detained him more than he would have hoped during this past year. However, your remarks on his good name are without foundation and I must counsel you – as a friend – not to expand on them lest you stray into slander.'

'It's not Oxley who needs protecting but the reputation of this Corporation.' Micklethwaite's voice was controlled yet icy. 'I need not remind you, Alderman, that the well-being of our town rests on that of our cloth trade and that the future of both rests full-square upon this body? We are hard pressed both at home and abroad, and discontent is growing again among the weavers. And they have still not forgotten our recourse to the dragoons back a while. Further bloodshed must be prevented and we can permit nothing – absolutely nothing – to undermine our standing in the community.'

Micklethwaite's supporters banged the table. The pretender had been put in his place.

'Therefore,' the mayor continued, 'I propose instead that Mr Walker, as an established and well-respected merchant, would be a far more circumspect choice.'

Crompton smiled benignly. 'Forgive me for speaking directly but is John Walker really the kind of man we need? Clinging to the ways of the past – is that all we aspire to? The future beckons, gentlemen. Oxley embraces it gladly and so must we. We face a stark choice: change or die.'

'You're right there.'

'Hear! hear!'

Some of the waverers had been swayed.

'Well then, "for King and the law", let the Corporation decide.' Micklethwaite was never one to allow long debate.

The hands went up.

'The vote appears to be tied,' declared the mayor, with thinly disguised satisfaction. 'In which case it falls to me, as chairman, to use my casting vote.'

At which moment the door of the council chamber opened and in walked Alderman Thomson.

***

She stood a few feet inside the narrow alleyway, with her cloak pulled up against the deluge, all but invisible to those passing by in the street. The flow of human traffic slowed to a trickle. Then she had the night to herself.

And opposite her, the house.

She noted all the little domestic routines: one room plunging into darkness and another brightening; smoke ascending from the one fire still alight – the study, in use long after the rest of the household had retired; the separate sleeping arrangements; the distance between the rooms; the distance between the people.

And still she watched. The fire had burned in her for so long now that these extra hours hardly mattered. She turned the thin, bone handle over and over in her hands. Now, at least, her waiting had a purpose. Wiping the blade dry on her cloak, she slipped it back inside her boot and stepped out into the street.

Now, at last, justice would be done.

***

As a skewer glides through roasted beef, the metal slid effortlessly between the sinews of the neck and up into the man's brain.

***

Mary Crompton sat in bed, planning the activities that lay ahead. It was going to be a busy Sunday. The door burst open.

'Ma'am! Ma'am!'

23

'Kitty, your manners!'

'Begging your pardon ma'am but it's the master.' At which the young girl put her hands to her face and dissolved into tears.

Mrs Crompton pulled a thick gown over her nightdress and swept down the corridor, with the sobbing maid trailing behind. In the chamber at the far end, Robert Crompton lay on his back, unmoving under the sheets. His head rested neatly in the centre of the pillow.

She laid the back of her hand against the bristly cheek. It was cold.

'Kitty, please would you send for Doctor Barnard.'

As the maid rushed gasping from the room, Mrs Crompton looked down at the bloodless face. The years had been kind to it. There were a few extra lines, of course, and the once jet-black hair was now silver throughout but it still had the same fine bone structure, still the same power to attract. As she knew to her cost.

In the silence and solitude that surrounded her, a faint smile rose onto her lips and into her eyes. It remained there for a few moments. Then she banished it and turned on her heels.

3

Tuesday dawned dark and overcast, and despite the clothiers in the taproom below, Charlie woke late. He darted through the kitchen of the King's Arms, where Beth Tinker was carrying a trencher laden with pork and cabbage out towards the taproom. He whisked a large piece of meat from the pile.

'I'll have you, Rossi!' she shouted as he sprinted from the door.

As he turned into Vicar Lane, he could see his first customers of the day standing in the rain.

'Damned impertinence,' growled the man as Charlie fumbled for the key. 'Fifteen minutes! You'll make no living treating people like this.'

He mumbled his apologies and ushered them up to his consulting room, where he invited Mrs Walker – a lady of overabundant proportions – to take a seat. Glancing disdainfully at the flimsy looking chair, she launched forth.

'It is the consumption. I have been bled. I have been cupped. I have been purged. My physicians, for all their ruinous charges, have failed to effect any improvement in my most frail condition. I have been at my wit's end for weeks. But then we saw your advertisement.'

'I am honoured to receive your trust.'

'We are Methodists, sir.' Mr Walker, who was as angular as his wife was round, had taken the seat that she had spurned. 'The Reverend Wesley places much store by these machines and it is on that basis alone that I am willing to entrust my wife to your care.'

'I see. Well, I am gratified nonetheless.'

'And there will be no contact whatsoever with my wife's person.' Walker scowled up at him.

'Nothing more, I assure you, than the tips of the conducting rods.'

'Only we have heard tales from Paris of this man, Monsieur Mesmer. They are barely to be credited: the lack of chaperones, the placing of hands, the swooning – unimaginable indecencies.'

'I fear that with his improprieties, Mesmer besmirches all respectable practitioners,' Charlie replied with some feeling. 'We harness nature's energies from the machine alone, not from our own persons. His so-called "animal magnetism" will soon be exposed for the dangerous quackery it is, mark my words.'

'I am reassured to know your opinion on the matter.'

He took a few more details of Mrs Walker's history and then directed her to stand on a glass-legged footstool.

'The procedure requires many dozens of applications, so I would ask you to be patient. The electrical fluid will flow from the neck down to the abdomen, where it will return to the Leyden jar. You will feel a certain warmth and an unusual sensation on your skin, but most people find it not altogether unpleasant.'

Almost an hour later, after much turning of wheels, adjusting of screws and applying of rods, he declared the process finished. Mr Walker jolted awake as his slightly perspiring wife stepped off the stool.

'Well, it is certainly a most tedious process' – she smoothed her gown – 'yet, compared to Doctor Jackson and his infernal heated cups, it is altogether less violent. Let us only pray that it proves to be more effective.'

'I beg you to give it time,' Charlie replied. 'A full course of treatment is required before the electrical balance is fully restored. However, over the coming days, I believe you can hope for some signs of improvement.'

'If so, we will be indebted to you sir – most indebted.' Mr Walker smiled at his wife who held out her arm. They bowed, as one. Charlie returned it with satisfaction.

An hour passed. He paced the floor. He looked out of the lecture room window once again. Where had the man got to? He turned away.

Behind him, the glass shattered. A brick flew past his head, smashed into the rear bench and dropped to the floor. He bent to pick it up and another crashed through, striking him on the calf. Angry voices drew him back to the window. A gang of men were standing in the street.

'You bastard!' they jeered.

Bewildered, he ran down the stairs and threw open the door.

'What the hell are you playing at?'

One of the men spat in his face. The others advanced. Instinctively, he raised the brick.

'Now then gentlemen' – a constable stepped between them – 'that'll be enough or I'll have you in the cells.'

'What's going on?' demanded Charlie.

'So you haven't heard?' replied the constable. 'It's the talk of the town. Alderman Crompton were found dead on Sunday – one of your customers, I believe.'

'Aye, and the owner of our mill,' growled one of the men.

'And this 'ere quack has buggered our livelihoods,' snarled another.

The constable raised a hand. 'Steady on fellas.'

'I'm sorry to hear that,' Charlie replied, 'but what's it to do with me?'

'The alderman's physician, Doctor Barnard, has laid the blame squarely on your nostrums, which were found at the bedside. He's

27

been denouncing you from the market cross this morning and pressed me to come here.'

'But that's absurd.'

'Be that as it may, I'll be having those potions.'

'You will not!'

'Look, just be grateful it's not the rest of your equipment. That's what Barnard's calling for.'

'But—'

'Come on, upstairs.' The constable turned to the men. 'And you lot make yourselves scarce. There'll be more than bricks coming through your windows if Josiah Armstrong gets to hear of this.'

In the consulting room, Charlie gathered his bottles and placed them carefully in their wooden carrying case.

'You know there's nothing in them really,' he sighed, 'nothing that could do any harm.'

'Now ain't that a surprise.' The constable reached out for the box.

Just then there were footsteps behind them.

'Thank you, Dawson, but I'm afraid you have been misinformed.'

In the doorway stood a portly man in his early fifties. He had a head of thick black hair with flashes of grey above the ears. His eyes bulged slightly and his nose was heavily veined.

'Alderman Thomson!' The constable was disconcerted.

'Indeed, hearing of your commission from Doctor Barnard, I thought I had better come and set the record straight.'

'I don't understand.'

'I am here to vouch for this gentleman's merchandise. I purchased the very same elixirs as Alderman Crompton and, like him, I have used them for several days. I can tell you that I have suffered no ill effects whatsoever and the alderman himself mentioned how beneficial they were proving. I'd have thought you'd have known better than to waste your time listening to Barnard's ramblings. It's him who needs taking in hand, not Doctor Rossi.'

'Well—'

'The Corporation is very grateful for the attentive pursuit of your duties. I trust that this' – he proffered a handful of coins – 'will more than compensate for your troubles.'

'When you put it like that...'

'I am in your debt.'

'Think nothing of it.' Thomson stepped onto the glass footstool. 'I apologise for my late arrival, only Alderman Crompton's death has required various adjustments to my diary.'

'I understand.' Charlie began charging up the Leyden jar.

Thomson watched the glass as it span. 'Barnard is a pest and a bore. I fear that he wages something of a crusade against anything that does not conform to his understanding of good physic. You are not the first to fall foul of his bigotry. Sadly, he takes it as a personal slight that Robert and I, and no doubt others of his patients, have been prepared to stray from his fold.'

'I see.' Charlie stood beside the alderman holding the glass conducting rods.

'Since my first two electrifications, I must confess that these damnable headaches have been noticeably less disabling. My wife is of the view that they are also less frequent. I do believe that there may be some merit in this thing after all.'

Charlie said nothing.

Thomson looked round. 'I suppose you must be wondering about that little charade with Dawson.'

'I don't deny it.'

'True, I may not have purchased any of your elixir but that's no reason to grant Barnard satisfaction. Besides, I find myself in further need of your assistance.'

'In what way?'

'It is a delicate matter. One on which I know that I can rely on your complete discretion.'

'Of course.'

'As a cloth merchant, business takes me away from home, sometimes for weeks at a time. You will understand, as a medical gentleman, the needs that must be satisfied if a man is to remain healthy and his mind is not to become unbalanced.' Charlie nodded but said nothing. 'Well, I fear that I have contracted something… unsavoury. I do not relish the reaction should Doctor Barnard learn of it. He is quite the puritan in all aspects of his life and he expects the same standards of the rest of us.'

As might your wife, thought Charlie, placing the rods on Thomson's neck.

'Well, Alderman, I am due a delivery of mercury in the next few days, although I will first need to electrify it in order to remove the worst of its less pleasant effects.'

Thomson scowled. 'Keep your twaddle for the plebs. It's just the mercury I need – and your silence. And for that I'll keep Barnard off your back.'

Red Hall stood near the edge of town, just inside the western toll bar. As Charlie approached, three stories of glassy eyes glowered at him from its red brick face – twenty windows on the front alone and not one of them bricked up. Putting his hand to his purse, he felt the few coins within. When the window tax barely registered in this empire of cloth, his rent seemed an utter irrelevance.

He raised his hand to the knocker but it swung away from him. Sarah Armstrong stood in the doorway, dressed in a thick coat and hood, and carrying a yellow patterned umbrella.

'Doctor Rossi – how delightful! Please do come in.'

As he stepped into the hallway, she bestowed on him a very solicitous smile.

'And how does your practice fare?'

He suddenly felt the need to confide. 'Thank you for asking. It begins moderately well, though today I have received something of a shock.'

'Ah, that would be to do with our dear Doctor Barnard, I suppose.'

'So you have heard.'

'Unfortunately I had reason to be in the vicinity of the cross this morning. I do wish it were possible to enjoy our market without being forced to endure his tedious opinions. Ours is a society where we are free to seek healing wherever we can find it. It is hardly as if our established physicians are able to offer much hope to the sick and dying. So why should we not look for help wherever it may be offered? He calls you a quack but only because he is afraid that you will draw patients away from him.'

He had rarely heard his views on the subject put so succinctly.

'However,' she continued, 'not content with slandering you in public, I fear that members of the Corporation have also received a letter from him. It is in my husband's study. Would you care to see it?'

She led the way upstairs to a large room that overlooked the street. It was sumptuously decorated, lined with heavily laden bookshelves, and dominated by a large oil painting of Josiah Armstrong, who stared down at the two of them from above the fireplace. She handed him the letter, leaning in towards him. Even in his agitated state he was all too aware of the delicate perfume surrounding her and the subtle colour of her skin. He tried to focus on the paper.

Barnard came straight to the point. His patient, Robert Crompton, one of their esteemed body, who had been in more or less perfect health, had been found dead in bed with a bottle of medicine beside him. According to Crompton's widow this had been bought at Rossi's first lecture and her husband had been taking it daily. It was without doubt the cause of his good friend's sudden and premature death. He therefore urged the Corporation to ban "this newly arrived electrical charlatan".

'Damn him!' Charlie cursed. The whole thing was ridiculous but gossip spread and mud stuck.

'Do not overly concern yourself with Doctor Barnard,' urged Mrs Armstrong. 'We are well used to him and his views in this town, and I doubt that many in the Corporation will take heed of his letter.'

Her smile was warm but he was increasingly conscious of the watchful gaze of her husband from the wall above.

'I came to settle my account for the coming week.'

'I am sorry but my husband is away in Wakefield. I am afraid that you will need to call again but it will always be a pleasure to see you, Doctor Rossi.'

***

Alderman Thomson sat at his study desk, updating his accounts. They were well overdue but he had been particularly busy. Trade was booming.

He looked up. His wife, Ann, had entered the study.

'George, I apologise for the interruption but you will recall that I shall be staying at the Forsyth's this evening.'

'Of course, my dear. Please give my regards to your cousin. I do hope that she has fully recovered from her palsy.'

'Oh, surely or she would not have invited me for cards. Her offer of a bed through the winter season is especially kind.'

'Indeed it is. Do thank her most sincerely for me.'

'You won't work too hard – you know how you suffer.'

'I know, my dear. But this new treatment does appear to be having some effect. It is just as well, for I have much to occupy me.'

He bent his head to his ledger. For a few seconds the only sound was the scratch of his quill. Then the door clicked to. Thomson smiled to himself. Yes, he had plenty to occupy him this evening.

***

'I'm wasting my time.'

'It can't have been that bad.' Sam Tinker passed him a pot of ale. 'Get that down you, Charlie, and you'll be right as rain.'

'No, just look at it.' He picked pieces of eggshell out of his hair. 'They'd heard the rumours and took the first opportunity. I knew it would be a rough night so I tried some new experiments but – I don't know – my mind just wasn't on it.'

'There's always tomorrow.'

'Aye, and the next day and the one after that, and all the while I'm fighting a losing battle. I've got the smart-arse travelling philosophers over here, queering my pitch with their la-di-da lecture series and the likes of Belteshazzar over there, fleecing everyone in sight. To be honest, I don't have either the knowledge or the showmanship. Not when folks are either wanting enlightenment or a damn good show.'

'And your lectures give them a bit of both. What's wrong with that?'

'Lectures!' He laughed bitterly. 'They're nothing more than a recruiting drum. It's the treatments that pay.'

'So you have to keep doing them.'

'And don't I know it!'

Sam meant well but, tonight, his relentless cheerfulness grated on him. He needed some space. He made his excuses.

The street was quiet, apart from a few sedan chairs making for the Assembly Rooms. Otherwise people were still in the taverns. He walked past them – the Leopard, the White Hart, the Boy and Barrel, the Bull and Mouth. They kept coming, lining Briggate like a row of stitches; a seam running up the centre of the town, joining it together. Or were they stopping it tearing itself apart?

Outside the Talbot, an elderly man stumbled as a broken paving stone tipped up and he fell face down in the gutter. Charlie helped him to his feet.

'God bless you, young man. And, to make sure he does, I'll buy you a drink.'

He tried to protest but the man grabbed his sleeve and dragged him back inside the inn. It was packed to the gunnels, the air thick with smoke and the stench of unwashed bodies.

'It's a re-match of the Wars of the Roses,' explained the landlady, cryptically, as she filled him a pot. Charlie frowned. 'You know, love, Lancashire and Yorkshire, only this time it's with armies of cocks.' She winked.

He turned to see, in the corner of the bar, two birds fighting for their lives. One had its beak dug into an eye. The other was lashing wildly with a spike-armoured foot. The cheering got louder. The half-blinded bird collapsed under a frenzy of stabs and slashes. It writhed, then twitched, then lay still. The victor pecked away at the bloodied head as cheers rang out and the lucky punters clamoured for their winnings.

'That's nowt but the first skirmish,' observed the old man. 'They'll wait till we're legless before the real battles begin. Saturday night prize – thirty guineas a time. Purse strings'll be loose enough by then. Are you in?'

He pulled a face. 'No, go ahead. I've had my fill of that.' The man disappeared into the throng, coin raised high in the air.

Life was precarious enough without stepping into that old snare. This time would be different. There would be no more debts.

He left his half-full pot on the bar and went back into the street. A few yards away, a young woman was being pestered by two men. Drawing closer he realised that he had seen the long hair and fierce expression once before: in the office of the *Mercury*. Tonight her anger was directed not at a hapless newspaper clerk but at the men who were manoeuvring her towards the deeper darkness of a side alley.

Charlie Rossi's natural gallantry didn't give his equally natural lack of bravado time to think. Coming up behind the men, he called out a challenge and grabbed one of them by the arm. The man spun and crunched a right hook into his eye, dropping him to the cobbles. A boot cracked into his ribs, then his shoulder. Pain seared through his body. The second man looked round and in that moment the woman took her chance. She brought her knee up viciously into his groin and the man crumpled to the ground. Then she gripped the shoulder of the other, who was still off balance from kicking Charlie, and drove his head into the rough brick wall.

Three men lay groaning on the pavement.

The woman bent down. 'Are you alright?'

'Never felt better.' Charlie tried to wink.

She laughed and walked calmly away down the street. Through his one good eye, he watched as she turned a corner and was gone.

**

George Thomson arched his back and slowly rotated his neck. The rest of the accounts would have to wait. Three hours earlier, he had summoned the domestic staff and given them the evening off. By now they would be lying somewhere in a drunken stupor, or shamelessly rutting among the tenter frames. He found the thought both arousing and mildly repulsive.

He closed the ledger, placed it back on the shelf and made his way downstairs. Opposite the front door stood his father's longcase clock. He watched as, almost imperceptibly, the hands approached the hour. He let his breathing settle into the soporific rhythm of the pendulum. One by one, he cracked his fingers. The clock began to chime.

A gentle rap on the knocker.

Pain stabbed at his temple. Clutching at the door handle, he swore under his breath. Bloody timing. The spasm passed and he turned the knob.

**

Beth Tinker looked up from filling a tankard as her new tenant staggered into the tavern. Her good-natured face couldn't disguise the steel in her eyes, which along with her ample frame and immaculate cloth cap and apron, proclaimed to the world that here was someone who could look after herself – and others.

On balance she preferred the 'drowned rat' look of Charlie's first night's arrival. His left eye was swollen and discoloured, he was holding his side gingerly and his other arm hung awkwardly. To add to that, he reeked of something, animal or human. She suspected it was both. Even her more inebriated customers moved aside to avoid any contact with this gutter rat.

'My, you're a pretty one.' She laughed, but there was kindness in her face.

She led him up to his room. 'Get your clothes off and I'll be back.'

A few minutes later, she kicked open the door as she carried in a bowl of water and a pot of ale. Charlie was grunting and groaning, in a feeble attempt to unbutton his shirt. She shook her head.

'Look at the state of you.'

She stripped him to the waist, pulled off his stockings and then grabbed the top of his britches.

'Hang on, Beth.'

'Don't worry, love, there's nowt in a pair of these that I've not seen a hundred times. I doubt you've got owt to surprise me.' And with that she yanked them off.

'These'll all need a good wash before they see the light of day again. And so will you.'

She began to examine him. The eye was closing up rapidly.

'That's going to need some attention, but I don't think your arm's broken.' She pressed on his ribs and he winced. 'And these are going to be painful for a fair while but there's nowt much me or anyone can do for them.'

She set to, carefully cleaning his face before washing down the rest of him. Producing a small pot of ointment, she began to rub it gently into the swelling around the eye.

'What's in it?' he asked.

'It's a preparation my mother passed down to me. And it came from her mother before that – her own mixture of plants and herbs. It'll take the swelling out of this eye as fast as owt I know.'

'Fast enough that I don't have to shut up shop for a few days?'
She raised an eyebrow.

'It's not the pain, or even my vanity' – he grinned – 'it's people consulting a black-eyed doctor who gets into brawls. I don't think that's likely to do my already fragile standing in this community any good.'

Beth smiled in return. 'Aye, love, you might have a point.'

She turned her attention to his chest and arm. While she worked, she listened as he told the brief tale.

'Sounds to me like they picked on one of our ladies of the night,' she observed.

'Not unless she's taken to advertising her services in the papers,' he replied dryly. 'I saw her at the *Mercury* a few days back. And she'd been giving the clerk there a hard time as well.'

'Well she knows how to handle herself, that's for sure. Those fellows will think twice next time. Mind you, it might've been a different story if you hadn't turned up.'

He sipped at his drink, washing away the foul taste of the street, while Beth stood back to assess her work.

'You'll live, though you won't be looking your best for a few days, which reminds me: I don't know what you did to Sam the other night, love, but whatever it were can I have the recipe?'

He laughed, a little gingerly. 'I can do better than that, Beth. I'll electrify you as well.'

Now it was her turn to laugh. 'Just you be careful, Charlie Rossi, or you'll be earning yourself a reputation.'

'I got one of those long ago.'

***

When the Thomsons' young maid entered her master's study the next morning, the room felt colder than usual. She moved with practised, almost instinctive, care through the darkened room to draw back the thick curtains and pull down the sash window. As she gazed into the garden, she saw, not the rain or the blackbird enjoying its hard-won breakfast, but the face of her young man pressed close to hers under the trees the night before. She relived their lips exploring each other and Seth's work-roughened hand against her nipple. She remembered the warm stirrings within and how he had pressed against her. But she had kept her head. If he really liked her, he could wait. She closed her eyes and tried to imagine how it would feel to let him enter her.

She turned from the window and let out a gasp, not of anticipated ecstasy but of shock. It was not unknown for her master to fall asleep at his desk but his presence in the room made her jump all the same. There had been none of the normal snuffles and snores. He was sitting in his chair, with his head resting back on his neck, his thick, dark hair dishevelled. She moved quietly around the desk to the door and then looked back. Had she disturbed him?

Bulging eyes stared through her, unseeing. A swollen blue mass of tongue protruded from his mouth, half bitten through near the base. Her master's face was a rigid mask of pain.

Her knees crumbled beneath her and she dropped to the floor, screaming.

4

'So where d'you get that name then?' Sam stretched his legs out. 'It ain't exactly Yorkshire.'

Charlie's head rested back against the courtyard wall, his eyes closed. The air in the yard was cold and crisp but, after two sleepless nights propped up in bed, he was glad of a chance to be outside. The winter sunlight bathed his upturned face.

'Come on,' coaxed Sam.

He sighed. 'My father was from Florence.'

'And?' Sam prodded him, playfully, in the ribs.

He yelped. '*And* he went to Edinburgh.'

'Why on earth would he want to do that?'

Charlie gave up and opened his eyes. 'Is there no end to your damned inquisitiveness? Because, it just happens to be the best place in all of Europe to train as a physician.'

'And he never went back – that'd be your mother then.'

'Aye.'

'The same old story, I suppose: brilliant Italian doctor swept off his feet by poor local beauty and so besotted that he barely managed to qualify.'

'Something like that.'

'Well, he must have been right proud of you, following in his shoes.'

Charlie didn't reply.

'Is that where you trained?'

Silence again.

'Charlie?'

'What?'

'Edinburgh?'

He studied his pot of ale. 'Aye, but… well, it didn't end happily.'

'You didn't finish?'

He snorted. 'I barely got started! My God it was mind-numbing. It was just a bunch of old farts, regurgitating dead traditions from a past age. And, anyway, a big part of me was there for something else.'

Sam grinned. 'Like father like son, hey?'

'Not exactly. A bit more… commercial.'

'Ah.'

'Except that I fell for one of them.'

'You wouldn't be the first.'

The back door opened and Beth's scowling face appeared.

'In case you've forgotten, Samuel Tinker, we've a tavern to run and a barrel what needs changing. And I'll thank you, Mr Rossi,' she glowered, as Sam slunk inside, 'not to encourage him.'

Charlie shrugged and closed his eyes again.

She had been three years his elder but thirty more experienced. He could still hear Helen laughing at him.

'You're sweet, but what I need is a gentleman of means, not some poor medical student. I need someone who'll set me up in a little place, where I can keep the bed warm for when he gets away from his wife.' The laughter turned bitter as she stepped into her skirts and pulled them up. 'But that's just a whore's fancy.'

'No it's not. You'll see. Once I have my own practice I'll have all the money you'll need.'

'Pah!' She shook her head in disdain. 'More like I'll be dead of the pox before you can even read a piss-pot.' Her eyes flared. 'And what good'll your fine medicine be to me then?'

And he knew she was right: what was the point of all this drudgery if he couldn't even save her?

He walked out of the brothel, crossed the street and stepped into a gambling den. To win her or to lose himself? He didn't know, didn't care. A cacophony of voices embraced him and drew him in. He pressed against the tight ruck of bodies and slowly they yielded. As he stood in the centre, he looked into the faces around him and saw ecstasy, excitement, terror, despair. He thought of the students sleeping through lectures.

These people are alive. This really matters to them.

He knew the bet was a waste of money; he couldn't even tell the two black mastiffs apart.

'Well, aren't you the lucky one,' shouted the purse-man over the din. 'You'll be robbin' me blind soon.'

The man dropped coins into his palm. Not many. Just enough to hook him.

His allowance lasted all of a month; his friends not much longer. All but destitute, he knew there would be no prodigal's return. He couldn't face his parents after all the sacrifices they had made. So he went back to the benches in the lecture hall. He found a few "gentlemen of independent fortunes", who had better things to do with their time and far more money to do it with. He started taking notes for them and so, finally, began to learn a little of his chosen profession.

But then the letter from home arrived and everything changed.

'And how's our injured soldier.' Beth breezed into his room the next morning.

He slowly levered himself up in bed. 'All the better for seeing you.' He grimaced as a stab of pain shot through his ribs.

She bent down to begin the daily examination of her patient.

'Well, that arm's on the mend and I guess your ribs'll get there by Easter.'

'And my eye?'

'Oh it's fine.' She waved away the question, her eyes fixed firmly on his torso.

He frowned. 'Is something the matter, Beth?'

'No, it's healing up nicely, love. It'll be right as rain in a few days' time.'

'Come on, not my eye – me. Is anything wrong?'

She looked up; concern now written on her face. 'Aye, well, I don't know how to say this, Charlie, but another of your patients has gone and popped his clogs.'

'What?' He swung his legs off the bed. 'Who?'

'George Thomson.'

'Thomson!'

'I know, love. He were found in his study the other morning and Barnard's been going for you, all guns blazing.'

'But I haven't sold him a bottle of anything… well, not yet.'

Beth shook her head. 'It ain't your tinctures, love. He's blaming that thing you do with your machine and he's hollering for you to be driven out of town.'

She rested her hand on his knee. His eyes burned into the floorboards. His chest rose and fell at speed. He pushed her hand away.

'Where do I find him?'

***

'Is he in?'

The maid's mouth flapped soundlessly.

'Barnard, is he at home?'

'Y-y-yes, sir, he is.'

'Tell him I want to see him.'

She recovered herself. 'Do you have an appointment, sir?'

'No I do not. Please inform him that Doctor Charles Rossi is here.'

42

He stepped up onto the threshold and she backed away.

'Well, I don't know… I suppose… if you would wait in here.'
She showed him into the parlour.

From the street, the house had been grander than he was
expecting for a provincial physician, but this room was simply
decorated and sparsely furnished with rough floorboards, a few,
almost threadbare, chairs and a modest table. On it sat the only
thing of real beauty in the room – a brass orrery. However, in no
mood to admire anything of Barnard's, he stood at the window,
watching a steady parade of wigs and bonnets pass by.

Behind him, door hinges squeaked and he turned to see the
thin, elongated figure of Henry Barnard. Cautiously, the physician
began to circle around him, weighing him up. Charlie turned slowly
on the spot, returning his stare.

The state of the man's clothes matched the chairs. His hair was
close-cropped for a wig, accentuating the sunken bones of his skull.
His long nose came to a precise point, while his pale eyes looked
equally sharp.

Barnard reacted first.

'My God, sir you have a nerve coming here. And look at you.
Have you taken up as a street fighter as well as a charlatan?'

Charlie spat his reply. 'If you must know I gained this' – he
touched his cheek bone – 'coming to the defence of a lady. But it is
you who have the nerve. By what right do you defame me in public
and libel me to the Corporation? Why are you so determined to
accuse me of murder, not once but twice? Who do you think you are?'

'I'll tell you who I am. I am the physician of Robert Crompton
and George Thomson. I am the one who had to examine their bodies
and comfort their widows. I, above all people, know that they were
in fine health until they began flirting with your quackery. And
now, within days they both lie dead.'

'So, did I poison them? Did I strike them down with lightning?
You have absolutely no evidence whatsoever for your charges and
yet you see fit to ruin me.'

'You talk of evidence but it is you who are in complete want of it. Where is there any evidence, even a shred, that this charade you perform is anything more than a vulgar and dangerous deception? And don't think to bamboozle me with your testimonies. You may seduce others with them but I know them for the worthless fictions they are.'

'What? You choose to ignore dozens of practitioners, decades of treatment and thousands of patients, all to preserve your status and your income?'

'Ha! The same old tune. You complain of slander and libel but it is you who defame the true physicians; you who libel us, who insult our knowledge, our competence, our integrity.'

'But it's true. You purge, you blister, you bleed and for what reason? Nothing but tradition. And how many have died from your blood-lettings? Tell me that. And you study piss-pots and cups of blood, and to what effect? Can you save more than a fortunate few? No sir, you cannot. You are as impotent in the face of illness as the ancients were and yet you resent those of us who offer people new hope.'

'Hope! What hope do their widows have? I treated their husbands for years – years I say – and they were both in vigorous health. You treat them for a matter of days and they drop dead. What other conclusion do you expect people to draw?'

'Vigorous health! You don't know the half of it. Thomson was incapacitated with headaches. Not to mention the pox.'

'How dare you!' retorted Barnard.

'Ha! You didn't know that, did you? You'd be the last one he'd tell, with your narrow-minded ways. And who's to say about Crompton? What else didn't you know? Or...' Charlie raised his finger as the possibility dawned, 'what *did* you know? Treating him for something else were you? Worried your own prescriptions might be at fault? And how convenient for you: a travelling quack arrives, just in time to take the blame.'

'That is a vicious slander!' exploded Barnard. 'I'll have you before the Quarterly Sessions for that. You speak of passing the blame, but it is you who bear it and the whole town knows it. No, sir, you have been exposed, at a terrible cost, but exposed nonetheless. When the Corporation meets again, have no doubt – you will be barred before any more fall victim to your damned quackery.'

'So that's what it comes down to, is it? Your patients die all the time, of illness or your own incompetence, but no one sues you or arrests you. Yet because of these two pillars of the community, and some warped vision of yours, I'm to be hounded out of town. Well, you will not be rid of me that easily. I shall not go without a fight. Be sure of that.'

'Indeed not. It is clear that you make a habit of it.'

Despite himself, Charlie clenched his fist.

'Henry?'

Charlie turned to see a thin, plainly dressed woman standing in the doorway. A young, blond-haired boy peered out from behind her skirts. She looked startled; shocked at the strident voices and unseemly conversation.

He strode past her. 'I was fighting' – he flung the words back into the room – 'for the honour of a woman.'

Barnard snarled: 'And I think we can imagine what sort.'

Charlie was still seething when he got to the market cross.

This was no good. He had to calm down. The Cromptons' home was only a few minutes away and he was going to need all his charm if he did manage to speak to the widow.

He turned into St John's church and sat down at the back. Pale sunlight streaked through the leaded windows, picking out motes of dust as they drifted in the gently stirring air. He watched his breath take shape in the cold of the nave and then fade away.

Damn it, Barnard wasn't going to get the better of him. He wouldn't – he couldn't – give up. The echoes of the past were too disturbing. And they were all around him – even here with the lion and the unicorn looking down from the painted chancel screen. He remembered the rhyme from his childhood: the Scottish unicorn beaten out of town by the English lion.

And when he had beat him out,
He beat him in again;
He beat him three times over,
His power to maintain.

His father had let himself be beaten out of their Northumberland village. He wasn't going to let it happen to him.

He didn't really blame his father for leaving. It was his patients. Of course, wracked by grief and guilt, his father had more often than not been in his cups but they should have tried to understand. After all he had done for them, they should have made allowances. Instead, they closed their all-so-respectable ranks. He could picture them, one by one, settling their accounts and walking away from his father's door to take their custom elsewhere. And then – the memory was still too vivid – arriving back from Edinburgh, to find his father a broken man: shunned and humiliated, with his confidence in shreds. He had tried to persuade him to begin a new practice elsewhere but it was a lost cause. Within a fortnight they were in Newcastle and all his father would take on was shoemaking – his own father's profession. It hadn't lasted long.

The rage was rising again.

He needed to get it back in its box, or at least channel it, if his precarious practice wasn't going to collapse even faster than his father's.

He shivered. Was this supposed to be a place of peace? If so, it was eluding him. He needed to get going. But his eyes still followed the shimmering dust. The light bathed him and a faint warmth spread over him.

What would his mother have said?

He tried to picture her but these days it was like looking through a sea fret. How could you lose your grasp on the face of someone you loved so much? He searched for the lullaby that she never gave up singing and caught a snatch of her voice. And then her mouth became clear – the gentle turn of lips as she smiled. Her eyes sparkled into life and she was looking at him. She opened her mouth to speak. They would be words of encouragement as always.

Then her face dissolved into Helen's and her voice into bitter laughter.

'Well, Mr Rossi. I must confess that this is a somewhat unexpected visit.'

Mary Crompton was not exactly what he had been expecting either. In a fine black gown with lace trimmings, she sat erect on a fashionable and brightly patterned settee. Her eyes suggested a keen intelligence but no outward sense of grief. Her demeanour seemed less one of mourning than of dignified pride. Sitting across from her on a matching settee, he noted the lack of his medical title but was at least grateful for the lack of open hostility.

'I appreciate that, madam. Nevertheless, I wanted to express my sincere condolences to you.'

Mary Crompton bowed her head slightly. 'I thank you for them. Yet there are not a few in this town who would be surprised that I have even allowed you through the door of my house.'

'Given the accusation levelled against me, I would not have been surprised, so I appreciate your graciousness in speaking with me. However, I wish to assure you that my preparation could, in no way, have contributed to your husband's sudden and untimely death.'

'Again, Mr Rossi, there are those who would ask how you can be so certain of your claim. Doctor Barnard is full of tales of other medications that have brought on similar, premature deaths.'

Her tone was almost teasing. Was he already a figure of fun?

'Without wearying you with the details of my remedy for the

gout, I can assure you that it has been widely used for several years and there has been not the slightest complaint from even one of my patients.'

Mary Crompton smiled openly at this. 'Indeed, I am sure that you are able to supply some very eloquent testimonies on its behalf.'

He took that on the chin.

'Compared to your grief, madam, the predicament I find myself in is as nothing, and yet it is difficult and delicate nonetheless. My integrity, reputation and livelihood are all under threat from accusations for which there is no evidence yet against which I find it hard to defend myself. I am as yet unknown in this town and my word counts for little, whereas Doctor Barnard is well known to you all. But is familiarity to be the arbiter of truth? Surely, in an age of enlightenment, we should look to facts not reputations.'

She dipped her head. 'A point well made.'

He felt encouraged. 'Mrs Crompton, Doctor Barnard has claimed that your husband was in perfect health, whereas I find myself wondering whether, in fact, this was the case. Forgive me, I appreciate that this may seem an intrusive question, but was there anything else which ailed him; something, perhaps, for which he had been receiving treatment?'

Mary Crompton regarded him thoughtfully.

'So you seek your salvation at the expense of our physician.'

'I can assure you, that is not my intent. I seek only to restore my own reputation. I do not desire his ruin, only the truth.'

'Although if your adversary were to suffer as a consequence you would not object.'

He looked down at the rug. 'Mrs Crompton, please – are you able to help me? Can you tell me anything which might shed light on your husband's sad demise?'

'Well, now, there was his gout of course. It could be most debilitating at times, though I don't recall ever hearing of it as a *fatal* condition. Oh, and the doctor was most assiduous in administering bleedings but he was always careful to leave Mr Crompton with more than enough in reserve.'

He looked up. Was she still playing with him?

'Apart from that... no, I'm afraid there was nothing. My husband was in as sound health as the doctor has claimed.' She picked up the bell from the side table. 'I fear, Mr Rossi, that you have wasted your time.'

He was still nursing his disappointment when he arrived at the Thomsons' house in Upper Head Row. As the door opened, he glimpsed a long black dress scurrying up the wide, ballustraded staircase, accompanied by the sound of sobbing.

At the mention of his name, the maid's eyes widened. She said nothing but, when she went to find her mistress, she left him waiting outside on the step. A few moments later, from round the back of the house a large woman with a shining, almost red, complexion appeared carrying a pair of wicker baskets. She paused for a moment, scowled ferociously at him, then snapped her head away and flounced off down the street.

He tapped away at the wrought iron boot scraper.

The girl returned. She was not smiling.

'Mrs Thomson is not at home to visitors.'

'Might I call again at a more convenient time?'

'I'm afraid not.'

'I wish only to extend my deepest sympathy to her.'

'My mistress will not be able to entertain you.'

'But, if—'

The door closed in his face. He took hold of the knocker again, then let it drop. He stood looking at the handle. His hopes, faint as they had been, had evaporated in a matter of minutes.

What could he hope to do now? Brazen it out or bow to the inevitable?

He turned away. A few yards up the street stood the Armstrongs' many-paned house. It reminded him, now, of the eye of a spider he had once seen through his father's microscope. This one was far from dead but had watched over his abject humiliation.

Well, he might as well make it complete.

Josiah Armstrong's portrait looked down at Charlie from the study wall but the man himself had not deigned to look up from his desk.

This whole arrangement was about rubbing his nose in it. It was like standing in front of his headmaster, waiting for the tawse. Well, he'd waited long enough.

'I've come to hand you my—'

'Ha!' Armstrong's smile was no more than a baring of teeth. 'It didn't take long for them to find you out, did it? The whole damned lot of you are nothing but a bunch of quacks but you really have excelled them all. Two dead in a week: is that your normal rate of success?'

Charlie clenched his teeth.

Armstrong took in his tenant's now yellowing eye. 'And I see it's not only my windows that people have been smashing.'

'I was coming to the aid of a lady.'

The merchant waved away the words. 'I couldn't care less what you were doing but you're a bloody fool. It's all grist to Barnard's mill. God knows what the Corporation's going to make of you. Or perhaps you're here to save us the trouble. Off to fleece easier sheep, are you? Well, it'll still cost you a week's rent plus one to cover damages.'

That did it. Something snapped.

'The Corporation can do what it bloody well likes, but I'm going nowhere. I may have been forced to suspend my practice but I will be resuming it forthwith and, rest assured, I will establish myself in this town, regardless of the calumnies made against me. And as an earnest of my success' – he slammed his purse down on the desk – 'a month's rent in advance. Truth will out!' He turned on his heels.

'Suit yourself.' Armstrong snorted and returned to his ledger.

Before he reached the front door, Charlie was already ruing his action. What was he thinking? He was only pouring good money after bad. He swore under his breath.

'Doctor Rossi.' Sarah Armstrong had come up behind him.

He closed his eyes for a moment and then, turning, bowed with the best smile he could muster. 'Mrs Armstrong.'

'How pleasant. Would you be so kind as to accompany me into town?'

Courtesy had its demands. He walked a while beside her in broody silence.

'Things do not improve for you, I hear. And doubtless my husband does not help matters.' She lightly touched his arm.

Charlie turned towards her. He was struck again by her warmth, her perceptiveness. What was she doing married to such an objectionable man?

He sighed. 'In truth, his opinions are the least of my concerns. I have spent the morning in a fruitless attempt to rebut the accusations against me.'

She raised her eyebrows. 'Is that so? By what means?'

'I had hopes of finding a perfectly rational reason for these deaths: some hidden illness perhaps, or another treatment gone awry. Anything that would allow me to defend my reputation and livelihood.'

'But without success?'

He snorted. 'Robert Crompton, so his wife informs me, was in fine health and Mrs Thomson won't even entertain me, though I can't blame her for that – the man who killed her husband.'

Sarah shook her head. 'No, Ann is understandably distraught but I doubt that in her heart she really holds you responsible.'

'You know the family?'

'A little – we are neighbours after all.'

'And did Mr Thomson keep in good health?'

She thought for a moment. 'You will understand that I wasn't privy to his confidences but I never heard him – or Ann – speak of anything. I'm sorry, Doctor, if that is of little comfort to you.'

He shrugged.

She smiled sympathetically. 'But please do not trouble yourself unduly. I am sure that these deaths were merely a most unfortunate coincidence and I trust that the sensible folk of Leeds will see them in the same way.'

They reached the corner of Vicar Lane and Sarah Armstrong said goodbye, leaving him a little brighter for the encounter. However, as he approached his practice rooms, on the ground, torn almost in two, lay the notice announcing the suspension of his lectures. Most of the writing had been obliterated by an ink-black bolt of lightning, zigzagging down to a tombstone that bore the words: "Dr Rossi – RIP".

He scowled. So much for sensible folk.

Stepping on the paper, he twisted his boot down into the dirt.

The handbill at the White Swan was still there. Well, it might take his mind off things. Besides, he needed a drink.

The landlord, a man of enormous height and girth, nodded Charlie a greeting and silently filled him a pot. He settled into a corner seat determined to enjoy it at a leisurely pace. After a few minutes he caught the man's eye.

'That's good ale.'

'Aye, I know.'

'You may be able to help me. I am looking for a young lady with dark hair. I think she could be with the conjuror you've got here – the Belteshazzar fellow. Do you know where I can find her?'

'And who is it who wants to know?'

'Only someone who helped her out the other night in the street – I got this eye for my troubles. I'd just like to make sure that she wasn't hurt.'

The landlord smirked. 'I see. That's how it stands, is it? Well, if it *were* her, she's here with her father. Isabelle they call her. But, by heck, she's a fiery one and no mistake, so you go careful now.'

'Is she in?'

'She may be. I'll see if we can find her for you. Mary!' A teenage girl hurried in from the kitchen wiping her hands on her apron. 'Can you see if Miss Broussard's around? Tell her there's someone here wants to see her.'

The girl hurried off and was back in less than a minute.

'She's in the Long Room but, I'm sorry Mr Cross, she says she's busy.'

The landlord smiled wryly at Charlie. 'Like I said – but go on if you like.'

Charlie downed the remains of his drink and the landlord's voice followed him through the door: 'Good luck!'

The room was at least twice as large as his own lecture room. Across its width, at the far end, lay a low wooden stage and perched on the front edge, holding a pistol, was Isabelle Broussard. She was looking along the length of the barrel, which was pointing just above his head.

She pulled the trigger.

He exhaled.

As she lowered her arm, she noticed him. 'Oh, it's you. I was kind of wondering.'

'Not enough to come and find out.'

She returned her attention to the pistol.

'If I knew you carried firearms I'd have saved myself the trouble.'

Her lips curled slightly but she didn't look up. 'I'm just getting it ready for tonight.'

She picked up a second pistol and began to work a small metal rod up and down inside the barrel.

'So what do you want?'

'Just to make sure you're alright. Those men must have given you a bit of a shock.'

'Not as big as the one I gave them.' Her eyes glinted.

He came forward to the front row of benches. 'May I?'

She shrugged.

He sat, watching her work. She wasn't exactly what he would

have called pretty: her features were too sharp, even hard and like the rest of her, her fingers were small and wiry. Yet even in this everyday task, their movements were rapid, forceful and full of intent. Her dark eyes were fixed on the pistol, as if daring it to resist her efforts. Here was a Leyden jar simply bursting with electrical fire.

She removed the rod and started polishing the pistol with a piece of cloth.

'How did you know where to find me?'

'I didn't but I saw you at the office of the *Mercury* last week, though I don't suppose you noticed. You only had eyes for the clerk.'

She tutted. 'Bloody idiot.'

'Then I noticed the handbill outside here. It seemed a fair bet and, hey, fortune smiled on me.' He grinned.

She didn't react.

Another silence.

'You certainly know how to look after yourself. Where did you learn to fight like that?'

'As a child – where I grew up you had to fend for yourself. No one else was going to.'

'London?' Her accent suggested it. She didn't reply so he continued. 'I guess you've come a long way since then. You could say that we're in similar lines: travelling and working an audience.'

She looked up quizzically.

'I'm an electrical healer: Charlie Rossi – or Doctor Rossi to the punters. I do beg your pardon' – he got to his feet – 'to the ladies and gentlemen of *distinction*.' He leant into a sweeping bow, only to freeze in a grimace of pain.

She shook her head, with a wry smile. He lowered himself back onto the bench.

'I give them a lecture or two on electricity and make sure that they get a bit of fun. And then, with any luck, some of them sign up for a course of treatment.'

'Ah,' she nodded. 'I've seen your puffs in the paper. You're the one who's been making a bit of a name for himself.'

'Aye, only it's the wrong sort of name.'

'It doesn't matter. It's all good publicity.'

'If only that were so.'

'Of course it is. You just have to know how to turn these things to your advantage. My father's had religious zealots accusing him of sorcery; magistrates charging him with vagrancy; and satirists taking the piss. All they end up doing is bringing out more people to find what the fuss is about.'

'That sounds fine but you weren't accused of killing two of your customers.'

'I'd polish some of mine off if I had the chance – the lecherous old sods.'

'Well these "sods" happen to be a pair of cloth merchants and both aldermen – pillars of the community apparently.'

She nodded grudgingly. 'That's a bit unfortunate for you.'

'You could say that. All I'd done was sell one of them something for gout and given the other a few electrifications.'

'There must be more to it than that.'

'I'm afraid there is: a lunatic physician whose sole purpose in life seems to be waging war against anything that smacks to him of quackery. Just at the moment that means ruining me.'

'Who's that then?'

'One Henry Barnard.'

She raised the gun again and pulled the trigger.

'The bastard.' She spat.

He was taken aback. 'You know him?'

'Never met the man but I wouldn't trust a physician – not if my life depended on it.'

'I don't know about that,' he reacted defensively. 'My father was a really good one. But you're right about most of them – they're little more than bigots and money-grabbers.'

'They're like dogs defending their territory.' She sneered. 'They piss on the walls of a town and say "Keep out!" to the likes of us.'

'That's about the sum of it.'

'So what are you going to do?'

'I don't know,' sighed Charlie. 'The whole thing's ridiculous. I'm mean, take the tincture: water, rum and herbs. How lethal can that be?'

'I think we must use the same supplier.' They exchanged a brief conspiratorial smile. 'What about the electricity?'

'Come on, I've seen your handbill. I won't be generating any more than your father is.'

'Alright, so the man doesn't know what he's talking about.'

'But if enough people believe him then I'm just going to have to cut my losses and move on.'

'You'll never get anywhere if you let people push you around. You have to stand your ground and you have to fight.'

'Don't you think I know it?' he snapped back.

They sat in silence for a few moments.

She pushed her hair behind her ears. 'I've got things to do.' She picked up a powder flask and began to load the muzzle.

It was time to leave. He rose from the bench. 'Well, I'm glad to see you've come to no harm.' He waited but she didn't look up. 'Goodbye, Miss Broussard.'

He was at the door when she spoke: 'The name's Isabelle. And thank you.'

'Now then.' Sam greeted him anxiously as he arrived back at the King's Head.

'Don't worry,' Charlie glowered, 'Barnard's still breathing… unfortunately. I didn't lay a finger on him.'

'Which is just as well,' grinned Sam, 'given your fighting ability. At least you've still only got the one black eye.'

'Ha, ha,' Charlie sneered and dropped into his usual settle.

Sam brought over some refreshment. 'Get that down your neck.'

'I don't know what got into me,' Charlie groaned. 'I mean, the man won't listen to reason. As soon as he opened his mouth, he was at me and then I couldn't help myself. What an idiot!' He banged his fist on the table. The other drinkers in the taproom looked round. 'I mean, why provoke him? I've only gone and made him more determined than ever to get me driven out of town. And to make matters worse I've chucked a month's rent at Armstrong just to prove a point.' He screwed up his face.

'So what now?' Sam asked.

'I don't know – hope the Corporation doesn't pay much heed to Barnard, I suppose.'

'They won't, not if they've got any sense. I mean, people die all the time. So what if two of them are your patients? It's just bad luck – a coincidence.'

'That's what Sarah Armstrong said.'

'Well, there you go.'

Charlie sipped slowly at his drink. 'And, when you come to think of it, there *are* quite a few coincidences here.'

'How d'you mean, Charlie?'

He leant forward. 'Like two deaths out of the blue – and they were also Barnard's patients, and both aldermen and cloth merchants. And they seemed to know each other pretty well.'

Sam frowned. 'That wouldn't be surprising now, would it? It's a small town. What are you getting at, Charlie?'

He sat back. 'Oh, I don't know – nothing. It's just getting to me.'

'Don't fret yourself. It'll blow over in a fortnight, you'll see.'

Charlie snorted. 'That's about all I've got.'

Sam pulled another face.

'Come on, Sam, you know what these newspapers are like: the worthies of Leeds being killed by a quack doctor? They'll have a field day. It'll be in London next week and round the provinces after that. No, Barnard's sticking his scalpel in good and proper. So, if I don't get the better of him soon, the glorious medical career will be well and truly buggered.' He shook his head. 'And God only knows what I'll do then.'

5

The shot shattered the silence, then the wine glass. A woman screamed.

'Madame, calm yourself. Bella is unharmed, as you can see. My dear…' Louis Broussard beckoned his daughter to the front of the stage.

Isabelle plucked the bullet from between her teeth and held it out, along with the remnants of the glass, for the audience's inspection.

'I'd love a shot at you.' The man made as if to take the bullet but grabbed Isabelle round the waist and pulled her towards him. She ruffled his hair with a wink. The man licked his lips. Dropping a shard of glass under him, she pressed him back into his seat.

'So you see, my friends, that the powers of magic can be harnessed for our protection. And now, through the hands of Belteshazzar, those same forces will be channelled for your healing. Which of you here tonight is in pain? It only needs a little warmth to release this mysterious energy.' Her father rubbed his hands together as a woman came forward. 'Come, allow me…'

A neck, an elbow, various knees, a back – all were presented, all declared to be wonderfully improved. Each time, the audience sent up a great cheer.

A large, middle-aged woman, wobbled drunkenly to the stage.

'And where is the pain, Madame?'

She grinned a vast, almost toothless, grin and pointed to her breasts.

'Get your hands on them!' the audience hooted.

He smiled patiently and sent her back to her seat.

'Shame!'

He signalled for silence. 'Tonight, my friends, you have been witnesses to the healing hands of Belteshazzar. Although the effects may wear off, you can purchase from me, in a few minutes, tinctures and medicines of lasting effect, the like of which will not be seen in this town for many years to come.'

'Oh aye, just like the last man!'

'But now it is my pleasure to reveal to you something truly miraculous. And for this I must tell you a story so strange that it will demand your greatest faith.'

This drew loud and exaggerated 'Oohs' from the audience.

'When I was still a young man I travelled throughout the Ottoman Empire. Those are dark and dangerous lands and time does not allow me to tell of all the hazards that I faced. After many weeks, I came upon an unending and ferocious desert, surrounded by barren and impassable mountains. For two days my lips did not touch water and I gave up hope of life itself. But then in the distance a beautiful oasis unfolded before me. Such are the deceptions which heat and thirst can play that, at first, I did not dare to believe my eyes. However, this was no mirage and I fell into those blessed pools with joy. I bathed for hours in their cool waters and from the palms I fed on the sweetest of fruits.'

'You didn't want to feed on mine,' shouted the woman with the toothless grin, to much laughter.

'I stayed there for a day and a night but the purpose of my journey weighed upon me. So I filled my meagre supply of gourds and prepared to leave that little paradise on Earth. I had only travelled for an hour or two when I came upon a man lying beside the trail, on the verge of death. He wore a robe, the like of which I had never seen. It was black and woven through with threads of gold, tracing pictures of strange birds and sea creatures. In one hand he held a staff, with the carving of a snake rising up its twisted shaft.'

'Bella can twist mine any day.'

Isabelle smiled sarcastically as her father pressed on. 'In his other hand he carried a large sack. Barely able to speak, he told me that he was a priest of a sect from a country far to the east. He begged me for water but I had barely enough for my own needs. However, he pleaded with me, offering a mysterious treasure in payment for restoring him to life. At this I finally agreed, knowing that I could return to the oasis, and after he had drunk his fill, the man was true to his word. He drew from his sack the strangest object that you can imagine.'

'One of my Fred's turnips!'

'No Madame, it was a hand – a bronze, metal hand – engraved with alien writing or symbols, I knew not which. He called it the Hand of Truth, and as I examined it he told me its most incredible story.'

'Oh, bloody hell, here we go again!'

'The Hand was thousands of years old and had come from the land of Babylon. It was none other than the hand that had written on the wall in the time of the prophet Daniel; the very one that had written the words of judgement which brought death to Babylon's king. What is more, the priest told me, at the right time, when it is surrounded by a company of true believers, the hand can still come alive – it can write once again to reveal the deepest thoughts of those who come to it in humility and faith.'

'What a load of tosh!'

'Like you, sir, I was amazed beyond words at this tale. But there were greater wonders yet to come. The traveller told me that, since the days of Daniel, the Hand of Truth had always chosen for itself a guardian. He had been the last guardian but his time had come to an end. The hand, he said, had now chosen me. If I was prepared to accept the burden of this calling then I would also need to take on a new name. It was the same name that each of the guardians had received, the very one by which Daniel, its first custodian, had been known. I must take for myself the name... Belteshazzar!'

In a flash, his old grey robe dropped to the floor, revealing a shiny black gown, covered in delicate golden thread. From within, he pulled a twisted wooden staff and held it aloft.

Isabelle always loved this moment. It was her father at his very best.

As stunned silence began to give way to applause, her father's voice boomed out: 'Mesdames et Messieurs, I Belteshazzar, the last guardian, present to you the Hand of Truth.'

He flung out the staff towards a small pedestal table in the centre of the stage. At the same moment, Isabelle whisked away the black cloth that covered it.

'Bloody hell fire!'

Resting on its side, like a discarded piece of armour, lay a life-size bronze hand. Its segmented fingers were loosely curled and across its back were etched black and silver hieroglyphs.

Her father continued. 'And now we must see if the Hand will speak to us. For this, it must be surrounded only by faith and so I regret that I must ask my assistant, Bella, to withdraw. Despite my best efforts, she remains sceptical, believing the Hand to be a channel, not of divine communication, but of demonic deceptions.'

The 'Oohs' returned.

'I am afraid that she is not alone. Therefore, if any of you share this opinion, I must insist that you leave us now.'

He paused for a few moments but no one moved. They never did.

Isabelle bowed to her father and stepped behind an ornate folding screen at the back of the stage.

'So then, my friends, let us proceed in a spirit of humble devotion and beseech the Hand to speak to us. Of course, I cannot expect your faith to be strong – in these matters you are merely children – and so tonight we will only be touching the fringe of this great mystery. But, as the reputation of the Hand spreads throughout this town, I trust that far deeper wonders will be witnessed in the days to come. Now, a volunteer…'

Shouts went up around the room.

Behind the screen, Isabelle lifted a hatch and dropped through it. Lying on her front, she wriggled forward towards the centre of the stage and then rolled onto her back. Faint light filtered through the narrow cracks above. Two levers descended through the floorboards from the bottom of the table on which the Hand was lying. A spider was busy between the handles. She swept it away.

In the room above, her father began his patter.

'Monsieur, I would like you to look at these cards. You can see that they are plain on one side and on the other they bear an image of an object, or creature, or symbol. Choose one of them but be very careful – not another soul must see it. You are happy with that? Good. Now, hold the image in your mind's eye and approach the table… slowly please… we are on holy ground. Now, lay the card face down in front of the Hand… Superb.'

Isabelle noted the code word.

'And now we must have faith: faith that the Hand of Truth, the Hand of Daniel, the Hand of Belteshazzar will live again. I beg you to remain quiet and simply believe.'

There were some sniggers but these were quickly hushed and the room fell to a watchful silence. Isabelle waited for a few moments and then gave both levers a twitch.

Cries of amazement rang out.

'Please, I beg you.' Her father hushed them.

The room settled again. She adjusted the levers more carefully, bending and stretching the fingers. There were a few more gasps.

'Praise be! The Hand lives!' called her father. 'Now all that is required is for me to place this quill between its sacred fingers.'

Isabelle waited a moment and then set to work. As usual the

fingers were jerky, especially at first, but some twenty seconds later it was done.

'Now, Monsieur, if you would please read, from the card, what the Hand of Truth has revealed to us.'

'Snake.'

'And will you please show us the picture on the front – the picture you have been holding in your mind.'

Applause exploded around the room, cheers rang out and the floor shook to the stomp of feet.

Now everyone wanted a turn. Isabelle knew that her father was choosing carefully, avoiding the drunk and overly excited. Next came an egg – 'Excellent' – then a mouse – '*Merveilleux*' – and finally a ball – 'Be careful'. Four was always enough to leave them wanting more.

Her work for the evening done, she wriggled back to the hatch, climbed up through and smoothed her skirts. Stepping out from the screen, she joined her father at the front of the stage as he was taking his bow. All that remained was the sales pitch for his patent remedies and, as people drifted forward, Isabelle thought with dark satisfaction of Barnard's utter inability to prevent them.

Clammy fingers grasped her ankle. She looked down into the inebriated eyes of their owner and smiled. The man leered back at her and his fingers began to crawl up under her petticoat. She squatted down and leant towards him.

'You'd like a feel?' She smiled invitingly.

'Not half.'

'Feel this!' She jabbed her thumb into his eye.

His friends were still laughing as she slipped out of the tavern into the dark.

***

Charlie stood in the empty lecture room. Not one single taker. It was probably too soon for the word to have got around. Or so he hoped.

'Is it on?' A young lad stuck his head through the door. A girl was just behind him.

'Not tonight, son,' he sighed, 'but you're welcome to come in and have a look.'

He let them charge up the Leyden jar and try raising a few feathers with their fingers. As he watched them playing, he remembered doing just the same at that age with his sister.

'I know what you'll like,' he said, with a grin. 'Come here.' The lad stood on the wax tablet. 'Take hold of these rods. Now, give her a kiss.'

'What?'

'Go on, don't be shy.'

Their lips got to within an inch of each other and blue flame flashed between them. They whooped.

'It's my turn,' laughed the girl, pushing the boy off the tablet.

As the lad leant towards her, she stuck out her tongue and the fire shot from the tip. They collapsed in giggles.

He and Sophie had been just the same. Only, in his case, out of the fun was born a passion – for the machine and the mysterious power it harnessed. And the passion had led him to the books. And together they had led him to… this mess.

'Alright, that's enough, off you go.'

'Thanks, mister.'

He pulled one of the books from the shelf. It was the inspiration for many of his lectures: an account of Benjamin Franklin's experiments. He turned again to the story of the great man flying his kite into a thundercloud and capturing the storm's energy in a Leyden jar.

That must have taken guts.

He flipped a few pages and read the report of Franklin electrocuting turkeys and serving them up as dinner for his audience.

The man had style. Enlightenment and showmanship in a seamless whole. That's what he was aiming for and, if he ever got close, it would be courtesy of his father's machine.

The candlelight picked out the rich grain of the wood and shone off the delicate, almost sensuous, curves of the glass. It was still a thing of beauty and wonder to him. It was that combination that had attracted him, just as it had his father – before he cast it off. He could remember the shock of seeing the jumbled pile in the hallway when he returned from Edinburgh. Every piece of medical equipment and every book, waiting to be sold off or burnt. And in the middle of it all, the chest containing the electrical machine. Like a scapegoat tainted by guilt and shame, his father couldn't bear to use it again. He couldn't take the risk that it might heal others when it had failed to save his wife. He knew he was to blame. He had been too busy to notice the pain she had tried to hide – the drawn lines of her face; the bones protruding from her already thin frame; the silent weariness replacing her natural joy. When he did finally notice, there had been nothing that he didn't try. He had bled her, cupped her, blistered her, electrified her. Yet it was to no avail and, with a cruel relentlessness, she grew thinner and weaker. And then, when she couldn't contain the pain any longer, he had been beside himself. He could barely live with his own impotence. At the end, all he could do was hold her hand, mop her brow and give her sips of water. For all his years of training and practice, that was all that was left to him.

A candle guttered and went out. He pushed the memories away.

He set off for the King's Arms. As the street joined Briggate, he saw a line of lights snaking along in the darkness and another childhood memory stirred: flickers in the hearth and his mother's hushed tones telling of the spunkies, Highland will-o'-the-wisps, appearing as link boys to lure unwary travellers to a watery grave. Had they now risen from the river marshes to entice the whole town to its doom? Then a more earthly fear gripped him: an all too human mob, inflamed by Barnard's rhetoric, intent on a fiery revenge, was heading for his practice rooms. Moments later, the fairies and fears resolved into a bizarre nocturnal funeral procession.

At its head, a black-suited featherman moved at unwavering

pace, as if responding to an invisible drum. The black ostrich plumes sprouting from his hat swayed in time to the silent rhythm. By contrast, the unsynchronised steps of the bearers bore witness to their struggles under the coffin; their dripping faces glistening in the torchlight borne aloft by the teenage pages on either side.

'A strange time for it,' he observed to an elderly couple, who had joined the onlookers lining the street.

'Nay lad,' replied the old man, 'that's 'ow the nobs do it 'ere, or else them who are trying on airs and graces. Though this one'll rest in St Peter's 'til tomorrow.'

Behind the coffin, a small, bird-like woman sobbed into a lace handkerchief. On either side, with arms linked through hers, walked Mary Crompton and Sarah Armstrong.

He was intrigued. 'Mrs Thomson?' he asked the man.

'Aye, poor lass.' The old man bowed as she passed.

The procession moved down the street and people tagged on the end, turning it into a jostling, noisy crowd. He joined them. Maybe he could find some way to speak to Thomson's widow after all.

But after only a few paces, from round the back of the White Swan, stepping into the torchlight, came Isabelle Broussard. Walking beside the procession, she paid it almost no attention. She moved with an air of casual, even imperious, confidence – almost as if she owned the place. After a hundred yards, she pushed through the mourners to the other side of Briggate and turned into Boar Lane. As far as he could remember, it was the same street she had gone up on the night of the attack.

He reached the junction. Mrs Thomson and her companions were continuing their steady progress down the hill.

Something nagged at the back of his mind. He turned the corner.

A three-quarter moon poked out from behind a cloud, silhouetting Trinity Church and Isabelle, standing a few yards further on, outside a large house. Adjusting her shawl, she glanced furtively up and down the street. He ducked down the side of the church.

A young man staggered out of the Leopard and crossed the road, unbuttoning the flap of his britches as he came. Reaching the church, he leant against the wall and steam rose in the moonlight. Letting out a grunt of satisfaction, he moved away unsteadily towards the market place.

Isabelle checked again before sauntering towards the front door of the house and then, veering to the left, she disappeared down the side.

He set off after her.

At the back, large outhouses clustered around the deeper shadow of the yard. Above him, a faint candle flickered in a top floor window. A servant on their way to bed? The rest of the shutters were closed. Was the kitchen door locked? He stood still and held his breath. A dog barked in the distance then all was silent.

What the hell was he doing?

He glanced quickly through the darkened panes of the outhouses before walking on into a long, walled garden. Each of the high walls was covered with espaliered fruit trees and, down the centre, the moonlight picked out a shrub-lined path. At the end, where it met the far wall, was a small gate. He walked towards it and lifted the latch.

It was bolted from his side.

6

'Man that is born of a woman hath but a short time to live...'
The priest wiped his nose on his mildewed sleeve. 'He cometh up
and is cut down like a flower.'

Even from a distance, Charlie could see stains down the man's
front and hear the slight slurring of the words. Several buttons on
his cassock were either undone or had given up the ghost under the
pressure of his fulsome stomach, which was erupting wherever it
got the chance.

'In the midst of life we are in death...'

Around the grave stood the remnant of the previous night's
procession: some thirty black-suited men in close ranks, including,
he noticed, Josiah Armstrong. A few yards off stood a small group of
women with, at its centre, the diminutive figure of Ann Thomson.
As the coffin descended into the ground, she let out a loud gasp and
began to sway but Mary Crompton and Sarah Armstrong, flanking
her once again, had her firmly by the elbows and she steadied.

'I heard a voice from heaven... saying unto me.' The Prayer
Book was having to compete with the sound of weeping and every
few words the priest glared across at the widow. 'Blessed are the
dead which die in the Lord... for they rest from their labours.'

He thought of Thomson's labours and how he had relieved his physical needs during them. That was common enough, he knew, even in good marriages, though there seemed to be no such ambiguity in his wife's affections.

'… the souls of the faithful… after they are delivered from the burden… of the flesh…'

The prayers stuttered to their conclusion and the priest walked off. After a few paces, he stopped, took out a small snuff box and snorted a pinch off the back of his hand.

Charlie frowned. As a child, his mother had taught him a love for the carpenter from Nazareth but not for most of the clergy with their privileges and idleness. How many tithes, he wondered, did it take to maintain this "man of God"?

He turned and noticed, a few yards behind him, a woman looking on from under a gnarled thorn tree. With her hood up, it took him a moment to recognise the fragile-looking lady whom he had rushed past in Barnard's house.

He walked towards her.

'Please forgive me if I am intruding – Charles Rossi, at your service.' He bowed his head.

She didn't reciprocate. 'Yes, I know.'

'I am afraid that I made an exhibition of myself yesterday,' he continued. 'Although I am at odds with Doctor Barnard, I wish to apologise for my unseemly manner in your home. I must have shocked you, especially in front of your son.'

'Doubtless my husband had provoked you.' Her tone was as inexpressive as her eyes.

She looked back towards the mourners. Some had moved across to Mrs Thomson, while others were drifting away.

'Your eye is somewhat improved.'

He was surprised: he had passed her so quickly in the doorway.

'Thank you. My landlady's medication has worked wonders. Perhaps I should ask her to give me the recipe; it might cause me less trouble than my own.'

She ignored the quip and turned away but a voice called out: 'Emily! My dear, how good it is to see you out.'

Coming towards them was a large, well-built lady who looked to be in her early forties. Her vast, powdered wig rose precipitously above her equally powdered but good-natured face.

'Elizabeth.' Mrs Barnard's response had more than a hint of reserve. 'It is indeed good to see you.'

'My dear, I have missed you. Taking tea together was such a delight. But how are you? You must be improved. Your being here testifies to that, surely.' The words came thick and fast.

'I am managing, thank you.' It was evident that Emily Barnard did not share her friend's buoyant assessment of her condition.

'And your dear husband? I trust he is well. Is he not here? George was his patient, I believe.'

'Unfortunately he was called away at short notice. He asked me to represent him.'

'Of course – a doctor's time is not his own. He serves at our beck and call, and he does serve us all so well. I, too, am here on my brother's behalf. James is away on business and won't be returning to Leeds until the morning. Oh, and doubtless you have heard the news: he has been elected as an alderman. Isn't that wonderful?' Pausing for breath, she appeared to remember Charlie's presence. 'But, my dear, you haven't introduced me.'

'This is Doctor Charles Rossi. Doctor Rossi – Miss Elizabeth Oxley.'

He bowed and Miss Oxley dipped her head in return.

'I am very pleased to meet you Doctor… Rossi…' The penny dropped. 'Oh, my dear. My dear, you don't mean…'

All her powder was powerless to mask the colour that rose throughout her ample face. However, she was spared further embarrassment by the intervention of another mourner.

'You're Rossi! My God sir, you have no more respect for the dead than you do for the living. How dare you flaunt yourself here, imposing upon Ann at such a time? You damned villain, I'll teach you a lesson and you'll need all your devilish quackery to fix it.'

The stranger was barrel-chested and had arms and fists that looked well suited to a prize fight. Lurching forward across the grass, he drew back his fist but, before he could throw the punch, two of his companions grabbed his arms.

'Come on Forsyth, calm yourself,' urged one of them. 'This is no place for a brawl. Look: Ann hasn't even left the churchyard. What would she say?'

Forcing his arms to his side, the men led the would-be assailant away towards the church gates. As they did, Forsyth craned back over his shoulder and shouted, 'Damn you!'

Elizabeth Oxley also took the opportunity of the fracas to make her escape, leaving Charlie and Mrs Barnard alone again. He raised his eyebrows in bewilderment.

'Forsyth is married to Ann's cousin,' she explained. 'They are her closest relatives.'

'Oh, I see.'

'Trouble seems to follow you around Doctor Rossi. If it hadn't been for his friends I fear that all your landlady's good work would have been for nought.'

'I think you may be right.' He grinned sheepishly. 'I am not much use in a fight.'

She looked at him properly for the first time. 'Unless, I hear, helping a woman in distress.'

***

Henry Barnard gazed into the depths of the fire and offered up the frustrations of the day to the burning coals. He picked up the poker and plunged it into the grate. He held it there, steeling himself to the heat.

'The trouble with patients is that they always think their petty troubles are an emergency.'

Emily Barnard looked up from her embroidery but made no response. From experience she knew that usually none was expected or wanted.

'Old man Pickering was so sure he was dying, when all that was required was an enema.' It had been a particularly unpleasant one. 'Or else they are hysterical. Mrs Lickiss – all that whimpering over having a few blisters snipped. I mean, how else does she expect me to bring her fever down? Pah! If I was foolish enough to believe in your God, they would make me a saint. Putting up with their quivering layers of fat, their obnoxious stools and odours' – he scowled – 'that must be close enough to a miracle.'

He looked at his wife but she didn't react. He clenched his fist tight against the burning pain.

'But it's medicine that is the real miracle – banishing ignorance and superstition. Of course, there is so much more to learn but it alone is the path to any "salvation". Your priests will soon be a thing of the past – their reputation is already in the gutter – and they will be replaced by the priests of a new age.'

The idea struck him as wonderful and he felt laughter welling up within but he controlled it, along with his hand.

'What they fail to grasp is that medicine isn't about those rather pathetic, malformed individuals but about Health – the perfect form of rational, harmonious well-being. That's the goal to which enlightenment beckons. All these people, with their insatiable demands, are merely steps on the road.'

Even so, how he wished he had more time for his astronomy. He longed for that, above all: to gaze up at the numberless stars; to lose himself under the silent, flawless movement of the heavens; to feel the anger ebb away; even at times to find contentment. Medicine was a master under whose yoke he laboured – he knew that only too well – but astronomy was the mistress at whose feet he gladly worshipped.

And if only the human world could reflect the order of the heavens. Surely that day must come. Rational well-being would triumph and, when it did, he would be free of his tedious responsibilities. But he mustn't lose his focus, not with these new threats all around. So for now, his astronomical pleasures must, like everything else, be rigorously rationed.

He snatched the poker from the fire and dropped it on the hearth. He breathed steadily over his scorched skin.

'I shall be going to Shadwell tomorrow.'

His wife looked up again from her embroidery frame.

'Of course, Henry. But why tomorrow?' It was unusual for him to vary his weekly visits to the family home.

'I wish to take advantage of these clear skies while they last and, besides, tomorrow is that damnable fair. I will not have our peace disturbed by the uncouth mobs who are allowed to run riot in our streets. You and Isaac will come as well.'

'But Henry... my nerves.' Since her pregnancy she had been excused the six-mile journey. 'I really think it would be better for me to remain.'

'Mrs Barnard!' He glared at her.

'I beg your pardon, sir.' She winced. 'As you wish, of course. May I ask at what time you plan to depart?'

'Three in the afternoon will suffice, before the worst excesses break out.'

His wife bowed her head once more to her needlework.

He picked up the poker again. If he couldn't order his own household, what hope was there? He plunged the rod back into the fire.

7

The calf's head stared at Charlie out of a giant pan of steam. A hog, turning slowly on the mechanical spit in front of the range, dripped fat into the tray below. On the central table, rabbits, pigeons and geese waited their turn and a young teenage girl sat filleting plates of carp and mackerel. On cabinet tops, curd tarts, custards and cheesecakes fought each other for space, while the floor was crammed with baskets of winter vegetables and fruit. At the far counter, Beth wielded a knife beside a platter of enormous and fashionable sandwiches.

Coming up behind, he gave both sides of her ample waist a squeeze.

'Morning, Beth. God, this place smells good.'

'Out, you rascal, or you'll find yourself served up on one of these.'

He grinned and deftly swept away the herring sandwich that she had just finished.

'If you don't mind, *sir*, you'll find that my *husband* has been expecting you since before dawn.'

Savouring his pilfered breakfast, he made his way outside onto the grass verge of Briggate. Purple and white bunting ran the length of the broad thoroughfare. Up and down the street, publicans and shopkeepers were setting out stalls or putting finishing touches to their windows. Near the greengrocer's opposite, a boy dodged out of the grip of a constable and hurtled down an alley. A band began tuning up in the distance.

Sam was standing beside a line of barrels, arching his back.

'Well, that's us nearly done. No thanks to you, Charlie.' He shook his head with a smile. 'I were starting to think you were going to sleep through the whole bloomin' day. Good job Tom were around.'

Sam nodded at a teenager who was carrying a stack of tankards out of the tavern.

'He's my brother's lad,' explained Sam. 'Agnes his sister's inside with Beth.'

Despite the mop of red hair, Charlie could see the large forehead and broad chin. This was a Tinker alright.

'He normally helps his dad with the weaving but he's not going to be needed for what Jake's got planned today.' Sam winked and raised an invisible tankard to his lips.

'Aye, he won't be the only one with a thick head tomorrow,' laughed Tom. 'There's nowt like St Blaise to liven things up a bit – not after the winter we've had.'

The night before, Sam had asked Charlie if he could give him a hand and, with no patients booked in, he had agreed. He was glad of the distraction.

'So who's this Blaise chap then?' He asked as they served the first customer of the day.

'Dad says he were some sort of bishop,' replied Tom. 'Invented wool combs and then got himself tortured with them. Just imagine that: having your skin scraped off you by dozens of nails.' He pulled a suitably pained expression. 'Anyhow, that's the point really: he's the patron saint of the wool combers. It's supposed to be their day, their procession, but everyone gets in on the act.'

Briggate started to fill up. Elbows jabbed and feet kicked as people claimed, and then defended, the best vantage points. Children sat on shoulders or sheltered under the folds of skirts. One rotund man sat astride the largest hog Charlie had ever seen. Flags and banners danced in the breeze while, from either end of the street, band music fought to be heard above the continual peeling of church bells.

The men were already drawing from a second barrel, when a cry went up: 'Here they come!'

Charlie leapt onto the trestle table for a better view.

'That's the guild master and his son, right up front,' shouted Tom above the din.

The leaders of the parade were dressed in scarlet coats and blue britches, with slivers of combed wool wrapped crossways over their chests. Behind them came a great purple banner bearing an image of the saint and then some lads of Tom's age, enthusiastically waving to the crowds with wool combs – square bats of wood that sprouted a mass of fine metal teeth.

'Some of the best apprentices,' explained Tom.

A military pipe band followed in their wake and the cacophony was completed by some exotically dressed Moors beating kettle drums. After them, a handsome couple, dressed as the king and queen, rode two magnificent horses and were guarded by a detachment of infantry.

Charlie pointed to a young man on a fine black horse, brandishing a sword, and surrounded by a group dressed in short tunics. 'And him, Tom?'

'That'll be Jason with his old fleece atop that pole.'

Next came the central figure of the whole show: Bishop Blaise, with crook and mitre, and a chaplain in tow. The crowds cheered even louder as he came past.

'I doubt they'd give a real bishop so much as the time of day,' called Sam.

'You're right there,' agreed Charlie with feeling.

Bringing up the rear was a vast horde from all the trades of the wool industry. Tom did his best to point them all out: crook-wielding shepherds and shepherdesses; more wool combers; wool sorters and wool staplers; comb makers, charcoal burners, spinners, weavers and cloth merchants. The list, like the procession, seemed endless.

'I've never seen anything like it!' he shouted from the top of his barrel.

'Aye, it's not bad,' grinned back Tom. 'But Bradford – now that's what I call a parade!'

Once the procession had ended, the crowd returned to the other activities of the day: mainly eating and drinking. Agnes joined the men and Beth's sandwiches were snapped up as fast as they appeared.

It wasn't until mid-afternoon that Sam gave the nod: 'You get off now, Charlie, and enjoy what's left of the day.'

'Thanks, I'll see you later for Beth's feast.'

He set off through the throng towards the Moot Hall where he could hear a band playing popular tunes. As he got closer the music blended with some high-spirited singing. He grinned as one ditty, about a blind milkmaid and a bull, had the better-dressed members of the crowd moving their children quickly away. The music took on a patriotic tone and he watched as two young men, egged on by the crowd, climbed up the face of the Hall. They reached a large niche containing a statue of Queen Anne and plucked the two Union Flags from around her. To loud cheers, they began waving them high above the heads of their friends.

'For England and King George!' called the standard bearers.

'Our lads and the army!' came the reply from below.

Then a shout: 'Death to the rebels!' And the chant was taken up by all.

He had already suffered enough from English jingoism. He moved on. Emerging from the press of the Shambles, he could see a stage set up beside the market cross. As he approached, a jester moved among the crowd, teasing the children. Three tumblers, dressed in blue and yellow, criss-crossed the stage with somersaults, flips and handstands. At the blast of a trumpet, one man sprang off a board to land, feet first onto the shoulders of another. The third followed, grasping the upright hands of the man below. He then flipped over and landed, faultlessly, on the middle man's shoulders. As the men jumped down, a lithe and scantily clad woman leapt up onto a slack rope. She walked, hopped, jumped, skipped, sat and lay down, and then, accompanied by many a wolf-whistle, walked on her hands from end to end. The crowd bellowed their approval.

He knew this was all by way of bait.

A fanfare pierced the air again and a momentary lull descended on the crowd. Then onto the stage, wearing a vivid green coat and britches, all trimmed with silver, and with two peacock feathers in a black velvet cap, strode the mountebank. With a flourish of the wrist, a bottle appeared at the end of his fingers.

'Is your throat sore from the excitement? Well I have just the tonic you need. Is your head pounding?'

'Give us a chance it's not even dark!'

'Then, with the remedy to hand, the gin'll not touch you.'

'I'll take the lot!'

'Or, gentlemen, are you in need of a little attention before tonight's big performance? I have exactly the thing for you.'

'Only if your rope dancer rubs it in,' someone shouted to raucous laughter.

Charlie had seen enough. The magical elixir was on offer again: the cure-all for every known ailment and some they'd never even heard of. In their high spirits and alcoholic haze they would be easy prey. Money was already changing hands. He spat and walked on.

More quackery.

As the flames took hold, the smell of burning flesh caught in Charlie's throat. The bonfires, which had appeared on the streets the day before, had grown overnight. This one had been supplemented by

78

some boot leathers, an old wig, shards of crockery and a chandelier. It had been topped off with a dead dog.

He looked on at the labourers, servants and destitute who had been drawn to the warmth. They were drinking, singing and laughing in the flickering light. Two nestled up close. Another pair slipped away into a darker alley. He shrugged. It was time to take pleasure while you could. Tomorrow would be here soon enough.

He turned back down hill, to join the other guests around Beth's sumptuously laden table. His mouth watered at the thought. However, as he passed the White Swan, people were making their way inside for the night's entertainment. He paused. Memories of an empty, moonlit garden wrestled with the prospect of Beth's cooking. For once, Beth lost.

In the Long Room, with the benches full, he joined others standing around the walls, next to two of the Moors from the parade. As Broussard began to ply his trade, money disappeared from a gentleman's pocket and reappeared in a lady's purse; a candle melted away into the conjuror's hand only to emerge from inside an empty box; Isabelle held up a series of watches, snuffboxes or combs from the audience and, one by one, her blindfolded father named them. It was not so much the illusions that fascinated Charlie as the showmanship; the way the man was working his audience.

'Mesdames et messieurs, our next experiment will require the help of the keenest eyes and truest of hands. Mine are beginning to fail, so tonight I must rely on you. Someone with no fear. Someone I can trust with my daughter's life.'

That drew some exaggerated gasps.

The Frenchman opened a box, which held a neatly arranged pair of pistols. He offered them to an army officer near the front.

'Like me, Monsieur, these weapons are not as young as they were and one fires slightly low. Would you find the one that I need, if you please.'

The man picked up each pistol in turn, looking along the barrel. He returned one to the box and passed the other back to Broussard.

'You are sure?'

'Of course, man, what do you take me for?'

Broussard charged it with powder, spilling a fair amount in the process. He then tipped a small bag of lead balls into the hand of the woman next to the soldier.

'Check these, if you would. They may be misshapen and I need the most regular one; the one that will shoot true.'

A man near Charlie snorted. 'She can check mine if she likes. They never fail!'

The woman held out a piece of shot. 'This one… I think.'

'Now drop it into the barrel, if you please. I do not trust my old hands,' he added with a smile. But it was the woman's hands that were shaking.

'Now for my final helper. And for this I will be guided by fate.'

He laid the pistol down on the table, pulled the blindfold over his eyes once again, and set off among the audience, passing up and down the rows. As he entered the row in front of Charlie, the conjuror stopped and turned. Stepping back out into the aisle, his head scanned the room. He raised his hand and laid it down firmly on Charlie's shoulder.

'You will be my eyes.'

Back on stage, the blindfolded Frenchman pointed the pistol vaguely towards where Isabelle was standing, holding a playing card just above her head.

'Now, Monsieur, my aim – or, should I say, our aim – is to hit the playing card. From now on, Bella and I are in your hands. Take my arm and be my guide. Then tell me when it is safe to fire.'

The crowd roared instructions. Charlie felt ridiculous. He knew it was a trick, so why was his heart racing? Why had his hands gone clammy? He looked along Broussard's arm from above and to the side, moving it inch by inch. It looked about right but he couldn't check both horizontal and vertical directions at once. If one was out, it had to be the horizontal. To shoot low was... but what was he thinking; this was crazy.

'Is it safe?'

'I'm not sure... I don't know... I think so.'

Broussard pulled the trigger.

At the sound, a spasm shook Charlie's body and he stepped backwards, almost off the stage. A woman behind him screamed. Broussard ripped off his mask. Isabelle stepped forward through the smoke. She held up the card. A bullet hole was punched through the bottom left corner. The room erupted.

Isabelle looked across at Charlie and winked. He smiled, embarrassed, took a deep breath and made his way back to his place.

Feeling a bit out of sorts, he watched as the conjuror began to relieve people of their pains. His hackles rose in an instant. Any fool must realise it was a liniment of fleeting benefit, rubbed secretly on the hands. It was the sort of trickery that mountebanks had been fleecing people with for centuries. He shook his head. Was it that much worse than the daily deceptions of physicians? Did it really matter, if people were happy to believe in it for a while? And what of his electrical therapy? Perhaps, in the end, all healing was no more than a medical sleight of hand.

He was drawn back into the room by the unfolding story of the Hand of Truth. Around him, people had gone quiet. He could see that Belteshazzar was a man who knew how to hold an audience in his palm and lead them where he wanted them to go. He watched as the Hand worked its magic. He recalled several similar automata in Newcastle some years before, though nothing used with such consummate skill, and he joined the applause without reserve.

The audience drifted away and he found a vomit-smelling settle tucked behind the taproom door. He sipped at his ale and waited.

By the time he had reached the bottom of the pot, there was still no sign of Isabelle. Picturing the room, he realised there was another door at the back of the stage.

'Damn!' he cursed aloud.

He checked back in the Long Room but Isabelle was still there, in animated conversation with her father. Before Charlie could withdraw, she saw him and beckoned.

As he came forward, he was struck by how different her father looked now. Short and thin, like his daughter, but frailer and more stooped; his face as grey as his hair. On the other hand, Isabelle seemed unchanged. She had the same fire in her eyes; the same intense movements.

'Papa, this is Mr Rossi – the one in the street.'

Charlie reached out his hand.

'Louis Broussard, at your service. I must thank you, Monsieur, for coming to the aid of my daughter. She tells me she would have managed on her own but I suspect that you were of more assistance than she cares to admit.'

'I could do no less.'

'And thank you for your assistance tonight. You have my daughter to thank for that but you played your part well.'

'You drew me in sir, as you did everyone. You have a gift – truly.'

'Ah, yes, I think you looked at it all through different eyes. As would only a fellow… performer? Forgive me, is that the word?'

'It will do – for now.' He couldn't help smiling. Broussard's English, despite its heavy accent, was pretty much flawless. Isabelle's father had the measure of the word – and of him.

'And will you also forgive the little deception with my "healing hands"?' asked Broussard with a chuckle.

'I suppose I have no alternative.' He found himself warming to the man.

'But what of your work? Tell me about your apparatus…'

The two men were soon in deep discussion, comparing the relative merits of ways to generate, store and apply electricity. It was quite some time before Charlie remembered about Isabelle and looked up from Broussard's machine. She was sitting on the end of the stage, kicking the side with her feet.

If she had intended to slip away tonight she would have done so by now.

Broussard noticed his change of focus. 'Ah but you did not come here tonight to talk to an ageing conjuror.' He smiled knowingly.

'On the contrary,' Charlie lied. 'I was hoping to have the chance to meet you. But you have reminded me: I am told the festivities conclude with fireworks. Would you and your daughter care to join me?'

'For myself, I fear that I need to rest,' sighed Broussard. 'But, *ma chère*, what about you?'

The only answer he got was a shrug of the shoulders.

People had disgorged from houses and taverns, and the streets were every bit as busy as they had been twelve hours earlier.

'The English do love their fireworks,' he observed as they wandered through the crowd.

'But you are not one of them?' queried Isabelle, stepping over a man who was lying comatose on the ground.

'Certainly not. I'm a Scot – well, Scottish and Italian – though I was brought up south of the border. So wherever I am, it seems like I'm an outsider. Part of me – all of me, sometimes – feels as if I don't belong.'

'I know what you mean,' replied Isabelle darkly.

He could imagine it: travelling around a country that was always suspicious of the French, and never more so than now they were supporting the rebels in America. He glanced at her. She was a virtual stranger but she might understand more about his way of life than all the townsfolk ever would.

They walked on in silence. It was, he felt, almost companionable and, as the first rockets took off, they looked skywards. High above them, the sky exploded in a shower of colour.

'Look at that!' they exclaimed together.

***

'Look at that, Isaac.'

Henry Barnard bent his son's head down to line up his eye with the lens of the telescope. It was a Newtonian one, named, like the boy, after its maker.

'That circle of light is Jupiter. It is a planet like the Earth. And it has moons going round it, just like ours. Who knows? It may even have creatures living on it as well. It is a world like ours but so very far away – a planet, a wanderer in the heavens. You see, the stars really stay in the same place. It is the Earth that spins and that is why the sky seems to change all the time. It is only the planets – Earth, Jupiter and the rest – which move around. However, even these keep to a regular path. So, you see how everything is ordered; everything is fixed.'

He wasn't sure how much of this Isaac was taking in but it was never too early to start his son's education; never too soon to challenge the view that the world was at the centre of things, nor the religious myths that traded on it.

Barnard's mother disagreed. Not about religion, though she found any discussion of the subject distasteful, but about inculcating natural philosophy into his son. They had clashed on the subject again over dinner.

'I don't know what you are thinking, Henry,' she had said curtly, 'taking the boy up on the roof in the depths of winter. He'll fall to his death if he doesn't catch it first.'

He waved away the remark. 'He will come to no harm.'

'Well, educate the boy if you must but for God's sake be practical. What a man needs isn't a head full of ideas but the ability to make money. Teach him how business works and then get him to knuckle down and make a killing. Would that your father had done the same with you.'

He sucked on his orange and let the criticism pass. Unlike his grandfather, whose dealings in the Caribbean had secured them the house and land at Shadwell, his father's enterprises had been a series of disasters, with ships sunk or pirated, and even a mutiny.

'Would that he had done anything, come to that,' carped his

mother, 'anything, rather than cavorting at his club or poking some pox-ridden harlot.'

'Mother!' He glanced at Emily but she was looking vacantly at the still almost full plate in front of her.

'Oh, spare me the sermon,' retorted Mrs Barnard senior. 'Where would you have been if not for my income? On the streets or in the workhouse. But instead you waste yourself at the beck and call of weavers and bricklayers, or squander your measly inheritance on telescopes.'

'We live comfortably enough.' He spat some pips into his hand.

'What, rattling around in that half empty kennel?'

'I choose my own way. Moderation keeps my senses sharp.'

'Moderation!' His mother laughed contemptuously. 'Pauperism I call it. I'd rather your licentious father than a hair-shirted monk. And why in God's name must you inflict it on a three-year-old?'

He leant forward. 'But think of it, Mother: to shape a young body, through diet and exercise, into mature and healthy manhood; to take the blank sheet of a mind and fill it, through study and exposure to the heavens, with the rational truths of enlightenment – surely this is a project worthy of a modern man.'

She snorted in disgust.

'Anyway,' he continued, 'the future belongs to science. Even in trade or manufacture, he'll need it. You'll see.'

Up on the roof, Isaac turned away, nudging the telescope with his arm.

'Don't touch it!' snapped Barnard, pushing his son aside.

The boy sat down by the parapet wall and began picking at the moss growing in the gutter. Barnard realigned the instrument and bent down to the eyepiece.

'Ah, Callisto… right on time.' He took out a notebook and jotted down the details. 'And Io should be along soon.'

The image blurred and dimmed.

'Damn it.'

He looked up. A bank of cloud was spreading across the sky,

obliterating whole constellations in its wake. The weather had let him down once more.

He cursed again. Why wasn't everything more predictable?

***

With the fireworks over, Charlie and Isabelle made their way back to the centre of town along Swine Gate, a narrow lane just north of the main millrace.

Four men stepped out of an alley.

'Well, if it isn't the bitch.' The brogue was Irish. A knife twisted slowly in the man's hand.

'And her pimp.' A taller man – Liverpudlian. A crowbar rested on his shoulder. He had a large scab on his forehead. The pair Isabelle had floored.

The Irishman rubbed his groin and leered at Isabelle.

'Now, if you'd only taken it the first time, darling, that little face of yours could have kept those lovely looks.' The knife traced a figure of eight in the air.

Isabelle's hand dropped to her ankle and returned with a stiletto dagger.

'What's this?' sneered the Irishman. 'We've got ourselves a wild one here, boys. Now, doesn't that get your blood pumping?'

Charlie turned and his stomach tightened: there were four other men closing in from behind.

'Sorry matey,' the Liverpudlian laughed. 'Should've kept your wits about you.'

Charlie cursed: a large group had passed them a few minutes earlier but he and Isabelle had been engaged in fierce debate.

The Irishman jabbed at Isabelle with his knife. She ignored the feint and then the crowbar arced down through the air. She ducked and the metal splintered a cobble. The Irishman's boot flew up towards her chin. Twisting to the side, she struck back, piercing the arm of his coat.

'Bloody whore,' hissed the man, backing off. 'Right lads!'

The six lackeys closed in round them, lashing out with their boots. Isabelle spun this way and that to fend them off. The two armed men looked on, laughing. They knew this couldn't last long.

Off to the side of the lane, Charlie spotted a narrow alley. He nudged Isabelle and nodded towards it. She grunted.

The man nearest the alley lunged. Isabelle grabbed his boot with her free hand and neatly upended him. The man's head smacked back on the cobbles. She sprang through the gap, lashing out with her dagger. The men on either side shrank back. Charlie was right behind her.

Ignoring turns to the left and right, they sprinted across a narrow footbridge over the millrace. Rounding a corner, another alley crossed theirs. They had stolen a few seconds.

'Right,' Isabelle hissed, directing them away from the centre of town. Even if it didn't fool them, the men would need to divide. The passage twisted and turned until they came to a fork. They went right again. A dead end.

'Hell!' cursed Charlie.

Isabelle jerked her finger to her lips, her eyes blazing. They began retracing their steps, trying a couple of doors but to no avail. At the junction, dagger at the ready, Isabelle snatched a glance round the corner, back the way they had come.

A man jumped her from the passage opposite, grabbing her wrist and yanking it back. Her fingers opened and the dagger dropped to the floor. His knee came up into her chest and she collapsed face down in the dirt. Charlie launched himself at Isabelle's attacker but two others plucked him from the air and slammed him back against the wall.

The first man picked up Isabelle's dagger and tucked it into his belt. He spat on the ground and then smashed a fist into Charlie's mouth. The next time it crunched into his stomach. Charlie doubled over. One of the men grabbed his hair, jerking his head back. A fist blurred in the air, and again.

Isabelle was back on her feet but shouts from the rest of the gang were getting closer. Although she had lost one weapon, she still had another. Grabbing the hem of her skirts, she pulled them up above her waist.

'Hey, boys, get your hands on this!'

Charlie's attacker turned around and let out a bestial snarl.

With her legs unencumbered, the kick that landed in the man's groin sent him screaming to his knees.

At the same moment, Charlie felt the pressure lessening on his shoulders as the men instinctively responded to Isabelle. He ripped his arms upwards and then jabbed his elbows outwards, slamming them with desperate power into the men's faces, catching one in the eye and the other full in the teeth.

Isabelle grabbed his arm and pulled him down the left-hand passage, away from the sounds of the approaching men. After a few twists and turns, they began trying doors and gates as they passed. Almost at once, Isabelle struck lucky and she eased the gate closed behind them.

With his hands on his knees, Charlie sucked in the air as silently as he could. His stomach and jaw throbbed violently and he swallowed a large globule of phlegm and blood. Stock-still, Isabelle was listening at the gate. Several pairs of feet ran past and then all went quiet. He looked up. They were in the corner of one of the largest tenter fields. The cloth-covered frames formed long corridors stretching away into the darkness. Along the boundary wall, several gates gave access from the millrace.

A few yards away, one of them burst open.

'They're here! In Low Tenter!'

Another gate opened and another, as the gang poured into the field.

Isabelle yanked at Charlie's sleeve and they zigzagged past several frames towards the centre. The moon emerged again, picking out the white cloths but also casting deep shadows. Gaining one of them, they dropped to their knees.

'Easy now, lads.' It was the Irishman. 'Take your time and we'll still have our fun.'

Isabelle checked round the frame and darted across the gap to the next shadow. Charlie was on her tail.

They waited, checked and went again.

A shout went up.

They turned and ran deeper into the field. Ahead, he could just make out the boundary wall on the far side. They cut right, into another long corridor, moving from frame to frame, shadow to shadow, all the time being pressed closer to the wall. Whenever they squatted down, he scanned it for gateways. There were none.

Eventually they reached the edge of the tenter field and looked out over open ground to a footbridge that crossed one of the smaller millraces. Charlie grimaced. If they made a run for it, they would be spotted but if they stayed here, the net would close.

Isabelle looked at him and nodded. They would go.

Keeping low, they dashed for the bridge. At once, the men broke cover, making for a second bridge to their right. Others emerged behind them, cutting off their retreat. Charlie and Isabelle crossed the millrace. Ahead lay another.

'Oh, hell,' breathed Charlie.

The gap was too wide to jump and, with wet banks, he wasn't about to try. To their right the gang were spreading out across the narrow finger of land, each now armed with a weapon, however makeshift. They were closing at a steady pace.

'Come on.' Isabelle's tone was more decisive than desperate.

With any hope of concealment gone, they jogged, side by side, down a track that lead south. After a couple of hundred yards, it ended at a large two-storey mill where the millrace met the swollen waters of the Aire.

Charlie tried the door. 'It's open.'

'Don't be stupid,' growled Isabelle.

'What?'

'We really will be trapped. It'll have to be the river.'

'That torrent? You must be joking. Anyway, I can't swim. You can risk it if you like but I'm going to have to take my chances in here.'

She shook her head. 'No way.'

Charlie shrugged and stepped inside, pulling the door to. Isabelle slipped through the gap. He bolted it behind them.

In the darkness, he could make out a dozen or more looms scattered around the ground floor and, directly in front of them, some large crates.

'Give us a hand.'

They dragged them across the entrance.

'That'll not keep them out for long,' said Isabelle, 'not with all these windows.'

He grimaced. She was right; they were enormous. 'I guess it depends how much damage they're prepared to cause. Anyway, we'll find out soon enough.'

Isabelle turned to him and touched his swollen, bloodied lip with her finger.

'You do keep trying to ride to my rescue and paying the price for it.'

He laughed. 'Well, I can tell you, from now on, madam, you're on your own.'

She smiled and planted a small kiss on his lip. 'Thank you.'

'Well, I owe you just as much,' he replied. 'You saved my bacon as well back there.' He could feel himself reddening at the memory.

'Don't worry about it,' she stroked his cheek. 'I just did what I had to do, which is what we need to do now. Come on, let's get upstairs. That's going to be our best hope if they do break in. They'll only have one way to come at us.'

The stairs were at the far end of the mill. As they moved towards them, the clouds parted again and a pool of moonlight illuminated the foot of the staircase.

He started. 'What the…'

Lying face down at the bottom of the stairs was the body of a man. Charlie hurried forward and knelt down. It was cold to the touch and stiff as he turned it onto its back. The face was badly bruised.

'Oh God! Not again!'

'What is it?' asked Isabelle.

'I don't believe it… I know him.'

At that moment, two of the windows, one on either side of the mill, came crashing in, scattering glass across the floor. Wooden batons and iron bars swept the sills clear and then, cursing and shouting, the men climbed through into the mill.

Stepping over the body, Charlie and Isabelle ran up the stairs. At the top was a small room – the manager's or owner's office – and inside was a large desk. They dragged it towards the edge of the stairwell. They tipped it up and slid it into the gap but the men had reached the top and effortlessly heaved the desk up and out of the way.

The first two to emerge were the Irishman and the Liverpudlian.

It was the Irishman who spoke: 'Well, well. You *have* given us the run around, so you have. But no matter. You've brought us here to this nice, quiet place. There's no one to disturb us, so we can take our time and, believe you me, we're going to.' He looked around the upper floor and nodded. 'Yes, I think we're really going to enjoy ourselves here.'

The hunt was over. The rest of the gang came up through the well and began to spread out down the sides of the mill, blocking access to the windows or any route back to the stairs. Slowly, the men moved forward.

Charlie and Isabelle fell back, taking cover behind one of the looms. The Irishman simply slashed at it with his knife, cutting right through the warp threads left by the weaver, and climbed through it, laughing as he came.

They darted behind another loom but this time the Liverpudlian set about it with his iron bar. The force was such that he snapped the side of the frame clean in two.

Slowly but surely the men pushed their prey backwards, leaving a trail of destruction in their wake. The rear wall of the mill was getting ever closer.

At the final loom, Isabelle looked over her shoulder.

'Charlie!'

He turned. Near the wall, fixed to the roof, was a hoist and beneath it was a hatch in the floor where fleeces and cloths were lifted up into the mill or lowered into the waiting boats. They must be directly above the river.

Isabelle dropped to her knees and raised the hatch. Realising what she was doing he shouted: 'But I can't swim!'

She pointed to an empty wooden crate by the edge of the opening.

'Grab that!'

And with that she was gone.

Letting out a roar, the Irishman surged through the loom but his feet tangled in the remnants of cloth and he tripped. With the Liverpudlian still on the other side of the frame, Charlie clamped his arms around the crate and dropped through the hatch.

As he hit the water, the force ripped the wood out of his grasp, slamming it into his chin. He tried to grab the crate again but it was gone. As cries of rage descended from above, the torrent swept him off into the night.

8

He came up a second time, gasping for breath. Icy water spewed from his mouth. He let out a howl of shock and fear. Kicking out, he tried to push himself towards the bank but he spun helplessly in the current.

The deeper darkness of the town bridge hurtled towards him and air exploded from his lungs as he was driven against the corner of an arch. Reaching for a joint in the stone, he clung numbly to the face of the bridge. Around him, the water surged into the gap. He stretched for a new hold but his fingers slipped and his hands dragged uselessly across the rough stone as the current sucked him into the gaping maw. Flinging out an arm, his hand closed on a branch. It was part of a tangled mass that had lodged against the stonework. He grasped at them with his other hand. They held.

He inched away from the arch and the drag lessened as the river pressed him against the side of the bridge. After a few yards, where it met the bank, the stonework turned a corner and came to an end. A warehouse towered over him and a wooden ladder rose from the river to the wharf above. With burning arms, he hauled himself out of the water and up the slimy rungs. Clambering over the edge, on hands and knees, he retched violently and collapsed onto the wooden walkway.

He opened his eyes. His whole body ached. He tried to move but was paralysed by a spasm of shivering. Then, into his mind, came an image of the gang sprinting along the riverbank. He forced himself to his feet. Another spasm overtook him and he retched again.

Ahead, a flight of stone steps led to the street. There was movement on the bridge and he flung himself flat against the warehouse wall. A silhouette appeared above the parapet and a head looked over.

It was Isabelle.

She waved nonchalantly and then walked on into town.

'My God, what have you been up to now?' Beth wiped her hands on her apron as he shuffled gingerly into the kitchen the next morning.

She strode over to him, scowling. 'I don't know why I bother, I really don't. I patch you up the best I can and you go and undo all my hard work. We keep a respectable house, Charlie Rossi, I'll have you know. Is it too much to ask that you just pay your bill and keep out of trouble like everyone else?'

Sam winked. 'Don't worry, she's only sore about you missing the banquet last night. Put her nose right out of joint!'

'Funny – that's the one bit of me that doesn't hurt.'

The men laughed and Beth shook her head, and smiled. 'What am I going to do with you? That ointment doesn't grow on trees, you know.'

She fetched it from a cupboard and started work again, while Charlie recounted the tale of the previous night's chase and the desperate escape in the river.

Sam frowned. 'My God, you were lucky to get out of that alive.'

'Anyway it's over now,' said Beth kindly, 'so put it out of your mind.'

'I would,' replied Charlie, 'except for one thing. I found a body at the mill and... well, you're not going to believe this but he was another one of my patients.'

Sam's eyes widened and he let out a low whistle.

Charlie raised his hand. 'Before you get too worried, there is one compensation – he was lying at the bottom of the stairs. So it looks like he'd just fallen down them.'

Sam sighed. 'Well at least they won't be pinning that one on you.'

Beth put a platter of beef and calf's trotters on the table. 'Here, love, get some of this down you – you must be famished.' She returned to the blackened range, spooning some fricasseed tripe into a bowl.

'Thanks Beth, you're the best cook ever. I'll never miss one of your meals again and that's a promise.' He speared a slice of beef with his knife and lifted it to his lips.

The door flew open and in burst a breathless Tom Tinker.

'They've taken our dad!'

'What the hell?' exclaimed Sam.

'They're going to hang him. I know they are.'

'What? Look, lad, sit yourself down and take it slowly.'

But Tom wouldn't sit. He paced up and down the kitchen, gesticulating wildly. 'Two constables – they kicked in the door and dragged him away.'

'For what?'

'I told you – for murder.'

'What murder?' asked Sam, bewildered.

'The murder at the mill – Oxley's mill – last night.'

The door slammed behind Charlie. Ahead, the passage was pitch black; the air, dank and stale. His chest tightened. The warder pushed past, carrying a grease lamp down the narrow brick stairs. Charlie followed close behind, focussing on the small flame. Halfway down, one of the bricks tipped up under his foot and he stumbled forward.

'Watch yourself,' said the warder over his shoulder. 'It may be "new" but, if you ask me, them that built it should've been first in line for these wards.'

At the bottom, the passage felt even more oppressive. The light disappeared without trace into the slimy black walls. A rat scurried past, brushing against his boot.

'That's the Rotation Office above,' explained the warder. 'The buggers up there will have their work cut out with hearings.' He rubbed his fingers together and grinned. 'St Blaise never disappoints.'

The warder was a small man yet with arms and legs far thicker than the rest of his body would have suggested. What was left of his hair was long and straggly at the back and sides. However, his clothes were clean and of good quality. Under his frock coat he wore a fine red waistcoat. From one pocket hung a substantial watch-chain.

He opened one of the cells. 'Newspaper and tobacco.'

There was a clink of coin and the cell door clanged shut.

A melee of shouts came from the door opposite.

'Stop your bleedin' hollering. You'll think it were heaven in here when you're dancing on air.'

He turned to Charlie. 'Them two go and attack a sedan, drive off the bearers and make free with the lady. But we've got them all in at the moment – the pickpockets and the drunks. One crashed through Draper Ainley's window and made off with a whole new wardrobe. He were still trying it on when the constable found him. And then there's the brawlers and the "disturbers of the peace".' The man laughed. 'Though God knows what kind of peace they were expecting at festival time.'

They reached the end of the corridor and the warder unlocked the door to his left.

Charlie nodded. 'I'm obliged to you, sir.'

The man looked meaningfully at him, blocking the way.

'Oh yes, sorry.' He fumbled in his pocket for a few coins and the warder moved aside. The key grated in the lock behind him as he stepped through the door.

The cell contained just two pieces of what could pass as furniture:

a single straw mattress and a bucket. The badly stained bedding lay against one wall and took up most of its length, and the stinking pail was tucked into the corner by the door. A shallow curved and barred opening below the ceiling on the far wall let in a little light, plenty of cold air and even more stench from the yard. A rat scuttled along the edge of the window and disappeared into a crack.

Despite the warder's forewarnings, Charlie was shocked. The little cell held four people: two men and two women. The older of the women sat under the window scribbling in a little jotter and kept her head down. The other, dishevelled and painfully thin, was slumped snoring in a corner. The men were both strangers to him but he would have recognised one of them anywhere. The broad family forehead and chin, as well as the flaming red hair of his son, proclaimed him Jake Tinker. The other man, according to Sam, was another weaver, Abe Robinson.

Charlie introduced himself and laid down Beth's basket.

'She's sent over the best bits left from last night's feast.' The men said nothing. Charlie frowned. 'So I'll pass on your thanks then shall I?'

'Aye, sorry,' sighed Jake. 'My head's splitting.'

'Well she's sent the hair of the dog as well.' Charlie pulled a bottle of wine from the basket.

Jake raised his hand. 'Nay, lad, it's not the drink. I kicked off when they tried to take me in and they gave me a pasting.'

'So what's this about?'

'Search me,' growled Abe Robinson taking a long swig of wine.

'Come on, what makes them think that you killed him – this Oxley fellow?'

'Well, I suppose we were sounding off about him in the Leopard,' Jake replied sullenly, 'saying somebody ought to do something. "Agitating" the constables called it.'

'But why?'

'Times are pretty hard, even worse for irregulars like us.' Charlie's frown deepened. Jake continued, 'Means we ain't served a proper apprenticeship. So we can't sell out of their precious Cloth Halls, though the Corporation, in its generosity' – he spat – 'lets us use a dingy basement down Kirkgate. But, it ain't easy for any weaving at home, though the Combination's a big help when times are really hard.'

'The Combination?'

'Aye, we all chip in when we can. Then, when we're up against it, the Combination shares out a bit. But if it ever tries to change anything, you can be sure as hell our beloved Corporation comes down hard.'

'That's true enough,' said Abe, grimly. 'We were just about making out and then this bloody war comes along.'

'What's that got to do with anything?' asked Charlie.

'My, you act bright enough,' said Abe, 'but you don't know much do you? What it has to do with it, is that since then we ain't been able to sell to the colonists. So, the price has dropped and, even with that, men can't sell much of their cloth. To cap that, the likes of Oxley have these fancy fly shuttles. So the looms get bigger and faster by the year and there's not enough wool to go round – not for love nor money.'

Abe fell silent. Jake chipped in: 'So you see, Mr Rossi, we're getting desperate. And I guess the ale got to us, loosened our tongues and we maybe said things we oughtn't to have.'

'But there must be others with these new looms. Why pick on Oxley?'

'Oh, he's a nasty piece of work that one, and no mistake.'

The answer left him none the wiser but he let it lie. 'So, what had you been saying?'

'Oh, I don't know. The usual stuff.' Jake slumped down onto the mattress and rested his forehead in his hands.

Charlie pressed: 'What, like someone ought to smash up his machinery?'

'Don't be daft,' scowled Abe. 'Well, not in so many words.'

'But you felt like it?'

'Too right we did.'

'And killing him?' He had to ask.

'Oh, aye,' Abe growled. 'I said, let's go up there and murder the bastard!' Then he sighed. 'Look, I'm sorry Mister, I'd have loved to give him a good hiding, that's for sure. But as for killing a man, well that's a bloody big line to cross, even when you've had a skinful.'

Charlie glanced at Jake who nodded in agreement.

'One other thing: what time did you leave the Leopard?'

'I don't know. It were pretty quiet, so it must have been after the fireworks.'

Jake's reply clinched it and, for the first time since he had entered the prison, Charlie smiled.

'Now, let me tell you some good news...'

From the top of the step, the doorman looked down at him.

Charlie's left eye was surrounded by a fading ring of yellow, his lower lip was swollen, a bruise ran under his chin, his knuckles were badly grazed, and his hesitant movements betrayed the tenderness beneath his clothing. He must have had all the appearance of a seasoned street fighter – not, he supposed, the sort of citizen who normally sought out the assistance of the town's mayor. However, the servant invited him over the threshold with no more than the raising of an eyebrow.

Left to wait in the hallway, the sound of muffled, angry voices reached him through the wall. After a few minutes, one man, now just inside the door, barked: 'You will bring it all down upon our heads!" at which point the servant reappeared, opened the door and Josiah Armstrong emerged. He glowered at Charlie before being offered his coat.

Charlie was shown into the mayor's study, the walls of which were almost completely hidden behind row upon row of books. Their leather bindings gave off a warm, familiar smell that instantly awakened a childhood memory: sitting on the floor of his father's study listening to the story of St Francis and the wolf, and feeling overwhelmed by the way that the holy man had saved the creature from the terrible retribution of the villagers it had been attacking.

Richard Micklethwaite was sitting by the window at a large oak desk. In his late fifties, he was tall and wiry, with a trim beard and grey hair, cropped short for a wig. On the desk's green leather surface sat two precisely stacked piles of papers and an ink horn. He rose in welcome.

'I see you also have a love of books.' He nodded at the shelves. 'It is the written word which distinguishes us from the beasts of the field. Do you not agree?'

It was not something that Charlie had ever given thought to but he murmured his concurrence. Micklethwaite beckoned him to the armchairs on either side of the fireplace.

'How may I help you?' the mayor continued. 'I cannot pretend to be ignorant of your troubles since your arrival among us. Do I take it that you are here concerning your controversy with Doctor Barnard?'

Charlie shook his head. 'It would be tempting to speak of that sorry affair but I am here on a different matter – one of far greater import.'

'Is that so? Well, then, it must be grave indeed.' There was the flicker of a smile. 'And what might that be?'

'The death of James Oxley.'

The mayor's posture sharpened. 'Ah, I see.'

'I am told that, because of the seriousness of the offence, you have taken a particular interest in the case.'

Micklethwaite nodded gravely. 'Just so. An assault against the life and property of one of our leading clothiers, an alderman no less, cannot be left for his loved ones to pursue justice as normal. Such a felony strikes at the heart of our economy and the fabric of our community. It is an attack on the whole town and so, as mayor, I am impelled to act on behalf of us all.'

'Indeed, sir, I appreciate these wider implications and your need to act swiftly and decisively.' Charlie picked his words carefully. 'However, I am obliged to inform you that the two men who have been taken into custody this morning are in fact wholly innocent.'

Micklethwaite stared at him. He resisted the temptation to look away.

When he spoke, the mayor's tone was cool and controlled.

'Tinker and Robinson were heard last night, by multiple witnesses, urging others to act against Alderman Oxley, his manufactory and his fly shuttles. This morning Oxley has been found dead, his mill severely damaged and many of the looms destroyed. If these men did not carry out the deed themselves then they are directly responsible for the crimes of others. Therefore, if you have further information, I should be grateful to receive it so that any other felons can also be apprehended. But, be in no doubt that all concerned – and I stress, *all* – will face the same justice.'

'Mr Mayor, do not misunderstand me. In the light of the information you have been given, the guilt of these two men must appear clear and straightforward. Yet, I assure you, they are neither directly nor indirectly responsible for these events.'

Micklethwaite's nostrils flared. 'Then please enlighten me.'

He briefly outlined the first attack on Isabelle and the events of the night before, ending with a detailed account of the events inside the mill.

'So you see, sir, whatever Robinson or Tinker may have said in the Leopard was totally unconnected to the actions of those who destroyed Oxley's property. And as for his tragic death, Miss Broussard and I can testify that he was dead before we arrived there, when Robinson and Tinker were only leaving the tavern.'

'And how might you know this?' Micklethwaite asked coldly.

'They told me so this morning in the prison ward, though the landlord of the Leopard has also confirmed it.'

'Well then, clearly those who had been inflamed by their words had left the inn earlier to carry out their violent purpose for them.'

'Yet, Oxley's body was cold and stiff. He had certainly lain there several hours – since sometime that afternoon, perhaps even earlier. Whereas according to the landlord it was well into the evening before they started their diatribe against Mr Oxley.'

The mayor steepled his fingers and held them to his lips for a moment.

'Of course,' Micklethwaite continued, 'we only have your word concerning the time of death. Sadly, neither you, nor Miss Broussard, are known to us and your reputations remain – how shall I put this? – in some doubt. As such, your testimony will carry little weight before the magistrate. In addition, I am led to believe that you are well acquainted with members of the Tinker family. The trustworthiness of your account would appear to be open to serious question.'

'I appreciate that, sir, which is why it is essential that those who *are* responsible for the destruction of Mr Oxley's property be found. As for his death, I believe that there is, as yet, no evidence of foul play and there are, surely, other far less sinister possibilities.'

'And what might those be?' responded Micklethwaite sharply.

'For example, it seems very likely that he died as a result of falling down the stairs by accident.'

The mayor frowned. 'And what possible reason could you have for making such a claim?'

Charlie hesitated.

'Well?'

'Well… I happen to know that Mr Oxley was suffering with bouts of dizziness.'

Micklethwaite let out a snort. 'Oh, I see. So, yet again one of your patients has met an untimely end.'

Charlie sighed. 'Regrettably so.'

'How many is that now, Rossi – three?' said the mayor, smirking.

'I realise that my discomfort may be a source of amusement for some. However, I would prefer it if we could attend to the matter in hand.'

'No doubt you would.' The mayor laughed again.

'Mr Mayor,' Charlie persisted, 'the gang must be found.'

Micklethwaite stroked his beard. 'Hmm, indeed so.' He sat back in his chair. 'You speak of an Irishman and a Liverpudlian. They are very possibly some of the labourers who worked on the canal. This end was finished a couple of years ago and most of them moved west. However, some have remained, looking for work where they can find it, on turnpikes and the like. I am told that there is a group of them out at Kirkstall, repairing the bridge on the Bradford road, some three miles west of here. Perhaps that might be a good place for you to begin your search.'

'*My* search? Surely you intend to send your constables to find them.'

'You don't seem to appreciate, Rossi – our men have no more authority than the average Parish Constable. Thus, they have no remit outside of the borough. Besides, you have doubtless seen them. Too many of them are old and frail. They would be of little use facing a group of determined, even armed, men such as those you describe.'

'And yet you expect me to walk into their camp and arrest them single-handed. Last night they were trying to kill me!'

Micklethwaite smiled, though his eyes had no humour in them.

'I rather fear that is your problem and not mine. In the wards, I have two troublemakers who need teaching a lesson. So, unless you can produce evidence to the contrary, I am sure that the court will be more than happy to convict them on the evidence provided by citizens of this borough. Their fate will dissuade others from following their seditious example.'

'But, surely, you don't want this gang to walk away scot free?'

'Not if what you say is true. But I am willing to leave that to you, so that you may prove – how shall I put it? – your good faith. In the meantime, I will have the body examined.' The cold smile returned. 'You never know, perhaps the alderman died of "natural" causes after all.'

The mayor rang for the servant. 'There *is* perhaps one thing that persuades me of your sincerity in this whole affair.'

'And what might that be?'

'That if Oxley's death cannot be pinned on Tinker and Robinson, then you can be absolutely certain that the people of Leeds will pin it on you.'

Sam banged his fist on the table. 'What a bastard!'

The kitchen of the King's Arms was full of Tinkers: Tom, his sister, Agnes and Lizzie, his mother.

'Too right,' brooded Charlie in the corner. 'He couldn't care less if they hang or not, so long as his beloved Corporation can carry on as usual.'

'Welcome to Leeds,' said Tom, smiling dryly.

'It's the same everywhere,' replied Charlie sourly, 'the middling sort protecting their own, and to hell with everyone else.'

Sam exploded again. 'But, God, that man – he sits there on his fat arse and expects you to track them down? Eight of them and they're probably armed… and he's not going to lift a bloody finger to help. If the Corporation goes on like this, Oxley won't be the last.'

'Tinker!' Beth spun round and launched an onion at him, hitting him between the eyes.

'Aye, easy now, Sam,' said Charlie.

'Well, you'll not go alone,' Sam growled, massaging his forehead.

'And you can count me in,' added Tom.

Agnes looked around the room, anxiously.

'Don't fret yourself, girl,' said her mother. 'You'll stay with your Aunty Beth. She'll be needing the help.'

'Hang on, Lizzie,' said Sam, frowning. 'No way.'

Lizzie Tinker was only small, hardly bigger than her daughter, but, standing in the middle of the room, every inch of her bristled.

'Try and stop me.'

'No, it's far too dangerous.'

'So you think you're the man for the job, do you?' She put on an affected voice: '"Can you sort out that trouble in the bar, Beth, as I need to go and change a barrel." God, you're no better than Jake.'

'Lizzie…' Beth tried to put an arm round her shoulders but

she pushed it away. She planted her hands on her hips and her legs firmly apart. Under her lace cap, Lizzie's face boiled.

'It's not enough that I'm married to an imbecile for a husband, who's drunk a week's earnings with that good-for-nothing, Robinson, or that he's made an enemy of the sodding mayor. It's not enough that he's going to get himself hanged and have us thrown into the workhouse. Now I've got his idiot brother trying to stop me saving him from the gallows. What the hell do you think you're playing at? Of course it's dangerous! But what makes you think you have the slightest say in the matter?'

She paused for breath.

Sam had paled slightly but managed to find his voice. 'I'm sorry, Lizzie, but it's not just me: Jake said to keep you out of it.'

'That daft apeth! I'll take no orders from him. What is it with the Tinker clan? When God were handing out brains you must have all been sleeping it off.'

'I know what you mean, love,' Beth tried to soothe her sister-in-law. 'They're not the brightest pennies in the purse, either of them. But think of Agnes: she's got her father in gaol and then the rest of you head off into God knows what. She needs you, Lizzie. She needs to know that you, at least, are safe.'

Lizzie looked at the men and shook her head. 'Pah! A fine hue and cry you'll make.'

The door shuddered on its hinges behind her.

***

On one side of the study sat Elizabeth Oxley, on the other lay the body of her brother.

She wasn't sure what was expected but this seemed to be the best place. Yet, it was repellent. Simply being in the same room felt like contamination. And the silence was so oppressive. It was a relief just to hear her own sobs. Once the funeral was over she would have the table burnt.

She raised her eyes to glance at the sheet shrouding the body. She couldn't bear to look at his face.

Cut short in his prime. His future snatched away. The chance of redemption denied – for, God knows, James's life didn't bear too much scrutiny. How cruel that death should come now, just when the mill and his appointment as an alderman had set him on the path to success and, surely, respectability. Joseph would have been proud of him.

The thought set her off again.

She would write and tell him but would it get through, wherever it was he was posted? Even if it did, there was little chance of a reply. Even less hope that he would return.

Her sobs grew louder.

They had both abandoned her – the brothers who were supposed to have looked after her. And now she might as well be walled up here like a nun, unless, at last, the whiff of inheritance brought suitors sniffing around. They didn't want her, that much was clear, but the money might get them drooling. At least she wouldn't be alone. Anyone would be better than that.

She wiped her cheeks again with the sodden, powder-smeared handkerchief. Moving to the table, she steeled herself to look down. The hideous face, half covered in bruising, assailed her. She had heard hardly credible stories of people placing a farewell kiss on the brow. A shudder ran through her at the thought. Even to touch the carcass was unthinkable. And staying the night was out of the question. She would go to her cousin's. The maid could keep it company. At least, tomorrow the carpenter would come and she wouldn't have to face it any longer.

There was a muffled sound of knocking.

She gasped and looked down at the colourless hands that protruded from the shroud. They lay, unmoving, on the table.

How foolish could she be? It was just a caller – doubtless come to convey their condolences. If so, she wouldn't be the only one wearing a mask.

Another knock came, this time on the study door. She turned as the maid pushed it opened.

'Doctor Barnard,' she said brightly. 'How good of you to come.'

***

Lizzie Tinker didn't stop until she got to the mill. Inside, the weavers were gathered around the bottom of the stairs.

'We might as well get ourselves down to the workhouse,' said a giant of a man, grimly.

'I don't know, Jem,' replied a short, plump man sitting on the stairs. 'Maybe Mr Joseph'll come back now. If he's still alive.'

'Pigs might fly,' replied the giant.

'Maybe his sister'll take over?' suggested one of the younger weavers.

'Stranger things have happened, Seth. There were a widow down Wakefield way what took over a mill. Made not a bad job of it, from what I heard.'

'Aye, but Elizabeth Oxley? Do me a favour.'

'That one ain't got a grain of sense in her head.'

As Lizzie approached, the man on the stairs greeted her with a curt nod: 'Lizzie.'

The others turned and she saw suspicion, even hostility, in their eyes.

The giant spat on the ground. 'You've got a bloody nerve, I'll give you that. If they give me the rope I'll string up your old man myself.'

'Steady on, Jem,' said the one on the stairs. 'It ain't her fault and she's gonna have it hard enough.'

'For your information,' Lizzie smiled sarcastically, 'Oxley were dead long before Jake and Abe started mouthing off at the Leopard. Now I realise that might take some of you a little while to work out, so let me help you: it means they never touched him. Alright?'

'Who span you that garbage?' snarled Jem.

'Only the people who found Oxley here last night.'

'What, the sods that smashed the place up?'

'Don't be so thick – the two that lot were chasing. They hid in here.'

'So why's Jake in the wards then?'

'Because stupid men' – she glared at them – 'believe the first thing they're told!'

'Easy now, Lizzie. We meant no harm.'

'No? Well, I'll give you a chance to prove it. He's still gonna swing unless the gang's brought in. They reckon they're out Kirkstall way – incomers, eight of them and they may be armed. So you just go and get your mates. We need numbers and we need them fast.'

The men glanced at each other. A few feet shuffled.

'Well?' She scanned the group, angrily.

'What's it to us?' replied Jem. 'We've had a bad enough day as it is. No point rounding it off by getting ourselves killed.'

'Aye, it ain't gonna save the mill.'

'It'll save my husband! Who happens' – Lizzie fumed – 'to be innocent.'

'Says you.'

'Says a man who's sticking his neck on the line for Jake even though he hardly knows him. And our Tom too, who's still wet behind the ears but more of a man than any of you lot. God, you're a shambles. You're neither use to man nor beast. I don't know why I'm wasting my breath.'

She spat her contempt and turned for the door.

***

Sam's cart left the claustrophobic streets behind and trundled past newly hedged fields, dressed in stubble. A group of deer peered out from a patch of woodland alongside the road, and rooks cawed in the bare trees. To their left, the River Aire snaked through the valley with its newly cut cousin flowing imperceptibly alongside. At any

108

other time, and despite the light rain, Charlie would have enjoyed the ride. Today, though, the jolting brought out all his aches and pains, aggravating his darkening mood.

As the road emerged from a large wood, Sam pointed ahead to where the turnpike crossed the river. A group of men were hard at work.

'Looks like we're in luck,' said Sam.

'Aye, if they're the right ones,' replied Tom, grimly.

Just then a whistle blew and the men shouldered their picks and shovels and, like a motley platoon, set off along a narrow lane that branched to the right of the main road. Sam kept them at a discreet distance.

As they rounded a bend in the river, a large ruined abbey lay behind a thin screen of trees. Even at a distance, they could see that the great east window of the church was missing and that the wall below it had been demolished. The lane ran straight through the gap and, as if being swallowed by some monstrous mouth, the line of labourers disappeared into the nave.

The bell tower, rising high above, had also seen better days – half of it was missing. Sam whistled. 'Well, would you look at that! I heard it had come down in a storm last year but, Lord, it's in a sorry state.'

Smoke began to rise from within the abbey walls.

'Warming up and drying out by the look of it,' he observed. 'Can't blame them for that.'

He pulled up alongside a dilapidated farm cottage.

'So, what do we do now?' asked Tom.

Sam turned to Charlie. 'Well?'

'How the hell should I know,' he snapped.

'Woah! What's up?'

'Well, let's see. I spent last night being hunted, beaten up, nearly murdered and almost drowned. And to be honest I'm not that keen on having to do it all over again.'

'I know,' replied Sam, sympathetically, 'but if that's all you thought you'd be miles away.'

Charlie snorted. 'I'd like to be.'

'Wouldn't we all,' said Sam. 'Look, you don't have to do this – you really don't. You've done more than enough already. I mean, if it weren't for you, Jake and Abe would be on their way to the gallows for sure. We wouldn't have a shred of evidence to get them off or even have a clue where to look for this lot. God knows what we're going to do when we meet them but whether there's three of us or only two ain't going to make much difference. So, if you want to sit this out, no one's going to blame you – least of all me or Tom.'

'Aye, he's right,' agreed Tom.

'I don't know,' Charlie shook his head. 'I guess what's eating me is Micklethwaite – I'm really only here because of him.'

'How do you mean?' asked Sam.

'He knew just how to play me. My reputation's on the line and if he'd told me to jump straight back in the river I'd have probably done it, if there was any hope it would win people over, or "prove my good faith" as he called it. He knew I'd stick my head back in the noose. As far as he's concerned, I'm only out here to save my own skin. And maybe he's right.'

'Aye, but you're still helping to get Jake and Abe off the hook.'

'That's the thing,' he grimaced, 'and I don't know how to say this but… well, part of me wishes they *had* killed Oxley.'

Tom looked aghast. 'What?'

'I know, Tom, it's just that, if by some miracle we do save them, then his death ends up on my plate and that's another nail in my coffin, and probably the final one at that. It's all wrong, but…' He put his head in his hands and groaned. 'I'm sorry, I'm not thinking straight. I'm dog-tired and every bone of me hurts, and I feel as if… well as if I'm being used.'

Sam put his hand on his shoulder. 'Look, Charlie, it's alright with us but it's your call.'

Smoke continued to rise above the abbey walls.

He heaved a heavy sigh. 'I'm sorry, Sam.'

'Right then.' Sam pulled a cosh from his coat, with a wink. 'Despite what Lizzie thinks, I do know how to keep an orderly bar.'

Tom followed suit, drawing out a large, wickedly tapering knife. Charlie looked at it quizzically.

'A burling knife,' explained Tom. 'Great for rooting out knots in cloth. Pretty handy in a scrap too. Or so I've heard.' He smiled sheepishly.

'Yeh, well, let's hope…' Charlie's voice trailed away.

'Aye, no problem,' said Sam, brightly, slinging a coil of rope over his shoulder. 'We'll see you later.'

The two Tinkers jumped down from the cart and set off towards the ruins. They kept away from the lane, staying close to the riverbank, where cattle looked on cautiously from their pools of mud. Turning away from the river, they began to pick their way through the ruins. Everywhere, the walls were overgrown with creepers and saplings. A few larger trees grew from cracks in the stone, steadily prising the joints apart. Several walls had already given up the ghost. Rounding a corner, Tom tripped over the lip of an old stone-lined coffin and landed face down in the dirt.

Sam grinned and whispered, 'Nay, lad, it'll not be that bad.'

They approached a low Norman archway, which opened onto a large grassy square surrounded by high walls. Sam motioned to Tom to stay back while he had a closer look.

In the centre of the cloisters, half a dozen men sat round a big fire on which a kettle was boiling. In the corner, to his left, another man, wrapped in a great overcoat, was resting against a yew tree.

Maybe the foreman, thought Sam.

On the other side of the square, to his right, two large sheets of tarpaulin hung down where they had been pegged into the mortared joints of the far wall. The man holding the kettle gave a shout and one of the tarpaulins lifted up as two more labourers emerged from a room set back off the cloisters.

Sam waited for a few minutes but no one else appeared. He crept back to Tom.

'Looks like there's just nine of them,' reported Sam, quietly. 'So if these are the ones who attacked Charlie…'

'… there's only the foreman to help.'

'Aye, lad, maybe.' He smiled ruefully. 'Well, we might as well get on with it. Let me do the talking and, if I say so, run like heck.'

Passing through the arch, they approached the man by the tree. He looked up and nodded a silent greeting.

'Would you be in charge here?' asked Sam.

'Aye, that I would.'

'We're wondering if you need any more hands.'

The foreman snorted. 'You can say that again – I lost five men overnight.'

'How so?'

'Some bleeding argument on the way back from town. God knows what it were about.'

Sam could imagine.

'Actually, that's why we wanted to talk to you. We think it was them who attacked a friend of ours last night – nearly killed him and the woman he was with. They smashed up a mill as well – windows, looms, the lot. And this morning, the constables have arrested two of our weavers. They were nowhere near the place but, likely as not, they'll still swing for it, unless we can bring in the real culprits.'

'Well, they'll be miles away by now,' replied the foreman, sourly.

'Aye, but there were eight in the gang, so maybe some of them are still over there,' he nodded in the direction of the fire. 'One's Irish and another's from Liverpool. They were the ringleaders.'

The foreman got to his feet, his face darkening. 'Hang on, how do you know this? Who says so?'

'I do.' Sam turned round. Charlie was standing behind him with a rusty-looking mattock in his hands. 'It was me they were trying to kill when they were smashing up the mill. But we're going to need some help to bring them in – from you and the rest.'

The foreman frowned. 'What, and lose three more men?'

'But save two others!' replied Charlie.

The foreman clicked his tongue, weighing his options.

'Well, then, let's see, shall we.' He called across the grass: 'Hey lads!... Doyle! Callaghan! Barton! This lot want to us to help take you in. It sounds like you've been naughty boys.'

A pile of picks were leaning against the cloister wall. The three men each grabbed one and, with their workmates, quickly closed in on the intruders.

Charlie gripped the mattock across his chest. Sam and Tom, flanking him, pulled out their weapons. They were outnumbered three to one but they stood shoulder to shoulder.

'Well, look at that – if it isn't Pimp Boy himself!' jeered the Irishman. His two companions laughed.

The foreman wasn't laughing. 'Alright, Doyle, what's all this about?'

'Well now,' the Irishman replied, 'this would be the very fellow who lost you your men last night – him and his whore. If it wasn't for them you'd still have a full crew.'

'Callaghan?'

'Just like he says, boss,' said the Liverpudlian.

'That's rubbish!' erupted Charlie. 'They set about us and when we escaped they hunted us down like animals, and when we hid in a mill they wrecked the place. We managed to get away and that must have spooked the rest of them. That's why they've scarpered.'

Some of the labourers eyed each other, uncertainly.

Barton, the third gang member, spoke up: 'Look boss, sure we chased them, but then his whore shows us her muff, right there in the street. I mean, what were we to do after that? If we got a bit excited it's down to her, not us.'

The other men laughed, knowingly.

Tom burst out, 'And right now my father's in Leeds gaol for your "bit of excitement" – that and a murder he didn't commit.'

'Murder?' The foreman swung round. 'What bloody murder?'

'Ain't nothing to do with us, boss,' growled Callaghan. 'When we got into the mill there's this man lying dead on the floor. For all we know, it was the pimp who killed him.'

'That's the God's honest truth, to be sure,' said Doyle. Then, looking at the three of them, he snarled, 'And now they're trying to stick the noose round our necks.'

'No, you've got it wrong!' cried Charlie but the labourers, eyes narrowing, closed ranks around them. He stepped back but his heel struck the cloister wall.

He glanced at the foreman. 'You can't let them…'

The man shrugged casually.

In a blur of silvery grey, Doyle's pickaxe arced towards Sam. Charlie thrust the mattock out in front of his friend. The pick smashed against it, snapping the rusty blade clean off. As Doyle drew back, Callaghan launched himself. Charlie braced the mattock handle above his head just as the pick struck home. The wood held but he crumpled to the ground. With the axe still hooked over the handle, Callaghan yanked backwards, ripping it from Charlie's grasp. Sam and Tom stepped in front of him but, seeing the short reach of their weapons, the three gang members laughed derisively. They raised their axes as one.

'Stop right there!'

A little woman, wearing a cloth cap, stepped out from one of archways on the other side of the square.

The men laughed. 'Hey lads,' leered Doyle, 'here's another bit of fun for us.'

'Lizzie, get out of here now!' screamed Sam.

And then the air was full of challenges as men charged out of every entrance around the cloisters. Some were carrying bars of iron or lengths of wood, many were wielding burling knives like Tom's.

With the tide turning, the rest of the labourers turned with it. Two of them grabbed Barton while another ripped the pick from out of his hands. However, Doyle and Callaghan twisted quickly away from their former allies and ran full tilt towards the far wall. Two of the weavers were blocking their path but with a few swings of their pickaxes they easily broke through. Reaching the wall, they disappeared behind one of the tarpaulins.

The chasers were only a few yards behind. Everyone except the foreman – who was sitting back down and lighting his pipe – had joined the hunt. Tom's whoops of glee brought broad grins to the faces of those around him.

Charlie ducked under the tarpaulin. Beyond was a large vaulted room, in the rear corner of which were a pair of tall, narrow windows. Running towards them, he could see that the ground outside was about four feet lower. It was enough of a drop to have taken its toll on Callaghan, who was hobbling after Doyle, but Charlie landed safely. Other weavers and labourers spilled out of the cloisters through nearby archways.

The fugitives made for the river and ran along the bank until they reached the point where a millrace split off. The flow of water through it was controlled by a line of wooden sluice gates that connected to form a narrow bridge over to a small island. Doyle crossed quickly, with Callaghan not far behind. Ahead lay a weir, which was swollen by the recent rains. Doyle trod carefully through the fast-moving water, reaching the other side without mishap. Callaghan followed but, whether because of his ankle, the force of the water or the slipperiness of the crest, halfway across he stumbled.

Looking on from the far side of the sluice gates, Charlie thought for a moment that Callaghan was going to be swept away but the man got back to his feet. Checking over his shoulder, the Liverpudlian saw that the first of the chasing pack was stepping out onto the weir. He threw caution to the wind and started to run. The bank was no more than a few yards away but after a few strides his long legs flew from under him. His head smashed down onto the ridge. At the weir's foot, the turbulent waters sucked him under.

Doyle, waiting on the far side for his friend, stood for a moment glaring at Charlie, his face contorted. He shouted something but it was lost in the rush of the weir. Drawing his finger across his throat, he spat and then sloped off towards the green pastures beyond.

The weaver out on the weir's crest stepped cautiously back to dry ground and the rest of the men spread out along the bank to look for Callaghan. He resurfaced, face down, a few yards from the foot of the weir, pressed up against an island of reeds.

The three Tinkers joined Charlie by the sluice gates and they watched as two of the labourers tried to retrieve the body. The men tied a length of rope to one of the pickaxes and then cast it towards their former workmate. Several attempts fell wide or short but eventually the pickaxe sank deep into the buttocks of the floating corpse. The men lining the bank gave a grim cheer. The Tinkers joined in.

'Well, we got one of them anyhow,' said Lizzie. 'Two, if you don't count breathing.'

'And we're alive to tell the tale,' added Sam. 'All things considered, I reckon that went pretty well.'

Lizzie laughed. 'Oh aye, I could see you had them eating out of your hands back there.'

Sam grinned. 'I know but, still, I'm glad you could join us.'

'Aye, thanks Mum,' said Tom. 'You saved our bacon.'

Lizzie allowed herself a satisfied smile

Charlie pulled a face. 'I'm sorry to spoil the party but six of them got away. Jake's not out of the woods yet.'

9

The overcast sky was darkening by the time Sam's cart trundled into Leeds, with Callaghan's body lying in the back and Barton and his captors walking behind. Some of the men began to peel off, saying their farewells.

'They'll have a tale to tell when they get home,' observed Lizzie.

'They're not the only ones,' said Sam. 'We've still got to run ours past the mayor.'

'No, Sam, this one's down to me... easy now Lizzie.' Charlie raised his palms in self-defence. 'Look, I doubt Barton's in any mood to open up and I'm afraid a bunch of Tinkers aren't going to carry much weight with the mayor. We need some other witnesses, one's he'll listen to.'

'I suppose so.' Lizzie nodded thoughtfully. She scanned the gradually thinning group of weavers. 'I'd go with Nathan Lee and Thomas Rooke – the others respect them and they're not slow coming forward.'

'Alright,' agreed Charlie, 'let's get this done.'

Once again, Micklethwaite's butler showed great composure when required to admit not only the "street fighter" but three other men,

117

one of whom was yanked over the threshold on the end of a rope. He silently ushered them into the parlour.

'Will the mayor be long?' asked Charlie but the man left the room without a word.

A longcase clock filled the silence as Charlie fidgeted nervously. Barton stared at the carpet a few feet ahead of him – his face and his thoughts unreadable. However, unabashed, the weavers began to explore the room.

'Bloody 'ell, these chairs'd fetch a pretty packet.'

'Aye, Nat, but have you seen this statue? Look at the tits on her!' The men smirked.

The clock chimed five and in walked Micklethwaite accompanied by another man.

'I think some of you know our magistrate, Mr Ibbetson.' Micklethwaite took a seat near the window, while gesturing the magistrate towards another, beside a small, rectangular table. The others were left standing.

Ibbetson was short, rotund, and very smartly dressed, or he would have been if his wig hadn't been set at a jaunty angle. It looked as if the mayor's summons had brought him out at pace.

'So, Mr Rossi, I see that you have been busy.' Micklethwaite surveyed the room. 'But what's this: a gang of one? Come, come – I distinctly remember you making allegations against eight men and I was under the distinct impression that you had set out to apprehend them all.'

Charlie let the sarcasm pass. 'Mr Mayor – Mr Ibbetson – as my companions here will bear out, by the time we found them, five had already fled. As for the remaining three, I fear that one of them escaped but the body of the other is in a cart outside in the street.'

'The body of the other one!' Micklethwaite laughed, coldly. 'Well, I suppose I should have known – death does seem to follow you around.'

Charlie bit his tongue and began to summarise the events at the abbey. When he mentioned the arrival of the weavers, Ibbetson, who had been making notes, stopped him in mid-flow and asked the other men to take up the account. Charlie hoped that they wouldn't be overawed. He needn't have worried. As they had so far been ignored by the mayor, Rooke and Lee pointedly introduced themselves and then gave a very adequate account of the capture of Barton, the drowning of Callaghan and the escape of Doyle.

'And what do you have to say to this account of the affair, Mr… Barton?' asked Ibbetson, checking his notes.

'It don't mean a bloody thing.' Barton's eyes were still fixed on the floor.

'I beg your pardon?' Ibbetson's head shot up. 'You are facing a charge of committing a most serious felony. I remind you, that your fate may well depend on your statement now and, I may add, on your demeanour.'

At last, Barton raised his head to look at the magistrate. 'Well, then, here's my "statement". I weren't nowhere near this mill they talk of – nor were the others neither. For all I know, this one' – he glanced at Charlie – 'smashed it up himself and wants someone else to pay for it.'

'So, if you are innocent, why did you try to run away from the abbey?' asked Ibbetson.

'And, what would you do, sir' – Barton's smile was as sarcastic as his tone – 'if a great horde sprang out of thin air and attacked you with knives?'

'Mmm. Indeed.'

The magistrate looked down and made some further notes. Micklethwaite sat gazing out of the window, absent-mindedly picking at his teeth.

Charlie groaned inwardly: it was just one version of events against another. Where was there any actual evidence? They needed something more for Jake and Abe to stand any chance of walking free.

A voice broke into his thoughts. 'I think this'll be of interest to you.'

All heads turned to look at Rooke, the taller of the two weavers, who had a wrinkled leather patch over his left eye. He was holding out his hand towards the magistrate. On his palm lay a gentleman's watch and chain. The casing looked to be edged with delicate engraving. He stepped forward and handed it to Ibbetson.

'I found it in Barton's coat. If you ask me, it were Oxley's. He'd flash it around at the mill. He were always checking to see how fast we were working.'

Ibbetson examined the surrounding filigree and then flicked the casing open to study the face. He nodded thoughtfully, appreciating the quality of what he saw.

'May I?' Micklethwaite held out a hand and Ibbetson passed it to him. After a moment, the mayor concurred. 'I would hazard that this is Oxley's. The engraving certainly matches his and it is most distinctive. Doubtless his sister can provide the final confirmation.' He looked at Barton. 'Not, I think, the watch of a common labourer.'

'I never took nothing. I've never seen the thing before in my life.' Barton looked from the magistrate to Rooke and back again, his voice growing louder, angrier, more desperate. 'That bugger's set me up!'

The magistrate raised his hand. 'I've heard enough. Barton, you will come before the Sessions on a charge of criminal damage to the mill of Mr James Oxley and of the theft of this piece of his personal property. Mr Rooke and Mr Lee, you will find two constables outside the front door. Please deliver the prisoner to them and may I thank you for your not inconsiderable assistance.'

The three men left the room with Barton shouting and cursing.

'Very well, Rossi, I suppose you have proven your point.'

'Thank you, Mr Mayor.' Charlie bowed slightly. Micklethwaite's concession had been grudging but Jake and Abe were free men again. Elation and relief flooded him at the sudden turn of events.

'Tinker and Robinson will of course be flogged.'

'What?'

'Incitement will not be tolerated. They will be made an example of.' Micklethwaite smiled his cold smile again.

'Indeed,' concurred Ibbetson, gravely. 'The law is here to protect us from disorder and the mob. God knows we need it, for they appear to require such little provocation to cause havoc. If it isn't the price of bread, it's the turnpike charges.'

'But surely—' Charlie tried to protest.

'*Or* the fall in weavers' wages,' Micklethwaite interjected firmly over him. 'You may think them all noble fellows, Rossi, but our streets have seen far too much of their rampaging in recent years.'

Ibbetson nodded. 'And those who create the spark are as guilty as those who burn down the house. So it must be stamped out before it takes hold. If we do not, then before we know it, I will be reading the Riot Act and there will be Dragoons in the street once again and even more bodies.'

'Precisely, Mr Ibbetson.' Micklethwaite steepled his fingers and nodded affirmingly. 'I am gratified to see that our sentiments are in such close accord. But your mention of bodies is, regrettably, a timely reminder. We still have before us the matter of Mr Oxley's death at the mill. You will be wanting Mr Rossi's... version of the events.'

Once Charlie had finished, Ibbetson sat back pondering, stroking the pen's feather along his top lip.

'So he was lying at the foot of the stairs, face down. Was there any sign of a struggle?'

'I really couldn't say. It was dark and we were in fear of our lives. I assumed that he'd stumbled and fallen down the stairs.'

'Ah, yes,' remarked Micklethwaite, 'his light-headedness.'

'Was Oxley suffering from some affliction?' asked Ibbetson.

'Apparently so,' replied Micklethwaite, with what struck Charlie as undue relish.

'I see... which could explain his fall. Has the examination of the body been completed?'

'Indeed it has Mr Ibbetson. Doctor Barnard...'

'Barnard!' Charlie exclaimed, his heart sinking.

'… Doctor Barnard has visited the family home this afternoon and reports that there are no signs of any violence to the body other than bruising, which he holds to be fully consistent with Oxley having fallen to his death.'

'Yes, I see.' The magistrate made some further notes and then began to fold up his papers. The matter was clearly resolved to his satisfaction. Micklethwaite, on the other hand, wasn't finished.

'Of course, the doctor was very concerned to hear that Mr Oxley had been one of your patients, Rossi.' Ibbetson looked up as the mayor continued. 'Yes, he was perturbed in the extreme that three of our most esteemed residents have now died in no more than a week, all following receipt of your treatments.'

'You speak of Robert Crompton and George Thomson,' said Ibbetson. 'I was informed that there were no signs of violence or malicious intent in their cases either.'

'Apparently not,' replied Micklethwaite, 'according to Doctor Barnard. Nevertheless, he is very greatly alarmed at the… let me call it the coincidence, that the three men had recently been under the care of Mr Rossi. So much so that he has asked that the matter be considered as a matter of urgency by the Corporation. After careful consideration I have acceded to his request.'

'But that's ludicrous!' Charlie burst out. 'There is no more evidence that I am responsible than there is of any foul play.'

'Perhaps not. But how many more such deaths can we afford? How many more aldermen can we risk losing? If we do not begin to follow London's example and start to regulate our medical practitioners then we may end up bringing them all into disrepute.'

'Disrepute! And what is this reputation that we need to defend it so earnestly?' He couldn't restrain himself any longer. 'We all know what it is: ignorance, incompetence and self-interest. These should be things of the past. If someone embraces new ideas and applies them to the production of cloth then we hail him as a man of enterprise and we shower him with honours. Yet, if a man applies new ideas to the production of health we castigate him as a quack and drive him out of town. People die every day at the hands of our physicians, our surgeons, even our apothecaries, and no one pays one iota of attention. No one summons the Corporation to protect our citizens from them, oh no. But if someone tries to show a better way then—'

'Enough!' Micklethwaite rose from his chair. His eyes narrowed. 'You overstep the mark, Rossi. There may not be sufficient evidence to pursue any charges against you – not yet anyway – but the Corporation may still be minded to prohibit you from practising in our borough. So have a care whom you insult. Now, I have other business to attend to and I will thank you to leave.'

Outside in the darkening street, the Tinkers were waiting for him. They had watched with satisfaction as Barton was dragged out, struggling and swearing, and hauled off to the cells and they had listened to the weavers' account of what had happened inside and thanked them profusely for their help. They couldn't wait to begin the celebrations – he could see that in their faces.

'I'm sorry,' he greeted them grimly. 'I did my best but they're still going to be flogged.'

'What?' Tom and Sam burst out together. 'Bloody hell, why?'

'I'll tell you why: they want to stamp out discontent amongst the weavers. So what do they do? They flay the skin off their backs.' He shook his head in disbelief.

'The malicious bastards,' snarled Sam. 'Just when you think you're coming up to breathe, they tread your face back in the muck. You'd have thought Oxley were a damned saint the way they carry on.'

Lizzie stepped forward, took Charlie's hands in hers and kissed him on the cheek. 'Thank you.'

'I don't know what for.'

'For saving the life of my idiot husband, that's what.' She smiled thinly. 'And saving the rest of us from the poorhouse.'

'You that did that yourself, really.'

'But without you we wouldn't have known where to begin.'

'Ma's right,' agreed Tom. 'Thanks, Charlie. If there's ever anything…'

He laughed ironically. 'Well, if you could just get yourselves elected as aldermen that should do the trick.' As they set off back to the tavern, he explained about Barnard and the vote at the next meeting.

'Aye,' responded Sam, dismissively, 'but the word is that Barnard's tried all this before and the Corporation's just chucked him out. He's no more than a bigot. No one takes him seriously.'

'Well the mayor's taking him seriously now. Our doctor friend has got himself a powerful ally.'

'God, he'll be even more insufferable,' groaned Lizzie.

'Oh, and you can guess who Oxley's physician was.'

Sam's eyes opened wide as he turned to Charlie. 'Three out of three, eh – is that your coincidences again?'

'I don't know,' he shrugged, 'but according to Micklethwaite, Barnard's been round to examine the body and – surprise, surprise – found nothing amiss.'

'You think he should have done?' asked Sam.

'To be honest I've no idea.'

'But you'd like to know.'

'Now that's a thought,' said Lizzie, slowly.

'What is?' Sam asked.

'Crompton and Thomson are already mouldering but I doubt Oxley's been coffined yet.'

'Lizzie, you're a wonder,' exclaimed Charlie, returning her kiss. 'It's not much but at least it's something to go at.' Sam was still looking puzzled. 'Do you know where he lived?'

'Aye, just along on Boar Lane,' answered Lizzie, grinning. 'Our Sally used to do for "Madam".'

'His wife?'

'Not likely. His sister. They lived together. Well, at least since Oxley returned a year or two back. Before that she were there with

Mr Joseph – the younger brother. Believe it or not, that one were actually alright.'

As Charlie turned into Boar Lane, it came to him where he had heard Oxley's name recently. It had been nagging at the back of his mind: the woman in the graveyard – the friend of Barnard's wife – Elizabeth Oxley. She had mentioned her brother as well. He puffed out his cheeks and shook his head. Given her reaction to him, how could he hope to charm his way past her now?

With his head buzzing, he arrived outside the house before he realised where he was. He looked around to make sure: the Leopard was a few yards along the road and behind him loomed Trinity Church. There was no mistaking it. It was the house where, three nights earlier, Isabelle Broussard had disappeared.

10

What the hell did Isabelle have to do with all this? He had felt an understanding growing between them, born of their common experience as performers and outsiders, and of being hunted the night before. But when it came to it, what did he really know about her? He shook his head, took a deep breath and walked up the path.

His knocking was eventually answered by a thin-faced, cloth-capped maid who peered out through a narrow crack. In the light of the candle, her eyes looked hollow; her face blank.

'Good evening,' he smiled warmly. 'Please excuse the lateness of the hour but I have come to offer my condolences to Miss Oxley at the tragic death of her brother.'

'I'm afraid...' the maid's voice was barely audible '... Miss Oxley ain't at home.'

'Oh, I see. My name is Doctor Charles Rossi and Mr Oxley was one of my patients. May I come inside for a moment?'

'But Doctor Barnard has already been.'

'Yes, I know but I was also treating Mr Oxley, for a condition which may have contributed to his death. I was hoping to examine Mr Oxley's body, so as to prevent such a terrible thing happening to anyone else.'

'But Miss Oxley ain't here,' she repeated.

He spoke as gently as he could. 'I realise this may seem unusual but I won't detain you long. I give you my word.'

The maid looked even more anxious.

'Please?' he beseeched her.

The door opened and the maid stepped back, allowing him into the hall.

'Thank you…?'

'Charity.'

He could now see that the maid was no more than about fourteen. She was shivering, despite being wrapped in a woollen shawl.

'You won't tell Miss Oxley, sir? You won't get me into trouble for letting you in, will you? Only, I'm alone here. Except for… him.'

'You have my word, Charity.'

He couldn't believe his good fortune. Not only was the lady of the house out but she would never even know he had called. Despite this, he felt for the young girl, who had been left to keep a solitary and unnerving vigil with her dead master.

The maid glanced towards one of the doors that led off the hall and her shiver became a shudder.

'He's in the study.' She backed away from the door.

Stepping into the room, he turned, inviting her to follow him but she shook her head.

'Please, sir, I'd rather wait out here, if you don't mind.'

'Of course.' He pushed the door to.

The body lay on a table in the centre of the room. Under the covering cloth it was dressed in a simple cotton nightshirt. Four large candles were set on tall, wooden stands, two at either end of the table. Out of the public gaze, Elizabeth had chosen cheaper tallow candles. Their smell, mingling with the odour of the body, caught in the back of his throat.

At first sight, the lighting appeared to be casting a dark shadow down the right side of Oxley's face but, drawing closer, he realised that this was a large bruise, running from Oxley's temple down to his jaw. It was made even uglier by the vivid contrast with the pallid hue of the skin on the other side of the face.

Looking down at the body, he recalled how he had first met the clothier at his practice. Oxley had breezed in announcing that one of his friends on the Corporation had recommended him, adding, with a sneer, 'Although I doubt this kind of quackery has anything in it.' Biting his tongue, he had assured Oxley that spells of dizziness usually responded well to electrification.

The man had been unremarkable in appearance. In his early forties and of average height, he was hardly slim, but neither did Oxley approach the vast proportions of many of the better-off members of society whom he often treated. His blond hair was short-cropped for his wig, with a small bald patch on the crown.

He pulled up the nightshirt, revealing some more bruising across the top of his chest and a small patch around his left knee. All this seemed to fit with the idea that Oxley had fallen down the staircase, smashed his face against the banisters, and landed flat on his chest at the bottom, perhaps snapping his neck as he did so. Nor was it hard to imagine Barnard quickly coming to the same conclusion. It would all have been grist to Barnard's mill: a dizzy turn aggravated by electrical quackery.

He rolled the corpse over, flinching slightly as he pulled at the lifeless skin.

There were no other marks on the body but on the back of the head something caught his eye. On the right side of the skull, back behind the ear, was a pronounced area of swelling and under the hair, the skin was badly discoloured.

This wasn't right. Not if Oxley had fallen forwards.

He pressed his fingers around the bones in the neck but could feel no obvious sign of a fracture. He ran his thumb up through the short hairs on the neck below the base of the skull. And there was something. It was only small but it felt rough on the surface of the skin. He drew one of the candles in closer.

Right in the nape of the neck was a thick little scab.

Had Barnard missed it? Had he noticed the swelling above it? Given all the bruises on the man's front, had he even bothered to look?

He went over to the writing desk. Beside a pile of unopened correspondence was an ivory-handled letter-opener. Returning with it, he carefully scraped the dried blood away. A sudden thrill surged through him. He was looking at a little wound, no more than half an inch across. A puncture wound – the sort of thing that a slim blade or a sharp spike might make.

All those coincidences…

With his heart pounding, he inserted the tip of the letter-opener into the wound. His hand was none too steady but, without much effort, over an inch of metal had soon disappeared inside Oxley's neck. He stopped, reluctant to force the blade further. He couldn't be sure how far the wound went in, but he could at least judge the direction. It was heading for the centre of the man's brain.

'Doctor Rossi?'

The maid's voice made him jump.

'Thank you, Charity, I'm coming now.'

He rolled the body onto its back, dragged down the nightshirt and smoothed it as best he could. Tomorrow the body and its tell-tale evidence would disappear into a coffin. Were his hopes for a way out to disappear with this corpse?

He stepped back out into the hall.

'Did you find what you were looking for?'

He nodded. 'I did indeed and I am indebted to you for your help.'

She smiled shyly and her face relaxed a little.

A thought occurred to him. 'But perhaps you could help me with something else.'

'If I can, sir.'

'Isabelle Broussard – is she a friend of yours?'

The maid looked puzzled as she shook her head. 'No, sir. Who is she?'

'Well, she has only been in Leeds for a week or two – a young lady, twenty years of age or so, with long dark hair. Might she have made the acquaintance of Miss Oxley?'

The maid thought for a moment before responding. 'No, I don't think so. No one like that has called on m'lady recently.'

'And Mr Oxley?'

'Oh, I couldn't say, Doctor. I don't know who he sees.' And then, hurrying on, she added, 'I mean that he's an important man and he meets many people, and sometimes I'm busy...'

'Yes, I understand.'

The maid was fidgeting with the front of her apron.

'I'm sorry. I have kept you long enough.'

'Do you have to go now, Doctor?'

Her question surprised him. How anxious the young girl must be feeling.

'Yes, I think I should. But surely your mistress will be home soon.'

'No, sir, not tonight. She is staying with Mrs Crompton.'

'Mary Crompton?'

'Indeed, sir. She is Miss Oxley's cousin. I don't think Miss Oxley wanted to spend the night here, you see, not with her brother being... in there.'

'And she left you here alone.'

The girl looked up at him and, in the brief silence that followed, her face began to crumple and she started to sob quietly. He tentatively reached out to place a hand on her shoulder. At the first touch of her shawl she drew back from him, wiping her eyes and sniffing. He took a handkerchief out of his jacket and offered it to her.

'Thank you... I'm sorry.'

'That's alright.'

'It's just that I don't know how I'm going to... she wants me to sit with him.' She was taking deep breaths. 'Only I can't.'

'I know.'

'It's so horrible.'

He nodded. 'I understand.'

More tears came. 'I can't bear it,' she whispered, and then, as a great sob escaped, she cried, 'I can't bear being with him.'

Her whole body shook with spasms and she bent double. He reached out to her and this time she accepted his help as he led her to a nearby settle. Sitting down, she clasped her hands over her mouth as if, shocked at what she had just said, she wanted to prevent herself from saying more. He waited beside her for several minutes until she had regained her composure.

'I should go now. Will you be alright?'

She nodded.

'Good. Don't worry, I'll see myself out.'

But at this, the maid in her stood up and went to open the door for him. As he said goodbye, she held the handkerchief out to him but he shook his head.

'You keep it, Charity.'

'What would we do without you, Charlie.' Beth smothered him in a bosomy hug.

His whole body ached and, as he sank into the carver at the kitchen table, a wave of exhaustion flooded over him. He said nothing of his discovery and Beth asked no questions. She merely laid the first platter of food in front of him: venison pasties. Then came roast mutton, stewed carp, carrot pudding... The aromas, tastes and textures all went to work and the quart of Sam's ale had never tasted so good.

'For two days, I've been chased and beaten up, interrogated and ridiculed, and do you know what, Beth? It feels good to be spoilt for a change.'

Beth beamed.

***

Henry Barnard picked up the blackened poker and prodded the glowing coals. They sprang into new life.

'Do you see that, Emily?'

His wife looked up from her embroidery.

'People have warmed themselves by fires since the dawn of time. To them it was inexplicable but to us it is a wonder laid bare: phlogiston. In Isaac's lifetime, we will unveil all its mysteries and, one day, we will chart every flicker on Earth and in the heavens.'

'As you say, sir, it is truly wonderful.'

'We will have stolen the secret of fire and what will your deity do about it?' Barnard snorted. 'What new glories will open up for mankind then?'

Emily resumed her needlework.

The coal crackled in the grate.

'It's over.'

Emily looked up, sharply. 'I beg your pardon.'

'After all these years – victory is in sight. Thanks to the mayor, the Corporation is taking up the fight and that is all I have ever asked. Now reason will triumph and order will be restored. Rossi and his ilk have had their day. Despite all the mockery and ridicule, all the self-interested blindness, I never gave up. "Persecuted but not forsaken, cast down but not destroyed" – isn't that the phrase, from that damnable book of yours.'

Emily rose from her chair. 'I will go and check on Isaac before I turn in. Good night, Henry.'

Barnard watched her leave the room. She seemed a little stronger.

Yes it was a good night. For once in his life, the day was ending free of frustration or resentment. He had fought and he had won – not just a battle but a long, long campaign. The deaths were regrettable, of course, but they merely proved the point. It had been, after all, a war.

The silence was broken by a sharp rapping on the front door. At this hour, it could only be some emergency, real or, more probably, imagined.

Damn them! Would they not let him have even one night of peace?

11

'Does the offer of help still stand?'

'Just name it, Charlie.'

Tom Tinker had popped in on his way back from the Cloth Halls. Charlie was relishing a breakfast of porridge, eggs and ample quantities of pork.

'There are some handbills at the printers that need spreading around. I'm open for business again but no one seems to know.' He held out a slice. 'You should try this.'

Tom pulled it from the end of the knife. 'Leave it to me.'

Charlie left the comforts of Beth's kitchen and set off for the prison. His previous visit had been to the cells but today he wanted the Rotation Office. It sat directly on top of them, like a lid on the town's cesspit. The front of the building looked fairly plain but, compared to what lay beneath, it was a palace.

Inside the entrance, so close that he could barely get through the door, sat a small clerk in a large, powdered wig, behind a very wide desk. The man looked at him over the rim of his spectacles.

'It's out of the question.' He looked disdainfully at Charlie's yellowing bruises. 'The magistrate is far too busy to see the likes... to see you. He will be *extremely* busy. All day.'

Charlie tried to smile. 'I appreciate that but would you please at least let him know that I need to see him as soon as possible.'

The clerk began twiddling his fingers. 'I don't think you heard me.'

'It is,' Charlie bristled, 'a matter of great urgency.'

'Well then, come back tomorrow but I can't promise anything.'

'Tomorrow may be too late.' He took a few coins from his pocket.

'Well...'

Settling down on a bench, Charlie prepared for a long wait. On the wall opposite hung a large map of Yorkshire. The county looked immense but the borough of Leeds was lost among countless other towns and villages. In his mind's eye, each name on the map became home to countless people, each with their own struggles – so much loving and hoping and hurting and dying, everywhere, each day. Could all those lives really matter? To themselves they might seem important but to him they felt vaguely tragic. He let out a long, slow sigh. In the face of this mass of humanity, what made him think that his own problems, his own ambitions and worries, were so important?

His melancholy thoughts were interrupted when a door opened and the warder emerged, escorting the thin woman who had been slumped in the corner of Jake and Abe's cell. She still looked very sorry for herself. Her face and hands were grimy and the front of her filthy skirts was almost shredded, as if a fierce dog had sunk its teeth into them and refused to let go. She was led away down the stairs to the cells and he wondered what combination of physical punishment and public humiliation lay in wait for her.

'Good morning, Mr Rossi.' Ibbetson's greeting took him by surprise. 'I think I can spare you five minutes.'

The magistrate led him into his chamber. The floorboards were bare and painted wooden panels covered the lower part of the walls. The only furniture was a small oak bureau and a simple chair.

'Am I right to assume that you wish to see me about James Oxley?'

'Indeed, I have some further information which is material to a fuller understanding of his death.'

'Is that so?' Ibbetson sat down at the bureau and drew a quill from the inkwell. 'Then we had better hear it.'

'Well, sir, after I left the mayor's house yesterday I paid a visit to Miss Oxley, to convey to her my condolences.' It wouldn't help his cause to mention that she was absent from the house at the time. 'While I was there I was given permission to view the body for myself. As I examined it, I found that...'

'You examined his body?' Ibbetson scowled.

'I did, yes.'

'Even though Doctor Barnard had already done so and had reported his findings to me, you took upon yourself the mantle of physician and presumed to interfere with the body?'

'I appreciate that my actions were unusual. However, if you will hear me out, you will see that they were more than merited.'

'Well, let's have it then,' said Ibbetson, shaking his head.

'You must remember that I had also been treating Mr Oxley and I had a legitimate interest in trying to establish the cause of death.'

'I was of the opinion that it had already been established.'

'A theory has been proposed, certainly. However, I was concerned to discover whether there was any substance to Doctor Barnard's accusation that my electrical therapy had played a part in his demise.'

Ibbetson smiled dryly. 'And now – let me guess – you have come to tell me that it didn't.'

'I have come to tell you that Oxley was murdered.'

Ibbetson looked at him incredulously. 'Are you serious, man? Oxley, murdered? On what evidence?'

He described the swelling on the back of the head.

'There is no way he could have got that falling down stairs. But if someone had hit him at the top and then he had fallen, all the bruises make sense.'

'And you think the fall killed him – snapped his neck.'

'That may be so but the person took no chances. There was also a deep puncture wound on the back of his neck.' He explained the details of the depth and angle of the wound. 'It was murder, sir. He was killed in cold blood.'

The magistrate set his pen down and examined his notes.

Charlie shuffled from side to side.

Ibbetson looked up. 'So you believe there were two blows: one to the back of the head and a second, up into the brain, which killed him.'

He nodded.

Ibbetson studied him, pensively, for a few moments and then shook his head: 'No. You have tried your best but I am afraid that you fail to persuade.'

Hope sank as anger rose. 'Why ever not?'

'Because, Mr Rossi, even if we assume the accuracy of your observations, there are simpler and far less sinister ways to account for these facts.'

Now it was Charlie's turn to be incredulous. 'And they would be?'

'The wound you describe will doubtless have been inflicted by a nail protruding from the woodwork of the banister as he hit his head against it. After all you have said that you were not sure how far it had penetrated. As for the blow to the back of his head, I see no reason to assume that this was caused deliberately. After all, how is one to recreate accurately the path of the body as it fell, or to predict precisely what it might have struck in the process? No, sir, we have the testimony of a respected member of the medical fraternity of this town and if anything were amiss he would certainly have reported it.'

'But that's just the point…' But the magistrate stood up and raised his hand.

'I am sorry, sir, but you have had more than enough of my time and I have listened patiently to you and given your remarks due consideration. Now, I have no more to say on the matter. I have a list of prisoners to see as long as your arm and their crimes are, without doubt, far less imaginary. I understand, full well, your desire to rehabilitate yourself in the eyes of our townsfolk but I am bound to say that you will not do so by wasting my time any further. I bid you good day.'

The narrow passage looked so different in the daytime. Doors that might have offered sanctuary to him and Isabelle, if they had only had the time and light to notice, now stood open to the cold morning air. Little children played on the steps. A dog sniffed at the waste that flowed down the alleyway. Two women argued over a basket of fish. A man lurched from wall to wall, already worse for wear on the results of his family's weekly weaving.

Charlie passed the junction where Barton had laid into him and then been floored by Isabelle. A knot gripped his stomach as the walls closed around him. Walking these twisting ginnels was like falling back into a nightmare.

With a sigh of relief, he opened the gate into Lower Tenter. Rows of frames stood like serried ranks of soldiers on parade: aligned, erect and unmoving. Five feet high and twenty feet long, they still wore their thick, frosty uniforms. Around the edge of the frames were driven dozens of tenterhooks – each one holding the woven cloth in place, keeping it taut while it dried. This morning the sheets were tighter than ever. He touched one of the cold, bent nails that protruded from the wood and thought of the wound in Oxley's neck.

Of course, he should have checked the mill first. It was obvious now. He had woefully overestimated his hand. For him, as an outsider, to have challenged the testimony of an important figure in the community, he would have needed far more evidence. And besides, the magistrate had a point: was there a nail? His gut instinct told him that the wound was no accident but he hadn't checked. It also told him that it was now going to take far more than the absence of any nail to persuade Ibbetson of Oxley's murder. And as for the other two deaths, instinct was all he was ever likely to have.

Leaving the tenter frames behind, he turned towards the river and the mill. The building impressed, even at a distance: high, red-bricked walls with massive rectangles of glass, extending the working day until the sun was low on the horizon. He thought of the many weavers still operating looms in the maze of cramped, dark passageways and yards. Surely the mill was a glimpse of what was to come. Manufactories were springing up all around Leeds and, before too long, ones far bigger than this would be flooding the world with cloth. Bigger, cheaper, quicker – that would be the future. It had already arrived in the fields and farms, and it was coming to cotton. It would come here too, soon enough. Jake Tinker and his friends would have no choice but to adapt to this new world or be swept aside.

Drawing closer, he could see that the broken shards had been swept out of the vast frames and two of the great windows stood completely empty, welcoming in the wintry air. As he stepped inside, the clatter of shuttles assailed him. Struck by wooden paddles, they flew backwards and forwards through the warp yarns, trailing the weft behind. Like clogs, dancing in a furious free-for-all, they beat out an ever-changing rhythm – now in time with their neighbours, now drifting apart, then synchronising again.

None of the looms at ground level had suffered damage and, after lying idle through the festivities, they were all being pressed back into glad, if chilly, service. A few men looked round as Charlie moved among them. They smiled or called inaudible greetings but no one stopped work for a moment.

He paused at the bottom of the staircase. Closing his eyes, he tried to visualise the position of the crumpled body. Instead, Isabelle's face came to him. He could feel her breath on his neck; the gentle pressure of her finger on his bloodied lip; her lips moist on his – all so unlike the hostility she directed at the world. His confused feelings welled up again.

Opening his eyes, he studied the floor. There was no sign of any blood, no hint that any crime had been perpetrated here. Slowly, he climbed the stairs, carefully scanning the banister on one side and feeling it with his hands. He was determined to expiate his premature visit to the magistrate by a thoroughness that none could question or criticise. So when he reached the top he came back down, repeating his scrutiny on the opposite side. He then made a third pass, attending to the treads and risers of the stairs. But there was nothing – not so much as a splinter.

On the upper floor, he looked into the office, where the desk they had used to block the stairwell had been pushed back into position. Up here, only a few men were weaving. Others were repairing looms: replacing broken woodwork or re-threading damaged warp yarns. Scattered around were empty spaces where an unfortunate weaver had given up hope of being able to salvage anything from the wreckage. He shook his head. Their future was bleak.

Once again, he moved among the men. Here, more were ready to talk – of the chase at the abbey or the wreckage at the mill – and they were glad to hear that Barton would be sent to the assizes.

'Let him swing, the bastard,' cursed one giant of a man.

'Aye, I hope he does,' echoed others.

Leaving them to their labours, he retraced the final few steps of that terrifying flight. Walking to the back of the mill, the hatch lay before him and above it, was the hoist. He stood, contemplating the narrowness of their escape. If Isabelle hadn't noticed the hatch, or they hadn't been able to lift it, or the men had been a little quicker, would he now be disfigured, or crippled, or even alive?

He watched his breath escape into the cold air and shivered.

And then he saw it.

Sticking out of a floorboard, just inches from the back wall, where Barton must have hurled it in a rage of frustration, was a slim bone handle attached to a narrow metal blade. It was Isabelle's stiletto dagger. He reached down and tugged it out of the floorboard. He ran the blade between his fingers. About four inches. Just long enough to reach the centre of a man's brain.

12

At his feet, the turbulent, murky waters surged past, carrying all before them.

Two years earlier, he had sat beside another river, in Newcastle, yearning to follow it out into the world. On the turnpike roads and green lanes of the land, he would be able to shake off the sadness and grief. He could start afresh.

The old urge welled up in him now. So what if his livelihood depended on stability and maintaining a practice? He wasn't cut out for staying put. To hell with Barnard and Micklethwaite and their power games, and to hell with Isabelle – whatever she was playing at.

He gazed vacantly into the icy waters as they hurtled past on their never-ending journey.

'I was wondering where you'd got to,' said Isabelle nonchalantly.

Did she care? It was hard to tell.

Despite the near freezing temperature, she was sitting on the step of the wagon in the yard of the White Swan. On her lap lay a curled-up black kitten. She was searching it for fleas. She pointed to the bruising under his chin.

'How did you get that?'

'The crate – when I hit the water.'

Isabelle laughed. 'That's what you get for not learning to swim.'

'Well I survived.' He shrugged. 'And how are you?'

'No ill effects, though it was a bit too close for my liking at the end.'

They began to talk of the dangers they had shared but after a few minutes he became aware of the cold seeping up from the ground.

'Forgive me, I'm keeping you here and you'll surely catch a chill.'

She shook her head. 'It helps me to think. In any event, with all the quacks around here, what could possibly ail me?' Seeing the hint of a frown on his brow, she teased, 'Oh dear, the gentleman takes himself seriously. That's a shame – I had begun to think him rather fun.'

Despite his mood, he grinned. 'Be that as it may, I would still be glad of somewhere a little warmer and more private where we might talk.'

'Well there's always our room upstairs' – she gave him a calculating look – 'but don't be getting any ideas in your britches.' Laying the protesting kitten on the ground, she led the way up the back stairs of the inn and along a narrow corridor.

The room was surprisingly small and it was made smaller still by the boxes taking up most of the floor space. Squeezed in amongst these were a large bed, a small square table, two rickety-looking chairs, and a washstand. The impression was of a home that was in the process of being moved into but he realised this was how the Broussards always lived – when they weren't sleeping under the wagon.

Louis was sitting, bent over a partly dismantled mechanical figure of a dog. He looked up.

'Ah, good day Monsieur. How are you? It is good to see you again. My daughter tells me that the two of you have been having some more adventures.' His eyes shone and he seemed unperturbed at his daughter bringing a man to their room. 'For myself, I am afraid the days of great adventures are over. I am reduced to repairing the tail of a dog that no longer wishes to wag in answer to my questions. Such are the joys that are reserved for ageing conjurors.'

Charlie smiled and Louis rose stiffly from his seat.

'Despite these unsurpassable pleasures I must go and attend upon our horses.'

Isabelle flashed a glance at Charlie. 'No, Papa, please. I will do it later.'

If Louis noticed the look he didn't show it. 'I need the fresh air and you do not need me under your feet.' And, with that, he was out of the door, leaving the two of them alone.

After a few moments, Isabelle broke the silence. 'You wanted to talk to me.'

'Ah, yes. Quite a bit has happened since the other night.'

He began to recount the events at the abbey the day before. She was quite animated when he spoke of the chase to the river, Callaghan's drowning – 'Serves the bugger right' – and Barton's arrest. However, her interest waned when it came to the magistrate's enquiries at Micklethwaite's home. There was a tight knot in his stomach. He couldn't put it off any longer.

'There's one other matter. I thought you would like to know about the man at the mill.'

For a second, she looked back at him blankly.

'At the bottom of the stairs – the dead man.'

'Oh, what about him?'

'Apparently, he was the mill-owner: a Mr James Oxley. Might you have met him... or known him, perhaps?'

She frowned. When she spoke, it was warily. 'And why, may I ask, would I know him?'

'I have no idea... I just wondered...'

He had rehearsed this conversation, on his slow, thoughtful way back into town, but now it was upon him he was floundering. He reached into his jacket pocket and drew out the dagger.

'I went to the mill this morning and found this.' He handed it to her. Her frown slipped away to be replaced by a smile of relief, even joy. Taking its bone handle she studied it, caressing the blade gently.

'Thanks, Charlie; it's good to have it back. It's served me well.'

'I also examined Oxley's body, last night, and his death was no accident, you know. He had a wound in the back of his neck.' She was barely listening. 'Someone had driven something up into his skull… something thin and sharp.'

It felt terribly clumsy but at least it was said.

Silence.

She looked at him, her face, for once, impassive and unreadable. The words, when they came, were not the volcanic eruption that he had been expecting but cold and abrasive.

'And what you're suggesting is… that you think that I might have used this… to kill him.'

'Well?'

'Well what?' The ice in her eyes matched her voice.

'Did you?'

'Please tell me: what possible reason could I have to murder a man I have never even heard of?'

'I don't know… but you tried to stop me going into the mill the other night.'

Her laugh was derisive. 'That's it is it – a guilty conscience? Forget about trying to keep you out of a trap that was almost the death of us both. You think I was frightened of seeing my victim's body again – that it would bleed and condemn me.' Her eyes narrowed. 'No, you can't really be *that* stupid. There's something else. There has to be.'

'Well, you do know him or at least have some acquaintance with him.'

'I have said not but, pray, do continue.'

'But you went to his house on Tuesday night.'

'I did no such thing.'

'You went to Boar Lane… made your way to the back of Oxley's house and then' – his voice trailed away – 'you disappeared.'

He steeled himself against the fire storm that was surely about to engulf him.

'Boar Lane? Tuesday night…?' Now it was coming. 'You *followed* me? You actually followed me? What the hell gave you the right to do that?'

'I don't know. You'd already been attacked, I suppose, and I wanted to make sure that you'd be safe.'

'You bloody liar!' She spat at him. 'Make a habit of following women, do you? You lecherous sod! Gives you a thrill does it – spying on us and fantasising about whose bed we're jumping into?'

'For God's sake, Isabelle. Look, I like you. That's all. It isn't a crime.'

'No it isn't. Not like murdering a total stranger. Not like shoving your dagger into a man's brain and then chucking him downstairs.'

'But he wasn't a stranger. Perhaps you hadn't met him but if you went to his house you *must* have known something about him.'

'I didn't go to his damn house! How often do I have to tell you?'

'But I saw you.'

'You saw absolutely nothing,' she snarled. 'If you had been there, you'd know that I didn't go and jump into his bed like a whore.' She took a breath and spoke slowly, as if to a simpleton, 'I climbed over the garden wall.'

He pictured the fruit trees with their espaliered branches. They were a ready-made ladder for someone as lithe and agile as Isabelle. His heart lifted.

'Oh, I see, thank God for that. So what *were* you doing?'

'There you go again! You just don't get it, do you? It's none of your bloody business. Now, get the hell out of here.'

Before he could respond, the door opened and Louis reappeared.

'Those horses have truly seen better days.' He shook his head. 'They can't pull the wagon much longer but I don't know where we shall find the money to buy some decent ones. Perhaps when we get to London our fortunes will improve.'

Isabelle, dagger still in hand, pointed it at Charlie, motioning towards the door.

Apparently oblivious of the atmosphere in the room, Louis continued, 'The stable boy tells me he has heard a rumour that the man you found the other night was murdered.'

Charlie sighed. 'That will be my doing, though I'm surprised the news has spread so quickly.'

Isabelle sat down and glowered out of the window.

'And why would you start a rumour like that?' asked Louis.

'Well, a man who's been murdered isn't one who died because of my treatment. But it's no idle rumour, sir. He was killed alright. Though not that Barnard would notice. He missed the signs or else paid them no heed. He's so set on convicting me of Oxley's demise, along with the other deaths, that he's blind to anything which doesn't reinforce his prejudices.'

'Doctor Barnard?'

Charlie missed the look of concern as the conjuror glanced at his daughter.

'Aye, he was Oxley's physician and he's certain the man simply fell to his death down the stairs.' He tutted. 'Well, more than that. Oxley was afflicted by bouts of dizziness. I was treating him for them and Barnard's convinced that they had been aggravated by my electrifications. The magistrate, I am afraid to say, rather takes Barnard's part and won't hear me further on the matter.'

'I am sorry to hear that, Monsieur.' Louis shot another look at Isabelle.

'Thank you... and just when I've something that could redeem my reputation in the eyes of the public and – more importantly – the Corporation. And I can't help wondering about the other men. Their widows have been no help at all and their bodies are already rotting in the churchyard but, like Oxley, they were under Barnard. I'll wager, in his determination to see me condemned, he missed things – things that would acquit me. Damn his incompetence... and his arrogance!' He bellowed with frustration, then fell silent, brooding on the injustices of life.

In an instant, Isabelle was out of her chair and striding towards the door. As she reached for the handle, Louis was behind her, a restraining hand on hers.

'*Ma chère.*' The concern in his voice was unmistakable.

She pulled her hand free, threw the door open and disappeared down the corridor. Her father sighed heavily as he watched her go.

Charlie grimaced. 'I apologise, Mr Broussard. I am afraid that I have inflamed your daughter by my conversation.'

'That may be so, Monsieur. That may be so.' Louis stood contemplating the empty corridor.

'In which case, should there be anything I can do to assuage her feelings…'

'Thank you but this is nothing to do with you.'

He could tell a rebuff when he heard one. 'Of course, I understand. I have already done far more than I should.' He bowed. 'I beg your pardon, sir, and bid you good day.'

Louis turned round. 'Forgive me, I did not make myself clear. I meant only to say that the reason for my daughter's departure has nothing to do with the argument you were having' – he smiled kindly, shaking his head – 'nothing at all. Please stay. I think, perhaps, that there are things which need to be said.'

'You are very kind but Isabelle spoke the truth. My regrettable situation has led me to intrude into matters that are no business of mine. I should take my leave.'

'Please, Monsieur Rossi, you have been through a lot with my daughter and I think you deserve some explanation for her behaviour. Why? Because, the fates have decided, for their own inscrutable reasons, to entwine your present and our past. And so our business has now, I regret, become your business.'

13

Isabelle left the White Swan and walked up Briggate and on past the workhouse, along Towns End. On her right, the fields stretched away towards a distant Sheepscar Beck. On her left was the Free School. Through a window she could make out a teacher conducting the, at that precise moment brutal, process of education. She shook her head in disgust. Life and her father had taught her all that she needed to know and far more than any schoolmaster or tawse would ever have done.

A few yards further on, she stopped outside the home of Mary Crompton. It was a fine, modern dwelling with an extensive, many-windowed frontage and pillared entrance. Out here on the edge of Leeds, raised above the river with its mists and floods, it proclaimed to the world the sort of prosperity that she would never know.

She passed down the side of the house to the yard behind. A large dog launched itself towards her, straining at the limit of its chain. She walked slowly but confidently towards it. The barking became a growl and then died away altogether. The dog lay down. Isabelle ruffled its ears. The back door of the house opened and a girl in her mid-teens emerged carrying several large bones.

'Ah, that's Archie. He's alright really but he doesn't like strangers, that's all. You must have a way with them.'

Isabelle nodded. 'I guess so. You just have to understand how they think.'

In fact, animals were something of a speciality for her.

'And these bones will keep him busy for a while yet.' The maid approached the dog who was now sitting absolutely still, with his eyes fixed on the approaching meal.

'Excuse me,' interjected Isabelle. 'Before you do that, would you like me to read them for you?'

'Oh, would you?' the girl responded enthusiastically. Then, dropping her voice, she continued: 'Though Cook doesn't hold with it at all. She says it's still the stuff of witches even if they *have* stopped hanging them.'

'Well don't you worry about old Cook and her superstitions. If you understand animals when they're alive, then it's a small step to understand what they are trying to say to us when they're dead. Those would be lamb bones, I think – and a shoulder blade as well – the very best for the task. My name's Bella by the way.' When playing a role, she preferred the name her father used for her on stage. 'What's yours?'

'I'm Kitty. Here, take it.' She handed Isabelle what was left of the shoulder of lamb.

Drawing the dagger from inside her boot, Isabelle scraped the meat from the bone, carefully dropping each morsel into Archie's ever grateful mouth. Then she held the bone up to the faint rays of light that were still reaching the back of the yard.

'Oh that's good… yes, that's very good.'

Kitty was looking eagerly over Isabelle's shoulder, as if in hope that the bones would speak to her as well.

'You see these clear parts? Well, they are a good omen – a sign of great happiness. I can't be sure but their shape suggests it will be with a man.'

Kitty gasped.

'But these shadowy bits…'

'What about them?'

'Well, if we were on a battlefield they would indicate defeat… and death.' Kitty gasped again, clutching at her neck. 'But given their position to one side and the way the light falls on them' – she was enjoying herself now – 'I would say that they indicate not a future death but one in the recent past.'

'Oh my – that's right! The master – Mr Crompton – he only died this past week.'

It always worked. The basics of the tradition were very ancient but the reading she gave had more to do with what the person wanted to hear, or, as in this case, what she wanted to hear from them.

'I see.' She chose a thoughtful tone. 'Yes, that must be what the bones are saying. Although it is hard to tell whether it was peaceful or…' She let the alternative hang in the air.

'Oh no, he died in his sleep. Though it were a terrible shock. I found him, you see. He were just lying there… so still, so pale.'

'Of course. It's just that there are these markings here. Can you see them? They can sometimes point to a different end and, as I am still learning the art, I would be glad to be certain of my reading. Are you sure that there was nothing that might suggest something else?'

Kitty paused for a moment, her eyes unfocussed, as she tried to recall the scene. She shook her head. 'No, I don't think there were anything.'

'No blood at all?'

'Oh, well there were the stain on the pillow but it were nothing – just a burst boil or something. It were only a little patch, under the back of his neck.'

'Well I am glad to hear it.' Isabelle nodded. 'That must be all the bones were saying. I must remember for the future so I don't alarm people unnecessarily.'

She handed the shoulder blade back to the maid.

'Now, shall we let Archie have his meal?'

***

'It began with passion and ended with grief. Perhaps it always does.' Louis had invited Charlie to sit with him at the little table. 'I met Thérèse in a village outside Paris. She lived on a small farm with her father, who shouted at her when he was sober and beat her when he was drunk. It was love at first sight, as you say, and at last she had found a reason to leave him. She crept away in the middle of the night, out into the lane where I was waiting. It was risky. If he had found out, who knows what he would have done. Then we set off for the Channel because I had heard there were fortunes to be made in London. And, yes, I was feted there for a time – the talk of the coffee houses. I even performed for His Majesty at court. But nothing lasts.'

Charlie snorted gently. 'I know what you mean.'

'So we made our way north. It was hard, as always, but I was glad to be on the road again. Then Thérèse told me that she was with child. I feared that there would be difficulties as she was so very thin. I could tell that she was worried too, though she was too proud to admit her feelings. The wagon became increasingly difficult for her, so, as the time drew nearer, we decided to remain here.'

'What – here in Leeds?'

'Indeed, this is not my first visit to the town, although back then I was not the great Belteshazzar that you see before you.' He smiled ruefully. 'I was known merely as "Broussari". We stayed at the Leopard in Boar Lane and life would have been quite tolerable but for a fly in the ointment. In those days, I fear that the puffs about my "healing powers" were even less modest than they are today and a young physician, who lived only a few doors away, opposed me bitterly, even picketing my shows.'

'Barnard?'

'The very same. Anyway, one night the baby came – the most wonderful gift that was given at the most terrible cost.' His brow creased at the memory. 'The blood wouldn't stop, you see. Thérèse was beyond my help, I knew that. So I turned in desperation for any help I could find.'

Charlie put his hand to his mouth in horrified realisation.

'I beat upon the door, begging him to come with all speed but he merely gloated. "What? Can it be that the wonderful Broussari needs my assistance?" While my wife lay dying, he stood in the doorway and hurled my puffery back in my face.'

'The man isn't human,' Charlie muttered, shaking his head.

Louis shrugged slightly. 'You might think so but he has his own demons – we all do. Well, when I got back, the sheets were utterly drenched. All I could do was hold her hand. It grew colder moment by moment. And then Barnard walked in. He took one look at Thérèse and shook his head. At least, at that moment, he had the courtesy to hold his tongue. It took no more than a minute or two. In the end she opened her eyes and looked at the little face at her breast. It was a look of such desperate longing. Then she breathed, "I wish I could have known her." A drop welled in the corner of her eye but she was dead before it reached her cheek.'

***

The late afternoon sun reached through the leaded window and reflected off a dozen copper-bottomed saucepans that hung from the pale blue walls. The smell of bacon wafted from a giant skillet on the range. The chain from the fan in the chimney turned the lamb on the spit. Otherwise, in the Thomson's kitchen, preparations for the evening meal were on hold.

'The right shows the future, the left shows the past,' explained Isabelle. 'Where shall we begin?'

'Oh, the future. Always the future first.'

The cook's hands were as crimson and bulky as their owner but with an added patchwork of cuts and burns, both recent and long forgotten.

Isabelle glanced briefly at the fleshy palm before exclaiming, 'What a mound!'

'Watch your cheek,' snapped the cook.

'No – see, this one here – it's the mound of Apollo, the mound of fortune. I've never known it to lie and I've only ever seen it as full as this once before.'

'Really?' The cook leaned closer. 'What happened?'

'Within a twelve-month, the woman came into a fortune on the lottery and entered upon a most genteel life.'

The cook squinted at her. 'Going to be a lady of leisure, am I then? That'd be more than welcome, I dare say, and to everyone else you tell it to – all those you take to be a simpleton.'

'Well, then, shall we put it to the test with the past?'

'Aye. Let's see how good your sight is there.'

She took the cook's other hand and studied the lacerated skin in silence. She began to frown.

'What is it?'

'I'm not sure. It's this fate line here.'

'What can you see?' Fascination was already replacing scepticism.

'It's all this hatching that's branching off, just to the side. Great sadness, certainly – it looks like a death but at some remove from you. Perhaps someone in this household?'

'Mr Thomson! Well I never.'

The cook gazed, wide-eyed, at her hand into which such a calamity had been etched and which could speak so eloquently of it.

Astonishment and relief mingled in her tone. 'Only a few days ago and such a terrible thing too. It were young Ruth what found him, weren't it dear?'

She looked towards the maid who was currently bent, elbow deep, over a washtub. Ruth nodded her agreement over her shoulder but didn't interrupt Mrs Dale's flow.

'He'd been there all night, you see, in his study, sitting at his desk. Mrs Thomson had gone to spend the night with her cousin at Hunslet and the master had said he wouldn't need us again – he must've been in a good mood. So I had a very pleasant evening down at the Three Legs with Emma from the Thorpes' over the road. You should go there when you leave, she'd love to have you read her palm. And Ruth were off to see her young man but the less said about that the better.' She winked. 'Anyhow, on the morning – Sunday it would be – Ruth goes in there as usual, walks straight past him in the dark and never sees a thing, opens the shutters and then gets the fright of her life. Here, Ruth, you should let Bella look at your hands. Think about it – what a tale they'd tell.'

'That must have been a terrible shock.' It only took the slightest of nudges to get the cook back on track.

'Shock? I should say so. There he were, sitting dead and cold, and staring straight through her, like he were looking at her from the other side. Enough to scare you straight into the next life and no mistake. Isn't that right, Ruth? Oh, and his tongue!' Her voice dropped to a whisper and her lips moved with exaggerated articulation. 'It looked like a piece of liver hanging out of his mouth. He'd bitten into it so deep that I swear I could have had it off in a flash with any one of my knives.' She raised her eyebrows and nodded. 'Aye, it were a shock to us all. The mistress were absolutely distraught of course. I suppose the shock were greatest for her.' She paused for a moment. 'Mind you, I did wonder about that.'

'What do you mean?'

'Only that she knew he weren't so well. I don't reckon there's any harm in me saying as much. I mean, it's not as if you'll be telling folk round here, will you.' Isabelle shook her head reassuringly. 'And anyhow, you'll have probably seen it already in my hands. No, he weren't a well man, the master. He had... well, you know' – more exaggerated whispering – 'a *condition*.' She paused to deliver several meaningful nods. 'I only know as much because I happened to be passing the drawing room the other day and I couldn't help hearing them. Not that I meant to, of course, but the doors in this house just aren't up to standard in my book. They're certainly not what they used to be when my mother cooked for the Arkwrights at Sherburn. She always swore that she couldn't hear a thing through those. Proper quality they were.'

'His condition?' cajoled Isabelle.

'That's right. There they were, arguing about it, you see. I couldn't make it all out – not even with these doors – but he's shouting that he was getting a remedy, there were nothing for her to worry about and he'd be right as rain in no time. And then she were in floods of tears and she's out of that room as fast as a cat to a bird, and it were all I could do to get out of sight round the corner. It wouldn't do for me to see her when she were in a state like that.'

'Absolutely not,' Isabelle agreed earnestly. 'But then you were going to have to see far worse, what with Mr Thomson's body. Not to mention all the work you'll have had, cleaning up after him.'

'I'm sorry?'

'Well there'll have been quite a bit of blood around the place.'

The cook continued to look puzzled. 'No, not really.'

'Oh, I thought with his tongue being like you said – on his face or his hair maybe.'

'No, nothing to speak of on his face. His hair were fairly messed about, which were a bit odd as he were quite particular, but then he had been up all night. No, it were his look that were the worst of it. What would you say Ruth?'

'I'm not sure, Mrs Dale.' The maid pulled her hands out of the water and turned towards them. 'It were agony for sure but almost more a look of… no, it sounds daft.'

The cook tutted. 'Spit it out, girl.'

'Well, I suppose it were shock really.'

***

'I named her after Thérèse's mother, who had died giving birth to her second child. I longed to keep her – she was my only link to my wife – but the life of a travelling showman is no place for a baby without a mother. I went back to London and took Isabelle to a foundling home, leaving Thérèse's ring and a scrap of cloth from her dress as tokens.'

'How long was it before you saw her again?'

'Seven years.'

'Why so long?'

'The war. It broke out a few days later and by then I was already back in France. All I could do was to wait until it was over.'

'That can't have been easy.'

'I have regretted it ever since and never more than when I saw the damage those years had done to my beautiful little girl.'

Louis fell silent, his eyes lost in memories.

Charlie waited, respecting the older man's pain. Eventually, he asked softly, 'Was it the anger?'

'*Oui,* Monsieur,' Louis sighed deeply. 'She would always have been strong and passionate like her mother but now she had learned that the world can be a harsh and brutal place and she treated it in the same way. And, of course, when she learned why I had left her in London that only magnified the bitterness. If she had turned it on me I would have understood but instead it was everyone else who had to suffer.'

Charlie smiled wryly. 'As the people of Leeds are finding out.'

Louis nodded. 'I knew that returning wouldn't be easy for either of us. Yet she was determined to come and I hoped that it might help us lay Thérèse finally to rest. But then she discovered that Barnard was still here...'

'So that's why she slips out after your shows.'

'I never ask but I can guess where she goes.'

'To his house?'

'I think so. She watches and she dreams of revenge. So when you followed her – I am sorry, I could not help overhearing – I believe that was where she was going.'

'And do you think I have just sent her off there again?'

'It seems likely, Monsieur, but I doubt that we will ever know.'

The black kitten followed Isabelle through the door, climbed onto the bed and lay down beside her. On the other side of the room, her father and Charlie had their heads together, discussing the tail of the dog that wouldn't wag. She stroked the kitten under its chin and looked across at the men.

'I imagine you were wondering where I've been.' Mild irritation mixed with triumph in her tone.

At last, the men looked up. 'That's true, *ma chère*. I cannot deny it.'

A deeply satisfied smile crept over her face. She took hold of the kitten, rolled onto her back and kissed it on its nose. 'Well, I have been showing Monsieur Rossi how to do it.'

'Do what?' asked Charlie.

'Find out what you want to know.'

'And what would that be, may I ask?'

She laughed and kissed the kitten once again. 'Anything you like but, in this case, getting some of the evidence you need to clear your name and to damn Barnard in the process. You see, you think you're just *so* charming that all you need to do is to come in here and accuse me of murder and I'll swoon at your feet and confess. And you think you only have to walk through the front door of the Cromptons' or the Thomsons', ask to speak to the lady of the house, and she'll tell you everything you need to know: all their goings-on, all the family's dirty little secrets, everything that gets whispered by the servants.'

She flipped the kitten over, dumped it unceremoniously on its back between her breasts, and began playing with its ears. The kitten took it all without complaint.

'You haven't got a clue, Charlie boy – not a clue.'

Now it was his turn to laugh. 'That's true enough.'

There was silence, as she teased the black ball of fur on her chest.

'Come on then, Isabelle. Out with it.'

'Crompton was murdered in the same way as Oxley, and Thomson met a violent end too, I'm sure of it. And the best bit is that Barnard missed them both.'

'I have to hand it to you,' Charlie shook his head, smiling at her tale. 'You know how to get people to talk. But you're wrong,

Isabelle.' She frowned. 'Aye, the best bit is that those servants don't have the faintest idea you were playing them.'

'Forgive me, Charlie,' interjected Louis, 'but I don't see that this makes things any better for you. A little blood on the pillow and a strange death mask is not the sort of information you can take to the magistrate.'

'I know but at least my instincts were right.'

'Oh really?' sneered Isabelle.

'Ah, yes.' He put his hands up. 'Look I'm sorry about that. Your father's right though. Now that my only "suspect" has managed to clear her name' – he grinned sheepishly – 'I'm a bit stuck on what I'm going to do next.'

Isabelle sat up. 'We.'

'Sorry?'

'Look Charlie, you're out to clear your name and I'm out to destroy Barnard. You need to show that the men were murdered. I am going to prove that Barnard's unfit to be a physician. So we join forces until we both get satisfaction.'

He nodded thoughtfully. 'You're on.'

'So tell me about these men.'

'There's not much to say really: three cloth merchants, three aldermen, three powerful men. Yet I can't help thinking that the answer lies somewhere in the connections between them.'

'Perhaps.' Isabelle sat cross-legged at the end of the bed, her arms clasped around her knees. 'But you've also got three widows.'

'So?'

'Thomson had the pox, you say.'

He nodded. 'He'd asked me for some mercury. I hadn't had time to get it but that'll be the remedy he was telling his wife about.'

'Only then she bursts into tears.'

'That's not surprising – she'd just learned of his condition.'

'Or because she realised that she's got it as well.'

'Surely not.'

'Come on, Charlie. You know as well as I do that half the men in this land think they can rid themselves of the clap by sleeping with someone who's clean.'

'I can't deny it.'

'So she breaks down in tears.'

'That seems to be her way. She was still weeping when I called on her.'

'Though I doubt the tears were for her husband.'

'That's a bit harsh isn't it?'

'What? Not grieving for a man whose been sticking his horn into some whore and then gives you the pox to make himself better? You must be joking. If he'd been my husband, I'd have killed him myself.'

'I don't doubt it,' laughed Charlie. 'Not for one minute!'

14

In the flickering candlelight, Charlie took a charge of gunpowder and packed it down into a small metal tube, then carefully screwed the tube to the floor. Raising the remaining wall, he lowered the roof of the miniature mahogany building into position. Attached to the outer wall of one of its gable ends was a strip of metal running all the way up to the roof. Here it ended in a spike that pointed sharply to the heavens. Halfway up the wall, the strip was interrupted by a small, square window. Tonight there would be no standard lecture. Tonight he would trust to his instincts. It was time for him to introduce his audience to the thunder house.

An hour later, he knew he had made the right decision. The benches were more than half empty but the noise in the room and the look on their faces told him that those who had come were here for one thing: a good night's entertainment at his expense.

Well, not tonight. Not after all that I've been through.

He didn't wait for the hubbub to abate. He filled his lungs and let rip.

'Ladies and gentlemen, I am no soothsayer, no cunning man, no prophet. I do not have the wisdom of the magi to interpret the heavens and see into men's souls. But, nonetheless, I know that you are here tonight with one thought, one solitary question in your minds: could this electricity' – he pointed to his charged-up Leyden jar – 'have killed Aldermen Crompton, Thomson and Oxley? Well, let it not be said on the streets of Leeds that Doctor Rossi is afraid of the truth. You shall not go away from here tonight disappointed. You shall have your answer. And it is this.'

The room went quiet. He had them now. It might only be for a moment but it thrilled him to have them hanging on his next word. He dropped his voice but not his firmness.

'Yes.'

'Murderer!' shouted someone from the back and the charge was taken up by others. Hell was breaking loose again but he merely smiled.

'Yes, ladies and gentlemen, electricity can kill – no less than fire, no less than wind or water. For these are elemental forces and they can all wreak death and destruction. But they also bring life. Indeed, they are essential to life. Our houses can be burnt to the ground but without fire we would not survive the winter. Gales wreck our ships yet we do not cease to breathe the very same air. And even as I speak, wooden pipes deliver water to the homes of the leading citizens of this town. Yet they do not fear that they will be drowned in their beds and we hail those who have made it possible as humanity's benefactors, not its destroyers. So, I tell you plainly, that even though it is the source of life and health, electricity can certainly kill. But I will not stop there. Tonight, ladies and gentlemen, I will show you how it kills.'

'Here he goes again!'

'Someone get the constables.'

He raised his hand. 'Fear not. You will all leave this room, not only safe but enlightened.' He turned back to the model house. 'Imagine, if you will, that this is your own home and overhead rages a fierce storm. All around are the crash of thunder and the flash of lightning. Nevertheless, you and your family are sleeping soundly in your beds, for you have taken precautions.'

He picked up a small, square piece of mahogany and inserted it into the "window" in the thunder house. It, too, bore a metal strip, so that now the strip ran, unbroken, from roof to floor. He reached for his conducting rods.

'Even so, ladies and gentlemen, it is only a matter of time before the inevitable happens and the lightning strikes your house.'

He placed one of the rods against the bottom of the metal strip and touched the other to the spike. Nothing happened.

'Bloody thing's broken,' growled a chap on the front row.

'No sir, your family is safe simply because this metal conductor has guided the electrical fire harmlessly into the earth. You have built your house on the rock of natural philosophy. On the other hand, your neighbour has seen your preparations and has ridiculed them. He has built his house on the sand of ignorance.'

He poked the wooden square through the window, breaking the strip of metal.

'Tonight, this man will pay the price for his foolishness. His family lies cowering in their beds. They are praying that the storm will pass over but, once again, the inevitable happens.'

He touched the rods to the two ends of the strip. As he did so there was a loud explosion. The walls of the house were thrown outward on their hinges and the roof was flung onto the floor. Black smoke drifted upwards and the smell of burnt gunpowder spread through the room. A middle-aged woman screamed and fled out of the door. Another dropped from the bench onto the floor. The rest of audience hooted with laughter.

He grinned to himself. Next time he needed to put in a little less powder.

'So as you can see, ladies and gentlemen, while lightning can kill, it can be made safe by the insights of natural philosophy. The same can be said when the electrical fluid is stored, not in the clouds, but in Leyden jars. In great quantities and in foolish hands it can indeed do harm and may even bring death. Yet, handled wisely it is not only safe but is the source of renewed health and vigour. Truly, if it were to kill you it would do so in an instant, whereas when it brings life it does so slowly and in harmony with nature. Therefore you have nothing to fear from this electrical machine.'

He then ran through his full repertoire of experiments and, for once, they all went off well. However, when he invited people to register for a course of treatments, it was as if the rest of the evening had not happened.

An elderly man on the back row called out, 'So you want us to be next in the churchyard do you?'

'I knew George Thomson,' shouted a woman, 'and he never hurt a fly!'

Something flew towards the Leyden jar. He plucked it out of the air.

All that they had just seen and heard counted for nothing. All their fears of the new or unknown surfaced again. Some people got up and left, muttering discontentedly. Others stayed for some target practice. He caught what he could and tried to block the rest. A potato hit the prime conductor, snapping it clean in two. He winced but at least he had a replacement for that.

Once their pockets were empty and the malcontents had drifted away, he locked up and slunk off into the darkness. In no mood for Sam's cheerfulness, he made for the river. On the bridge, he stood gazing down. Below him, the black, icy waters hurtled past.

Was it time to join them?

'Now then.' It was Rooke, heading into town. Charlie acknowledged him with a nod. 'You look like you could do with a drink.'

'And a few.'

'Come on, I'm off to the Talbot.'

The tavern was as boisterous and fetid as on his previous visit and once again the cocks were fighting for their lives. Charlie ordered a gin and then another.

'I know one of the owners in the next fight,' said Rooke,

downing an ale. 'From what I hear it's a killing machine. Sure fire winner.'

'I've lost more money on those than I care to think of.'

'Well, then, it's time for your luck to change.'

Charlie felt his battered purse. The takings from the evening's lecture were barely sufficient.

He nodded, grimly. 'Aye, you're right – it's long overdue.' And, knocking back the gin, he followed Rooke into the throng.

***

The river thickened with every flailing stroke. Then he remembered that he couldn't swim. He couldn't fight anymore – he was just too tired. He surrendered to the reddening waters. As he sank once again, he cried out for his mother and a stream of blood poured into his lungs.

He woke with a gasp.

***

Sunday's dawn was another one layered in thick frost. In the warmth of Beth's kitchen, Charlie rested his chin in his hand and groaned.

Sam grinned. 'A good night?'

'I'm afraid not and it wasn't the drink, either.'

'So at least there's nothing to stop you enjoying your breakfast.'

Despite himself, Charlie smiled. Here was someone he didn't have to perform for. Here was someone he had didn't have to question, argue with, tread carefully around, or – in the case of Isabelle – do all three at once. Setting his money troubles to one side he briefed his friend on Oxley's death. Sam greeted the news with a low whistle and shook his head in wonderment as he heard about Crompton and Thomson.

'And you say this lass is giving you a hand.' Sam winked.

He returned it. 'Well, you know.' Sam was fishing but he wasn't going to share the sorry tale of his own suspicions, nor what Louis had told him about Isabelle.

'So what are you going to do now?'

'I don't know – find out what I can about the three of them, I suppose. It's in there somewhere. It has to be.'

Sam asked for some help in the brew house and they chatted freely as they moved barrels around. Sam's main news was that Jake and Abe were to be flogged the next day and then released.

'Fifty strokes each. Lizzie won't be getting much work out of him for a while after that. Though I dare say she'll be glad to see him home, even if she does give him a few extra lashes with her tongue.' Sam smiled grimly. 'Anyhow, at least Beth's ointment will do its stuff.'

'I can testify to that.' Charlie felt his chin, which was still colourful but no longer sore. 'But fifty lashes. That's harsh.'

'It's no more than you'd expect from a man like Micklethwaite. Still, I'll say this much for him: he saw to it that our Adam got to choose the King's shilling rather than the convict ship or the drop.'

'Oh, really?' Sam had only mentioned their son in passing before.

'Aye, well you see, he took to a bit of poaching out at Allerton with another lad. And one night they were rumbled. The other one got clean away but not Adam. He goes and trips over some tree root or other and gets himself caught, the daft apeth. Anyhow, Micklethwaite got the magistrate to offer him the army. He likes doing that, our mayor. He sees it as his patriotic duty to fill up the ranks. So our lad ends up dodging Yankee musket balls – and now it'll be damn French ones as well. Still, there's a few from the town over there: lads in trouble with the law, like Adam, or drunk enough or stupid enough to believe the recruiting sergeant. And the weavers' troubles mean even some of their boys have taken the shilling. Then there's a couple of officers too.'

'Such as?'

'Well, I'm not sure where Oxley's brother is but there's the Armstrongs' boy for sure.'

'What Sarah's lad… and old man Josiah's?' Charlie added quickly.

Sam gave him a knowing look. 'You want to watch that roving eye, Charlie, or you're going to find yourself in even deeper water.'

He held his hand up. 'I know, Sam, don't worry. I'm not as stupid as I look.'

'Well that's a relief.'

***

'Does it always hurt?' Kitty's question was barely audible even though Isabelle was right next to her.

They were sitting together in a settle, in one corner of the Talbot Inn. Isabelle told the first man who had bothered them where his tankard would end up if he persisted. Another saw a sudden flash of steel from her boot before he backed off. Now the women could talk.

'No, of course not,' she reassured the maid.

Isabelle had ducked out of sight when Kitty appeared from the Crompton's house, heading into town to enjoy her free Sunday afternoon. Isabelle followed until, at the window of a dressmaker's shop, she could draw up alongside.

'You'd look so lovely in that.' What had caught Kitty's attention was a particularly fine-looking open gown. 'Thinking of your new man?'

'Bella!' Kitty greeted her like an old friend. 'Am I that obvious? So it's not just bones you can read.' They both laughed.

Over a couple of drinks at the inn, Isabelle had transformed effortlessly from fortune-teller into confidante.

'It hurts a bit the first time.'

Isabelle remembered it well. The son of an innkeeper in King's Lynn had got her merry on his father's cider and then had taken her against a stack of barrels in the brew house. He was fat and rough but she had been a very willing participant. She had needed to know what it was like, this thing that she had seen and heard so many adults doing – all the groping and grunting, thrusting and panting.

'Yes, I know that Bella,' Kitty said, a little indignantly. 'Jimmy Robinson did pickle-me-tickle-me once.'

Isabelle nearly choked on her ale. 'And what might that be?'

'You know. It's what my old grandma used to call the business.'

Isabelle laughed and shook her head. 'Oh, Kitty, you're such an innocent.'

'I am not so.' The girl looked down at her mug. 'I only wanted to know if they always hurt you. Men, I mean.'

'Well sometimes they do. If they're too quick or a bit rough; if there's not enough fun beforehand and you're not ready for it. But when you are – God, it's a fine thing and no mistake.' Other memories came to mind.

Kitty noticed the far-off look in her eyes. 'So have you done it much?'

'A bit – when I feel like it, that's all.'

She had felt like it in the mill the other night with Charlie. Oh, he was nice enough but that wasn't it. Her blood had been up for a fight. There was the danger, the thrill of the chase, even the fear. She had felt so aroused that she could have had him there and then on the mill floor and to hell with their pursuers.

Kitty was watching her with wide eyes, in awe of this free spirit and her worldly experience.

'Don't worry,' Isabelle said, kindly. 'It will all come soon enough. You just wait for your young man to arrive.'

They both took a long drink and Isabelle wondered how best to turn the conversation onto the right path.

'So they didn't hurt you, then?'

'Kitty, what is it? What's the matter?' The girl was clearly anxious about something. 'Did that Jimmy do you some real harm?'

'No, it's not that.'

'Well, what is it then?'

'Nothing really, I just want to know.'

Isabelle nodded sympathetically and waited. As always, it worked.

'You see… she always used to cry.'

'Who? Your mother?'

'No!' she hissed. Kitty looked around and then dropped her head and whispered. 'The mistress.'

Isabelle's face remained concerned, her voice solicitous, but inside the blood was pulsing again. 'Mrs Crompton?'

The maid nodded. She spoke quickly now, though still in hushed tones. 'My room's on the top floor, you see, just above hers. And the master would come to her and then I'd hear her crying out, yelping and – after he'd gone – sobbing.'

Isabelle frowned. 'That must have been awful.'

'I tried to stop my ears. I couldn't bear to hear her like that. And she was kind to me and tried to hide it. In the morning, as usual, I'd go to her but she'd tell me she wasn't going to be wearing her stays so she'd not be needing my help dressing. And she tried to keep herself covered up but sometimes, under her shift, I saw them – the bruises. Never on her face, but on her shoulder, her arm maybe, even her bosom… God knows where else.' She was silent for a few moments. 'I only want to know. He won't be like that, will he – my man?'

Isabelle didn't know which troubled her more: the young girl's fear or her hope. 'No, of course not, Kitty,' she assured her. She prayed that she would be right.

15

The heavy prison door grated backwards. Into the low sunlight stepped the prisoners. They were squinting, pale-faced and dressed only in shirt, boots and britches. Each was flanked by a pair of constables.

Lizzie glanced enquiringly at one of the guards. He nodded. She walked towards her husband.

'Morning, love.' Jake greeted her with a weak smile. It was overtaken by a shiver. 'Damned weather.'

'To hell with the weather,' replied Lizzie. 'You're a bloody idiot, Tinker.' She shook her head. Then she kissed him. 'And so am I.'

The party moved off up the road and rounded the corner into Briggate. Ahead of them, outside the town hall, some fifty people were waiting. A couple of street vendors moved amongst them, while children chased each other around the adults' legs. Seeing the prisoners, the crowd gave an ironic cheer and parted to let them through.

To one side stood a horse and cart, with the driver sitting up and ready; to the other side, the pillory. Clamped in its embrace was the woman who had shared Jake and Abe's cell. Her face was smeared with a mixture of rotten eggs and offal. In the centre, on the town hall steps, stood the mayor and the magistrate.

Micklethwaite, in his best wig and black frock coat, raised his voice above the crowd.

'Citizens of Leeds, once again we are gathered to witness the administration of justice, without which our town, indeed our whole kingdom, would collapse into anarchy. These men have encouraged the wanton destruction of property – the looms of Mr Oxley, who has been so suddenly and so tragically taken from us.' Several people turned to look at Charlie. 'The future prosperity of our town and of all our people lies in the kind of improvements that Oxley's mill is bringing to us. Times change and we must change with them.'

The noise in the crowd rose and the mayor scowled.

'That may be hard for some of you,' he continued, louder, 'but it is necessary, just as this punishment, which may seem hard, *is* necessary. In years to come, your children will be grateful for our resolution today. So let this be an example to you all. And let it be a warning.' He nodded to the constables. 'Carry on gentlemen.'

One of the men shoved Abe Robinson in the back.

'Come on, you know the form.'

Abe moved forward and stood behind the cart. He began to undo his shirt but his fingers kept fumbling with the buttons.

'For God's sake,' growled the constable. He stepped in front of Abe and ripped the shirt open. Abe took it off and threw it on the back of the cart.

The constable climbed onto the tail board and Abe leant over it, holding his hands out. The man bound them together at the wrists and then lashed the rope to an iron ring fixed to the wooden floor. Picking up a whip, the constable jumped back down and took up position behind the prisoner. He took a step to the side and threw his whip arm high and wide. The leather thongs, hanging from the wooden handle, dangled in the dirt. He looked over his shoulder towards the mayor.

Micklethwaite smiled coldly. 'You may begin.'

The constable threw his whole weight into the spin. The cat's tails whistled through the air and their tips struck home on Abe's skin with a dull crack. It reminded Charlie of a slate being snapped in half and it was immediately followed by three other sounds that mingled in a sort of bizarre ricochet: Abe's screech of pain; Ibbetson's call of 'One'; and the horse's whinny. Unnerved, the animal lurched forward, yanking Abe down onto one knee and ramming his chest into the back of the cart.

'Easy girl,' soothed the driver. 'Not yet.'

'No,' Sam spat. 'The bastard likes to see blood before it gets going.'

As Abe got back to his feet, Charlie could see that his back was covered by thin, white, criss-crossed lines where the skin had been raised. The constable bobbed his head from side to side as if assessing, with satisfaction, the start of his handiwork.

The crowd fell silent as they waited for the next stroke. Charlie could hear the blood pulsing in his ear. A pair of dogs snarled at each other and then the constable spun again.

'Two.'

Abe's cry was not so piercing this time but Charlie could see that he was biting down on his lower lip. The white lines had multiplied. By the count of ten, there were flecks of red on them. By twenty, the skin had started breaking open and trickles of blood were clear to see. The sweating constable took a breather and passed the cat to his colleague.

'Right you are, gentlemen,' called the mayor.

The driver snapped the reins and the cart rolled slowly down Briggate. Behind Abe and the constables came Jake, his head hanging, his eyes fixed on his feet. The mayor and magistrate followed on, chatting casually between lashes. Behind them, Charlie and the other Tinkers walked sullenly among a portion of the crowd – some had already seen enough and were drifting away. Bringing up the rear was a grey, thin lady, with hair and clothes to match.

'Abe's woman,' Lizzie murmured.

Clusters of people lined the streets or turned as Abe passed by. Some jeered but most stood in silence. Every thirty or forty yards another lash was added to the count. Before the bridge they turned up Swinegate, pausing at the lane that led down to Oxley's mill. Some of the weavers from the mill, Lee and Rooke among them, had gathered there. The giant, Jem, laughed disdainfully, cleared his throat and spat in Abe's face but the rest of the men merely watched grim-faced. The cart moved on, looping back into Boar Lane. It passed the Oxleys' home – no one was waiting outside – before pulling up at the Leopard. The final lashes were to be administered at the scene of the crime.

'Forty five.'

Abe's back was a mass of pulpy lacerations. Blood had soaked into the top of his britches. The constables' faces and sweat-soaked shirts were speckled red.

Charlie had seen all this before, mainly in his drunken youth, when he had joined the jeering crowds. But here in cold sobriety, watching someone he knew being flayed, he felt sick with rage.

'Fifty.' The magistrate's call came at last.

'And count yourself lucky, Robinson,' added Micklethwaite, disdainfully. 'At least you're alive to feel it.'

As soon as the rope was untied, Abe's legs began to shake. The thin woman hurried towards him and took hold of his arm but he shook her off. He steadied himself against the cart for a moment before moving slowly away. The woman walked silently behind him.

The cart now wheeled around and Jake was pushed forward, stripped to the waist and tied in position. A fresh pair of constables stood ready, one poised with cat in hand. Micklethwaite stepped forward and held out his hand.

'If you please.'

He took the whip and tugged at the thongs. Two of them came away.

'As I thought – this one's barely up to the job any more. You have another I presume.'

The constables glanced at each other.

'Well?' demanded the mayor.

'Aye sir,' said one of the men, hesitantly. 'Only, you see, I got it from my mate in the dragoons, and it's… well, it's barbed.'

Micklethwaite nodded, approvingly. 'A bit of military discipline – just what we need in this town.'

Lizzie opened her mouth to shout something but Sam laid a hand on her shoulders.

'Don't make it any worse than it is,' he muttered, sourly.

Micklethwaite gave the nod. 'Proceed, gentlemen.'

The man didn't move.

'I said, proceed.'

The constable shrugged and pulled the whip off the back of the cart. He unrolled the thongs. Tied to the ends were small bits of wire. The man readied himself and then spun. The tips struck home. Jake's scream sent a flurry of crows up from the roof of the tavern. By the count of twelve, blood was already flowing freely down to his waist and the cart set off.

By the time they reached the group of weavers, most of the men took one look at his back and his blood-soaked britches, and turned away. Even the giant, who had a mouthful of phlegm prepared, merely spat it on the ground. As the cart turned into Briggate, Jake stumbled and was dragged up the hill on his knees and shins. After a few yards, the flogger called a halt and got him back on his feet, only for him to go down again a minute later.

They reached the town hall with more than ten lashes to go. By now, each time the whip was flung back, flecks sprayed those standing nearby. Charlie felt something land on his cheek. He wiped it away. He looked down. On the back of his hand was a small piece of flesh. He shut his eyes and flicked it to the ground. The dogs had returned and were scouring the earth. He kicked one away.

Eventually, there was silence and the constable dropped the

whip to the ground. One of the dogs started licking the thongs. Charlie looked up at what had once been Jake's back and shoulders. The only things that weren't red were the swollen, white sinews protruding from the lacerations.

The constables wiped themselves off and then untied him. For a moment Jake's legs held but then he crumpled to the ground. Lizzie ran to him and dropped to her knees. She cradled his head in her lap, whispering to him through her tears. Sam and Tom waited alongside, until, at a glance from Lizzie, they put their hands under his armpits and raised him slowly to his feet. He locked his knees and brushed their arms away but as soon as he took a step forward his whole body started to shake and the men grabbed him again. As they shuffled off towards the King's Arms, Charlie looked on in impotent rage.

A voice sneered, 'Doubtless you think you can heal that as well.'

He turned to see the tall, thin figure of Henry Barnard; his face oozing disgust. Something snapped and Charlie launched a fist at the physician's head. Barnard's cane flashed upwards and Charlie's hand smashed against the brass knob.

Nursing his knuckles, he growled, 'I'll thank you to keep your damned opinions to yourself.'

'And I'll thank you to keep out of our town. Perhaps you should stick to pugilism. I am sure that what you lack in skill would be more than made up for in temperament. Who knows? With practice you may even earn a living at it, which is more than can be said for your infernal quackery.'

Charlie raised his fist again.

'If I were you, Rossi,' interjected Micklethwaite, as he approached the pair, 'I would not draw any more attention to myself so far as the law is concerned. Your future here already hangs by a thread, so tread carefully.'

'I don't give a fuck what you think!'

Micklethwaite laughed, derisively. 'You will Rossi. Before long, you will.' He turned away but then swung round again. 'Oh, and I hear you have been trying to persuade Mr Ibbetson that we have a murderer in our midst. I have but one thing to say to that: you will desist from such a malicious and frankly ludicrous allegation or else you *will* suffer the consequences. I trust I make myself clear. Now, I am due at Oxley's funeral.'

'As am I,' said Barnard. 'Perhaps I might walk with you.'

They set off towards St Peter's, heads together. The rest of the crowd were also drifting away. Charlie was soon alone but for the woman locked in the pillory. He sat on the bottom of the steps, seething. He looked at the woman. She was in a terrible state: still wearing her filthy, shredded gown and with several new projectiles plastered over her. He got to his feet, took out a handkerchief and walked over to her. He wiped around her eyes, her mouth and then the rest of her face. Screwing the cloth into a ball, he threw it into the gutter.

'You're a good man, sir, and no mistake,' she croaked. 'But you wouldn't have a drink on you as well, would you?'

He shook his head and left her to what remained of her humiliation.

A few yards down the road, he found Isabelle leaning against the wall at the corner of Kirkgate.

'I'm sorry about your friends, Charlie.'

He grunted.

She touched him on the arm. 'The rest of them have gone down to the prison to give Barton a send-off.' She tossed a mouldy apple in the air. 'He's away to the assizes. Are you coming?'

He shook his head. 'I'll see you later.'

'Come on. It'll make you feel better.'

She was right. It was what people came out for on days like this: to know that, for once at least, some poor sod was worse off than you.

'Oh, to hell with it, why not?'

He would despise himself for this tomorrow. But not today.

Hampered by his manacles, Barton struggled to climb onto the back of the cart. His guards – the two constables who had flogged

Abe – grabbed him from behind and hefted him up. He tripped over the edge and landed face first. As he pushed himself to his feet, a piece of rotting fish flew through the air and struck him in the eye. All around the cart, the crowd jeered and then the air was thick with blackened fruit and slimy vegetables. A volley of horse droppings found its mark. Barton tried in vain to wipe some of it away. Next to Charlie, a woman held out a basket of eggs.

'They stink like hell,' she shouted above the din. 'Help yourself.'

He grabbed two and sent them flying at Barton's head.

The constables allowed the crowd a couple of minutes to indulge themselves and then clambered aboard alongside their charge. At a stroke, the abuse became merely verbal and Charlie turned to give Isabelle a look of grim satisfaction.

It was then that he saw him. On the far side of the crowd, a man was watching the proceedings from out of a narrow alleyway. A bulbous nose and heavily pock-marked cheeks showed under a wide hat pulled down low over his eyes. It was Doyle. He was certain.

He was shocked at the brazenness of the man. What the hell was he up to? Planning some sort of rescue? He wouldn't put it past him.

He grabbed Isabelle's arm and hissed, 'Doyle, there, in the ginnel.'

At that moment, as if he had heard, Doyle looked straight at them and gave an ugly leer.

Taking a lungful of air, Charlie bellowed, 'Felon! Felon!'

Most of the crowd never even heard him. Those close by looked towards the alley but Doyle was already gone.

He shouted again, pointing in angry desperation, 'Another of the gang! He was there!'

Those around him merely shrugged and went back to baiting Barton. He had no takers for his hue and cry – none except Isabelle. They set off down the alley but soon the passage forked. A woman, who was sitting on her doorstep, spinning, claimed to have seen nothing. He started to argue with her but Isabelle pulled at his arm.

'We don't have time for this!'

They trusted to luck and turned left. As they approached the next corner Doyle was there again, standing calmly, as if waiting to see whether they were on his trail.

'He's playing with us,' growled Isabelle.

'Or it's a trap.'

The Irishman disappeared round the corner and they picked up their pace. They emerged onto a wider street with several more alleys branching off it, in different directions. Doyle was nowhere to be seen.

'Damn,' cursed Isabelle.

Four men were coming towards them from Kirkgate.

'They were at the abbey – some of Lizzie's lot,' said Charlie. He called to the men. 'Did you see him? Doyle – the one who got away – coming out of the alley here – did you see him?'

'Aye, there were some fellow but I didn't make him out,' replied one.

'Which way did he go?' demanded Isabelle.

'Down there,' pointed another. 'South, towards the river.'

They set off again and the men, unbidden, joined the pursuit. The passage twisted and turned. Again Doyle was waiting thirty yards ahead. Seeing the larger group, he pointed at Charlie and shouted, the sound bouncing off the narrow walls:

'I'm coming for you, Pimp!' He spat and was gone.

They followed but within seconds they came to another alley that crossed theirs. Left would take them towards St Peter's, while right led back towards Briggate.

'I think we should stick together,' said Charlie, a little unnerved.

Isabelle waved her hand. 'No, he could have gone anywhere. You two make for the church. You two head to Briggate. We'll go straight on. He may be waiting for you, so when you see him, holler. And take care.'

Charlie and Isabelle ran into the alley ahead but within yards the passage split again. They chose at random and again they came to a fork. This part of town was like a warren, and once again those they asked proved to be either unable or unwilling to help. They stopped, catching their breath.

'Nothing from the others,' puffed Charlie, 'but we'll be out of earshot now.'

The chase was over and he began to be aware of the walls of the ginnel looming over him. He could feel his chest tightening.

Isabelle turned to him. Her face was flushed and her eyes burnt fiercely. She took a step nearer. She opened her mouth slightly as if she was going to say something but then laughed to herself.

'Forget it.' She shook her head. 'Never mind, Charlie, he's not worth the sweat.'

'So what now?'

'We get to Oxley's house before the funeral's over.'

He pulled a face. 'You know, I'm still not sure about this.'

'Look we agreed. It's all we've got.'

'I know but…'

'It's simple – Crompton abused his wife and Thomson infected his with the pox. Oxley's going to have his own dirty secrets that tie him in to this.'

'We don't know that for sure.'

'There's a pattern Charlie,' Isabelle flared, 'only you won't see it. God, what is it with men?'

'Have it your way.'

They walked on in silence.

'Anyway,' Isabelle's tone was gentler, 'you'll get to do some digging of your own.'

He snorted. 'If Micklethwaite gets to hear of it, I'll have been digging my own grave.'

His hand had barely left the knocker before the door opened. He was glad to see that the maid looked in brighter spirits than at his last visit.

'Good morning, Charity.'

'Good morning, sir. I'm sorry but the mistress is out again – it's the master's funeral.'

'Oh, that is a pity. I had been hoping to express my condolences to her. Nevertheless, while I am here, perhaps I might trouble you for the return of my handkerchief. I find myself somewhat shorter than I imagined.'

'Certainly, sir – I laundered it just in case. Please come in a moment.'

He stepped inside the hall and the maid scurried off. She returned, a few minutes later, looking a little flustered.

'I am sorry to have kept you, sir, only there's a lady at the kitchen door promising to read my palms and I know you'll think me a silly girl but...'

'Of course not, Charity. We all live in hope of better times ahead and if learning about them can bring them here sooner, well then, what's the harm? Don't worry – I'll see myself out.'

He thanked the maid and opened the front door. The girl flew back to the kitchen. Quietly closing the door again, he moved across the hall to Oxley's study.

Inside, the room appeared larger. Gone were the tall candle-stands and the table on which the body had been laid out. Gone, too, were the dark, claustrophobic corners and the sickly-sweet smell of death. In the light of day, the furniture scattered around the room looked sparse, old-fashioned and past its best. The portrait on the wall was of an older man. He guessed it was Oxley's father. This room looked to be of his making and his son had not had the time or inclination to put his own stamp on it.

He looked at the books on the shelves: old histories, some works on natural philosophy, a copy of Adam Smith. Sitting down at the desk, he started going through the drawers. They were stuffed with unused stationery and old newspapers. He flicked through the papers: reports of Parliament, murder trials, shipping arrivals, quack remedies, turnpike announcements, a lost battle in the colonies, performing pigs. He didn't really know what he was looking for.

On top of the desk was the letter opener that he had used on Oxley's wound. Unopened correspondence lay beside it. The man had been away on business – his sister had said so in the graveyard at Thomson's funeral. He had been due back on the day of the festivities, the day of his death. No one had touched the letters since then.

He picked up the envelopes, shuffled through them, then opened them carefully in turn. Most concerned matters of business. One was an acknowledgement of an order for thirty new flying shuttle looms. Oxley was clearly not content with a single mill. Another was from his brother:

Dear James,

I trust this finds you with good health and success. Since October, the 90th have been filling up their ranks and we are now at full complement. They are a pretty desperate lot but no worse than the usual sort I suppose. How they, or any of us, will fair in a scrap we shall have to see. In any case, we now have our orders and 'the Yorkshire Volunteers' are bound for the West Indies. By all accounts it is a hellish place: swamps, insects and appalling heat. I'm told that most die of illness and it is a lucky man who returns. I have no concern for myself. I only beg you, once again, to honour your promise in any way you can. As I write this we are about to weigh anchor. I bid you farewell and God's blessing.

Your loving brother,
Joseph

Unlike the others, the final letter was local, coming by the Penny Post. He slid the blade under the seal and unfolded the paper. It simply read:

Crompton is dead. Do we continue? G. T.

He studied the note for moment, then tucked it into his pocket, tidied the desk and slipped quietly out into the street.

'And they have the nerve to call it justice!' Lizzie was spitting with rage when he arrived back at the King's Arms.

'And it ain't just the Corporation.' Sam screwed up a fist. 'It's the whole damn lot – the courts, the mill owners, the military and them lot down in London.'

'Oh those bastards know how to scratch backs alright,' snarled Lizzie, 'and they're always the backs of the likes of us.'

'That's all these laws are for – keeping the middling sort happy and to hell with the rest of us,' Sam smashed down on the table. 'God, I'd like to give them a taste of the cat – or something stronger. Whoever's doing them in has got the right idea.'

'Samuel Tinker!' erupted Beth from across the kitchen. 'Don't be so stupid. Have you not learnt a thing? Fancy doing a bit of rope dancing, do you? No? Well shut your trap and get out.'

Sam slammed the door behind him. Beth went back to dressing Jake's wounds.

'Can you keep your arms up for me, love.'

They had sagged again. Sitting on a stool by the fire Jake was gazing vacantly at the pale blue wall. He had barely spoken. Beth glanced anxiously at Charlie.

'He'll be fine in a few days. Your ointment will see to that.'

'Aye, I know Charlie. His ain't the first back I've had to tend to but it's different when it's your own kin. And sometimes the back's the easy part.' She grimaced. 'Anyhow, that should do you for now.' She lightly touched Jake's cheek.

He looked up. 'Thanks, Beth.' It wasn't much more than a whisper. 'And you too, Mr Rossi.'

'Don't mention it, Jake.'

The door from the yard opened and in walked Isabelle like she owned the place. Beth raised her eyebrows.

Charlie grinned. 'It's alright, she's with me.'

Beth shook her head and smiled knowingly. 'Come on Lizzie, let's get your man to his bed. Any fool can see these two have got some business and we wouldn't want to get in their way.'

When they had gone, Isabelle smirked. 'As easy as shelling peas.'

'And?'

'Oxley was having his way with her. One more tale of master sleeps with maid, the poor young lass.'

He shook his head. 'I must admit, I did wonder – when she couldn't bear to be in the same room as him. I thought it went beyond your usual dread of corpses. It was almost like revulsion. I mean, a man like that forcing himself on her. My God, she must have loathed him.'

'Now that's where you've got it wrong. She didn't hate him, Charlie. The poor, deluded girl was besotted with him. She knew no better and he took full advantage. That's why she couldn't bear to see his body – she thought it would break her heart.'

He stroked his chin. 'So that puts paid to your idea.'

'And why would that be?'

'Well, even if Crompton and Thomson's wives wanted them dead, why would a girl who loved her master?'

'Not her but someone who knew what he was up to. Look, Charlie – the Cromptons are friends with the Thomsons and related to the Oxleys. And their smutty little goings on weren't all that secret. So what you've got here is an avenging angel... and I'm not sure that I blame her either.'

'A woman?'

'What? You think a man's going to kill for that sort of thing!'

'You never know.'

Isabelle snorted disdainfully.

He shrugged. 'Well, I still don't reckon you have this right.'

She looked to the ceiling and sighed with exasperation. Charlie took the note from his pocket and passed it to her.

'I found it on Oxley's desk, though he was dead before he had a chance to read it. It has to be from Thomson.'

'Maybe.'

'Now who's being bloody-minded?' he retorted. 'Look, the three of them clearly had some agreement, some pact, that was... I don't know, secretive. If not, why such a terse note? And "Crompton's dead" – it's almost as if he knows this might have been going to happen; as if there was a risk they were taking and he's checking to see that Oxley's still prepared to go on with it.'

Isabelle pulled a face. 'Or else it's a normal business arrangement and he's a man of few words. You may not have noticed, Charlie, but round here they don't all have your gift of the gab.'

He couldn't help grinning. 'I'll give you that. But I reckon you're still barking up the wrong tree.'

'Look, Charlie, your average man is going to beat someone to a pulp or blow their head off. Sliding a dagger or whatever into men's brains, so smoothly that no one notices – that's a woman's work.'

'What if it's not your average man? What if it's... I don't know, some sort of assassin.'

Isabelle snorted. 'Don't be daft. This isn't London or Paris. We're not talking about cloak and dagger killers stalking the corridors of power. All you've got to choose from are some not so subtle Yorkshiremen. No, it's a woman – and some woman! She made them pay for not keeping their pricks in their britches.'

Charlie closed the door of his practice with a feeling of mild satisfaction. Both of his afternoon patients had arrived for their appointments. Maybe all was not yet lost but he had other things on his mind and set off to find somewhere quiet. Pushing through the Shambles and on past the market cross, he turned into St John's churchyard. Up ahead, a woman was standing beside a grave. Under the hood of her dark red cloak he recognised the features of Sarah Armstrong. As he drew closer, he realised that the grave was that of a child.

'Good afternoon, Doctor Rossi.' She composed her face into a faint smile.

'Mrs Armstrong.' He bowed. 'Forgive me for intruding.'

'No matter, I was just leaving.'

However, she gave no sign of doing so. Instead, she held him in a steady, thoughtful gaze. He returned it calmly. As if having made a decision, she broke the silence.

'Matthew was my first-born.' Her voice was quiet but firm. 'A group of older boys bundled him over in the street. When he fell, he struck his head on a post. The next day he complained of headaches and the morning after that he never woke up. He had just had his fourth birthday.'

'I am so very sorry.' He really was. 'I can't imagine how awful that must have been.'

'Thank you. You are kind but do not forget that the vicar was there to comfort me with the assurance that "The Lord giveth and the Lord taketh away".' The bitterness in her tone was evident. 'He was also certain that I would not feel the loss so grievously because I had my second son to attend to. He was a truly understanding gentleman.'

'No less than I've come to expect from the clergy.'

She raised her eyebrows. 'So you have also suffered loss?'

'My parents – my mother died of tumours and my father found that he couldn't live without her. You can imagine that the Church's tender compassion in our time of need was something that I shall never forget.'

She nodded, understandingly. 'Would you care to walk with me for a while?'

In spite of himself, he found that he did care to.

They walked in silence until they joined the street. As they did, flakes of snow began to fall around them. Some settled on her hood.

'I was told that your other son has taken a commission.'

She sighed. 'My husband was never blessed with the most sanguine of humours, Mr Rossi, and Matthew's death made him more severe than ever. He strove for even greater success in his business affairs and formed a settled opinion that his remaining son should join him in them.'

'But he didn't share his father's ambition.'

'William, I have to say, takes more after his mother – he has always preferred actions to auctions.' She smiled wryly. 'That much has been clear since his childhood but my husband refused to acknowledge it. When William asked to join the army, Josiah was incandescent. William pleaded with me to intercede on his behalf and eventually I consented.'

'You didn't agree with his choice either?'

'I am his mother, Mr Rossi.' There was a fire in her voice. 'To lose my other son…'

They walked on through the thickening snowfall.

'In the end, Josiah relented but his terms were harsh: no monies would ever be forthcoming to raise William above the rank of ensign.'

Charlie knew that, as a result, the young man would continually see wealthy junior officers promoted ahead of him.

She continued, 'I believe that, in his more charitable moments, Josiah hopes this will frustrate William to the point that he will resign his commission before any harm comes to him. That is certainly my hope.'

They arrived outside Red Hall, stopping at the already snow-covered gate. Sarah Armstrong turned to face him.

'I suppose that you will be calling tomorrow with your rent. My husband is away on business but I will be at home. I should be pleased to receive it from you in his stead.'

He knew that he was always skating on thin ice in Sarah's presence. Was that the sound of it cracking?

'As it happens, I gave him a month's rent only last week.'

On balance, he felt it was as well that he had.

16

The Coloured Cloth Hall was unlike any other building that Charlie had been in. The courtyard where he was standing was vast: more than thirty paces wide and fully three times as long. The façade of the halls surrounding it had the appearance of an immense arcade in which he could count over seventy pillared archways. Above the central arch at the far end, a clock struck seven, heralding the start of trading, while a bell rang out from a cupola mounted above it on the roof.

With its classical style and huge scale, it occurred to him that what the burghers of Leeds had created was not so much a market as a temple – a temple to the god of woollen cloth. The blanket of virgin snow, which had been laid over the courtyard during the night, had already been trodden down by countless devotees as they made their way into the hallowed halls. Now the bell was calling those within to begin their holy rites.

This impression was only reinforced when he went inside. Like some enormous clerestory, great leaded windows in the upper half of each archway flooded the hall with soft morning light. What was most striking, though, was the lack of noise. Two lines of low wooden tables, piled high with coloured cloths, stretched away into the distance and hundreds of clothiers and merchants were engrossed in bidding and bargaining. Despite this, throughout the hall there was an almost reverent hush. If the building was designed to be a temple then the atmosphere within was like that of worship.

'Surprising, isn't it?' Tom Tinker spoke quietly in his ear.

'It certainly is, Tom.' Charlie greeted him with a gentle pat on the back.

'And yet, by half past eight they'll have sold thousands of pounds of cloth, twenty thousand perhaps. Mind you, if you'd been here before the war, it'd have been thirty or even forty thousand.'

Charlie whistled softly.

The previous evening he had asked Tom for another favour and, as he surveyed the merchants in the hall, he pondered the task at hand.

'I need to find out what those three men were up to – what rumours have been going round about them – anything at all.'

'No problem, Charlie. I've asked a couple of mates to give me a hand. Might as well use their sympathy while I've still got it.'

'You've got your head screwed on alright. Taking after your mother, I don't doubt.'

'So she tells me.' Tom grinned. 'Well, I'll see you by the gates when it's over.' And with that he was off. A moment later, Charlie followed him into the throng.

Merchants were moving this way and that, examining the goods. Some of them were carrying letters from clients, bearing patterns that they were matching to the colour of the cloths. Time and again, he saw a merchant lean over the table and speak into a clothier's ear. There was a bid, a negotiation and maybe an agreement, all in a matter of seconds and all done in a virtual whisper.

High up on the wall, large letters proclaimed that he was currently walking down 'Mary's Lane'. He passed through a door to find himself in 'Change Alley' – a hall, running alongside the first, which was every bit as large and busy, yet just as oddly quiet.

At the far end, there was another name over a door and he squinted to read it.

'That's King Street.' He turned to see Nathan Lee, one of the men who had come to the mayor's house with Barton. 'There's five halls all told – two on this side, two on the other, and King Street across the top – with three hundred tables each, on a good day.'

'Seeing it,' said Charlie, shaking his head in wonderment, 'you begin to realise what cloth means to this town.'

'And it's only the half of it,' Lee replied. 'There's the White Cloth Hall as well – and then there's all the irregulars.'

The two men chatted together as they walked through the halls. Lee was a small man, bald and bearded, with blue eyes shining out from his ruddy face. He pointed to one of the endless tables.

'Them are broadcloths – "Yorkshire Dozens" we call them – a week's work for a man at home. In the mill, we turn out at least twice as many and the edges don't get spoiled by the shuttles neither. And them over there are narrow cloths – half the size.'

Other piles of cloth, all looking the same to Charlie, were revealed to be 'bays', 'kerseys' – 'very popular with the army' – 'half-thicks', blanket and hose. Lee's desire to teach soon exceeded his own to learn but, even so, he warmed to the man's cheery nature.

'By rights there shouldn't be so much here. It's only piled this high because of the war. And now, with the Frenchies getting stuck in, it's not just the colonies that are closed to trade – reaching the Mediterranean is a bit dicey too. Half a dozen merchants went under last year and things are tight for most of the weavers. Still, we'll be around long after the war's been and gone.'

'But what about you? Did you lose your loom the other night?'

'Not quite. A bit damaged but it's going to be rough for all of us. I don't doubt that Miss Oxley'll try to keep the business going though she ain't up to it by a long chalk. We can't afford any more bad news but weavers are a hardy lot. It'll take more than a few ne'er-do-wells to finish us off.'

'That reminds me – I never got to thank you for your help the other day. Without the two of you, I reckon Barton might have walked free. It's a good job Rooke found that watch.'

Lee grinned knowingly.

Charlie frowned. 'What?'

'Nothing… well, only that Rooky didn't just search Barton. He were also the first to find Oxley's body.'

'What? You mean he planted the watch!'

Lee shrugged. 'Maybe. Maybe not.'

'Haven't you asked him?'

'And why would I do that? Barton's going to swing, that's all that matters isn't it?'

'Yes, but if he didn't take it…?' His normal sense of justice was struggling to cope with the possibility.

'Look, he were there at the mill, he trashed it and he wrecked our looms – Rooky's too. The watch were the clincher. Who cares how it found its way into his pocket? Do you want him to get off?'

'No, of course not. It's just that…' Lee was still grinning at him. 'Oh, to hell with it – it serves the bugger right.'

'That's the idea.' He started to laugh and Charlie, letting justice take care of itself for once, laughed with him.

They carried on walking. He saw Tom at a distance and wondered how he was getting on, then shook his head as he realised that he had been missing a golden opportunity to make some enquiries of his own.

'Nat, can you tell me about Oxley?'

'Which one?'

'Well, all of them I suppose.'

'Right then – Mr Marmaduke, now he were a proper gent. He built the manufactory – one of the first round these parts – and started taking on journeymen. That were in the sixties when the fly shuttles started coming in. Well, he died a few years back. Then it were young Mr Joseph that took over. What can you say about him?

Nice enough fellow but no head for figures – not a clue – and things started to slide. Then one day, about two years ago, Mr James turns up. There'd been some falling out with his father and he hadn't been home in years, so they said. Anyhow, all of a sudden, he appears out of nowhere and takes over the mill.'

'And what was he like, this James?'

Lee thought for a moment. 'A very different story to his younger brother, that's for sure. If Joseph got his father's character, James got the brains – so far as business was concerned anyhow. Things really picked up and at first we're all happy. But apparently not James Oxley. What with that infernal watch of his, he kept on at us about how much we produced. God, he had a temper on him at times. It didn't seem to matter how fast we wove, he were never satisfied. Ambitious some would call him – greedy's more like it. I heard talk that he were out to start another mill, even bigger than his father's.'

'Did you hear anything else?'

Lee snorted. 'You'd have had to be deaf not to! One for the women – upstairs, downstairs or off the street – he weren't fussy by any account.'

'Anything else? Anything unusual.'

'Nah,' Lee shook his head. 'Nothing. Anyhow, what's this about?'

Charlie was wondering how to answer when a bell rang out.

'That's trading done for the day,' explained Lee. 'They've got five minutes to finish their deals or there'll be fines to pay – five pounds for every five minutes over.' Clothiers were already hefting cloth onto their shoulders. 'They'll carry it round to the buyers' homes,' Lee continued, 'and then head for a tavern. I reckon I'll be off to join them.'

Charlie thanked him and stood watching for a few minutes as the halls emptied. Then he wandered back to the main doors where Tom was waiting.

'So what have you got for me?'

'I don't know, Charlie. Might be owt or nowt.'

'Let's have it then.'

'Well, the word is that over the last year the three of them had grown right close, dining each month and always at Oxley's place, which is odd when you think about it.'

'Why's that?'

'He were a clothier – alright a big one but the likes of Crompton and Thomson

are usually stuck up about that sort of thing. Beneath their dignity as merchants to mix with someone who actually gets his hands dirty. But those three were thick as thieves. I mean only the day before Crompton's death, Oxley were elected as an alderman. Crompton proposed him. The mayor were dead set against it and it were touch and go. They say Thomson arrived in the nick of time to swing the vote.'

'And what about their business affairs?'

'Well, Oxley's never showed up at the Cloth Halls for ages. He must have been selling straight to merchants. Some think Crompton and Thomson were buying all his rolls. They've certainly cut back on their purchases hereabouts, but no one's sure.'

'Would that be unusual?'

'Not especially – there's a fair number of merchants who buy direct, at least for some of their pieces.'

'I see. Is that it?'

'Sorry, I'm afraid so.'

'No, Tom, you've been a great help.'

'You reckon?' Tom's tone suggested he felt otherwise. 'You heading back?'

There was no reply. With a shy half-smile and a nod, Tom Tinker left Charlie to his thoughts.

***

When the Cloth Hall Deputy arrived to lock up, he twice had to ask the young man with the dark curly hair to move out from under the entrance. With barely a grunt of acknowledgement, the stranger sauntered off in the direction of the river. The Deputy shook his head: he'd better watch where he were going, that one, or he'd be walking into the middle of a Press Gang and then he *would* have something to think about.

With an ease of movement that had never ceased to impress the old Deputy, the two great gates swung shut. The large metal key, so cold to his touch today, turned smoothly in the lock. He set off home to warm himself with a glass or two of his favourite spirit. Behind him, the great Cloth Hall stood empty and silent; waiting until the next holy day.

***

The weavers greeted Charlie with the silent nods and grim smiles that spoke of an increasing familiarity. He climbed the stairs to the mill's office. Looking out through its windows at the few men still working on the upper floor, he could picture Oxley standing there with watch in hand, scrutinising his journeymen's work rate.

He turned his attention to the shelves. There were invoices from staplers for the purchase of wool; records of payments made to the weavers; and a number of sales ledgers. He looked through these briefly. They went back as far as the start of the mill by Oxley's father but the most recent was over a year old.

In the centre of the office was the large writing desk and on it lay a wooden box. It was about eighteen inches wide and a foot deep. The sloping lid was engraved with an image of what looked like the Golden Fleece hanging from a harness. He tried the lid. It was locked.

He searched his coat pockets for the small screwdriver that he had used to assemble the thunder house. He checked through the windows but the weavers were all focussed on their looms. Wedging the screwdriver under the lid against the lock, he pushed down on it as hard as he could. It refused to budge. He looked around the office. Propped in a corner behind the door was a black, wooden walking stick with a large metal head. Picking it up, the weight surprised him. He gripped it halfway down the shaft, tipped the box on end and swung the bulbous knob down onto the screwdriver.

The lock, and the wood around it, shattered and the handle of the screwdriver splintered. That stick packed a punch.

He sat down and raised the lid.

The box contained just three books. The first was a novel: *Memoirs of a Woman of Pleasure*. He had heard of this. *Fanny Hill* it was now being called. It had been withdrawn, soon after its publication fifty years earlier, when the author had been charged with 'corrupting the King's subjects' but there were plenty of pirated copies around. He grinned to himself: if you owned one of these you would probably be well advised to lock it out of sight of polite society. He resisted the temptation to delve into its covers and put it to one side.

Next was a diary. Oxley had started it after his return to Leeds two years earlier. Flicking through the pages, he noticed various references to Joseph: 'J glad to relinquish business'; 'J miserable as always'; 'J away to London. Glad to be shot of him.' And then in the previous August, after a gap of over a year, there were several more entries: 'J returned. No change'; 'J talks of taking a commission'; and then 'J has entrusted me with such a treasure. Gave him my pledge. What a wonderful diversion it shall prove.' Several weeks after this final mention of Joseph, Charlie found: 'Evening with "FH" at last. Very diverting.' As he turned the pages he found other references to 'FH' yet always, he noticed, on a Saturday.

Reading on, he came to numerous accounts of the monthly dinners with Crompton and Thomson. He skipped over the endless lists of the food and drink that were consumed – standard fare in these circles – but amongst them were scattered references to the topics of conversation. Since the middle of the previous year, there were several entries concerning what Oxley referred to simply as 'the enterprise': 'At last, proposed the enterprise to them. Shocked, as expected, but to their credit they did not rule it out'; 'Both still lukewarm about the enterprise'; 'C coming round but T remains unsure – thinks he has too much to lose'. Then in October: 'Offered the inducement to them. Snapped at it like pigs at the trough. Both on board.' This was followed by: 'To Hull and the Continent to make arrangements. DLC slippery but amenable. All agreed but a very close thing in the end.' Several entries in November and December indicated that everything was going 'as expected'. January's meal had been accompanied by much discussion of 'the prize': 'After three months they considered they had earned it. Thought it wise to consent at last. Could barely contain themselves when they heard the full account.' There were only a few other entries after that, mainly about Oxley's imminent trip to Derbyshire in preparation for the building of a new mill.

He set the diary aside and lifted the last book out of the box. It was a sales ledger for the previous year. Even to his inexpert eye, it was clear that something had changed in the final quarter of 79. Up to that point, the entries showed a very diverse spread, both in terms of the material being sold – most of the types of cloths that Nathan Lee had pointed out were recorded – and also the number of merchants traded with. However, since the middle of October, the mill had been turning out almost nothing but kerseys, of either twenty-seven or fifty-four inch widths, and the column for purchasers contained just two names: Robert Crompton and George Thomson.

He closed the ledger.

The boards behind him creaked and a shadow spread across the desk.

As he turned, his head exploded in pain.

Shadow turned to blackness and he collapsed to the floor.

17

The blurred image of a beetle scuttled in front of his eyes. Timber planking grated harsh against his cheek. He touched the back of his head and winced. His hand came away sticky. Grabbing the edge of the chair, he hauled himself up into it, his head pulsing with pain. He bent over the desk, resting on his forearms, breathing heavily.

On the surface lay a large black book. He stared blankly at it for a while before remembering what it was. Opening it, he ran his reddened fingers down the ledger's spine   along the ragged edges of three torn-out pages.

He looked out through the windows. Around the upper floor, a handful of men were weaving. A few were still trying to mend their looms. Two sat in a corner sharing a bottle. He looked behind him. The black walking stick lay on the floor by the door.

'I have often thought there are easier ways of making a living,' said Louis, wiping blood from the back of Charlie's head, 'but I wasn't thinking of getting killed every other day.'

'I wish I *was* making a living,' Charlie replied, 'but actually I'm doing this for the fun of it.'

Isabelle laughed. She was sitting cross-legged on the bed, juggling some apples. Louis patted him on the shoulder and returned to arranging cards for the evening show.

'Alright, Charlie,' said Isabelle, 'so those three had something going on, I'll give you that.'

'And someone else knows about it,' he pressed the damp cloth carefully to his head, 'or maybe they're even involved.'

'So where do you go from here?'

'I wish I knew.' He watched as Isabelle threw two apples high while taking a bite out of the third. 'But it wouldn't hurt if I could get a look at either Crompton's or Thomson's records.'

'That'll be straight forward then.' Isabelle smiled sarcastically.

He returned the look. 'Could we try the ruse that we used at Oxley's house?'

'Not a hope. They already know who you are: the man who probably killed their masters. I doubt you'll even get over the threshold, let alone be left on your own.'

'Aye, you may be right.' He sighed. 'And of course we don't even know where the men's studies are.'

'Now that's something I *can* help with,' replied Isabelle. 'Unlike you, I am more than welcome downstairs.'

Louis looked up from the table. 'Don't forget, *ma chère*, that you would be more than welcome downstairs with me – that is, if you can spare any of your such valuable time before our next performance.'

He ducked as one of the apples flew towards him.

After an hour's rest, Charlie set off through the thickening snowfall for his practice rooms, where he treated one patient and waited in vain for two others. By four o'clock he was back in the Broussards' room.

'How did it go?'

Isabelle shrugged. 'Straightforward. Crompton's study is on the ground floor at the back of the house. Thomson's is on the first floor at the front. So, Crompton's it is.'

He frowned. 'What do you mean?'

'I mean' – she explained with exaggerated patience – 'that if you want to get into one of their rooms it is going to have to be Crompton's.'

'I gathered that, thank you. But you make it sound as if the "how" is a formality.'

'Well, the back door is bolted at night but there are sash windows on the ground floor so we use one of those – straight in, straight out.'

'Excuse me?'

'I don't think I want to hear this,' said Louis, heading for the door. 'I'll be in the Long Room.'

Isabelle sighed. 'Look Charlie, you tell me that you want to get into Crompton's study and I tell you how. If you have some other idea, then fine.'

'Yes, but breaking and entering!'

'There won't be any need to break anything. Those windows are child's play.'

'You've done this before!'

She merely shrugged, lay down on the bed and closed her eyes.

He shook his head. 'You're completely mad. I'm in enough trouble as it is.'

'I wasn't planning on getting caught.'

'Oh, really,' laughed Charlie. 'Well, that's a great comfort.'

He sat down on the end of the bed and looked at her lying there with her hair all splayed out. She truly was a law unto herself. She was so confident of her own abilities. There was no trace of the self-doubts that beset people like him. When it came down to it, he didn't doubt her either – she could get them into that house. In fact, he was coming to realise, when she set her mind to something, she didn't let anything get in her way. And, after all, they only wanted some information. It wasn't as if they would be stealing anything. But no, it was far too risky. The consequences of being caught didn't bear thinking about. It was out of the question.

'I suppose we can always nip out through the window if we have to.'

Isabelle opened her eyes and grinned at him. 'That's the spirit, Charlie.'

The backyard of the Cromptons' was bathed in snow-light. The moon lay largely hidden behind clouds but the snow underfoot seemed to be giving off all the light that it had soaked up during the day. Charlie shrank from it in the pale shadow of one of the outhouses. He glanced nervously up at the array of windows looming above him.

Archie's tail thumped the snow as Isabelle approached. She held a large bone out and it beat even more enthusiastically. The bone had come courtesy of Beth, along with a quizzical look. Charlie had winked and left before she could ask any questions. With the dog happily gnawing away, Isabelle beckoned him to the rear wall of the house. He darted across to its dubious shelter, sure that at any moment a curtain would twitch or a shutter be folded back.

They crept past the back door and the first of three large ground-floor windows. They stopped at the second. Isabelle pushed upwards on the lower frame. Nothing happened. He tapped her on the shoulder and she stood aside but his efforts only confirmed that the window was locked. Letting out a sigh of relief, he turned away – to find Isabelle holding up her dagger. Moving back to the window, she pressed the tip of the blade between the two frames, carefully working it upwards until only the handle remained visible. Gripping tightly, she pushed sideways against the lock. Very slowly, her hands moved as the lever swivelled on its pivot. A moment later, the lock came free. With the stiletto back in her boot, Isabelle slid the window upwards in one steady movement. At the sound of the wood squeaking, he looked up at the windows again, but there was no movement; no light appeared.

In one smooth, silent action, Isabelle sprang over the window sill and dropped out of sight. He shook his head. What lay in her past? And what was he doing in the company of such a woman? He took a deep breath, clambered up onto the sill and gingerly lowered himself into the room.

Thick material brushed against his face, smothering his mouth. He pushed down the urge to get back to the fresh air and fought his way through the curtains. The darkness beyond was absolute. A memory broke through – the acrid stench of urine – and demons rose in the dark.

Focus, for God's sake.

Reaching into his pocket, he drew out a tinder box and a sheet of sulphur matches – 'spunks' his mother had called them. He knelt down and opened the box. Taking out the flint and steel, he tore off half the matches and dropped them back in the box. Looping three fingers through the 'D'-shaped steel, he struck down on it with the small piece of flint. He flinched at the sound of each strike but after only three attempts the sulphur caught on the shower of sparks and the waxy splints began to burn. From another pocket he took out a small grease lamp and lit it. Isabelle crouched down beside him and lit a lamp of her own. They stood up and looked around.

An exceptionally long mahogany dining table dominated the room. The lamplight glistened off an array of silver candlesticks and tureens lining its waxy surface. Their grim expressions stared back at them from a large mirror on the opposite wall.

'What the…' He swore under his breath.

They were in the wrong room. He looked incredulously at Isabelle.

She raised her arms in bewilderment. 'Kitty said it was the second room along,' she breathed.

'But there are two windows in this room,' he hissed back. Behind them, a dresser filled the wall between the two sets of curtains. 'So we needed the *third* one.'

'Sorry,' mouthed Isabelle.

For a moment they stood in silence, each weighing the options:

retrace their steps and try their luck with the other window, or press on. He made his decision.

'We're here now.'

Isabelle shrugged apologetically. 'It's your show.'

They moved to the door. Isabelle looked at him and he nodded. She blew out her lamp and he sheltered his with his hand. She laid her hand on the knob. It turned without a sound and she pulled the door smoothly towards her. He gave silent thanks that Crompton seemed to like everything in his life well-oiled.

Immediately opposite, across the hall, was the staircase. They waited.

Silence.

Turning left they crept down the corridor towards the study. Once inside, Isabelle relit her lamp, passed it to Charlie and then dropped into a large armchair. He moved towards the window, in front of which was Crompton's desk. Like the dining room furniture, this was an impressive piece, some six feet long, and made, he guessed, from walnut. He sat down in the fine swivel chair and ran his fingers across the red, tooled leather of the desktop. It had belonged to a powerful man and a man with aspirations to more power. Not a man to take lightly. And yet someone had got the better of him – swiftly and ruthlessly.

On either side of the desk were four drawers and he set about examining their contents: Corporation papers, receipt books, newspaper cuttings, correspondence. It was all meticulously ordered. He worked quickly through it and had reached the last drawer when Isabelle laid a ledger in front of him.

'Is this what you're looking for?' she whispered in his ear.

He picked it up. It was the sales ledger for the year.

'Where did you find it?'

She pointed to the shelves that lined the wall adjoining the dining room. He nodded appreciatively. Opening the book, he scanned the few pages that had entries. Although some of the transactions appeared unremarkable, the majority of the rolls –

all kerseys – were being sold to just one person: 'van de Kruisen'. He replaced the ledger and found the one for the preceding year. Working back from December, the same pattern was evident but in the middle of October it came to an abrupt halt. Before then, Crompton was selling a far greater mix of cloth and van de Kruisen's name disappeared from the records.

He beckoned Isabelle over and silently pointed out the contrast. She nodded thoughtfully. And then all hell broke loose in the yard. Something had disturbed Archie. He froze, hoping that the dog would quickly settle but the barking was relentless. Isabelle's eyes communicated the same silent thought – someone must surely come. He shoved the ledger back on the shelf and stuffed the papers into the drawers of the desk. Isabelle, listening at the door, gestured for him to hurry up. He carried the lamps to the door and blew them out. Stepping into the corridor, they felt their way along the wall towards the dining room.

Footsteps sounded on the stairs. The faint glow of a lamp shone round the corner and spread along the passageway.

'Damned dog!' grumbled a woman's voice, thick with sleep.

Isabelle pushed Charlie back towards the study.

The light was spreading towards them. A large woman stepped into the hallway.

He pulled the door to.

Had she turned? Were they trapped? He could still smell the smoke from their lamps – a dead give-away.

Isabelle dragged him from the door towards the window. In the darkness, he felt for the chair. He edged his way around the desk and reached through the curtains for the lock.

'No time!' hissed Isabelle in his ear. 'And the noise.'

Reluctantly, he crouched down beside her in the gap behind the desk. Archie still bayed in the yard.

'What're you playing at?' the woman's voice growled from outside.

'Sounds like the cook,' whispered Isabelle.

Charlie closed his eyes and groaned. 'We left the window open.'

'Well, we'll know soon enough,' she muttered.

He took a deep breath and held it, fighting to keep his chest under control. He strained to hear beyond the blood pulsing in his ears. The dog's barks and the cook's curses gradually became more intermittent and, finally, stopped. There was a dull thud of a door closing. He exhaled. Isabelle stood up. As she did so, she dragged the curtains slightly aside and a thin shaft of moonlight shone into the room.

'Hang on.' Charlie touched her hand.

On the back of the desk, behind each set of drawers, there were two doors, each with a small round knob. He remembered a desk like this, although much less grand, from his childhood. His father would sit at it, working, and he would squeeze himself into one of the little cupboards at the back, making his father promise not to give him away to his sister.

The first cupboard was empty but inside the second, wrapped in a piece of cloth, was a small leather case.

'Come on,' Isabelle urged.

'Just a moment.'

He took out his tinderbox and lit his lamp again. Laying the case on top of the desk, he unhooked the clasp and drew out a bundle of letters. He unfolded the top one. The address was Amsterdam; the date, 11th October 1779. He scanned it quickly.

Sir,

I am in receipt of your letter of the 5th inst. at the hand of your colleague. I concur with your view that commerce must progress whatever the fate of nations may be. Rest assured that my services are at your disposal and I am happy to proceed with all necessary discretion.

The prices you propose form a basis on which we may proceed, although fortunes in the field may bring some variation. Your goods will certainly find a ready market. The need for such cloth will sadly always be with us.

I am your faithful servant,
Jean de la Croix

'Got it!' He nodded with satisfaction.

'Right, now let's get out of here,' urged Isabelle.

He pushed the letters back into the case and slipped it into his pocket.

Opening the door a fraction, all was dark. They crept cautiously back to the dining room. Isabelle went first, dropping silently through the window onto the snow. Charlie followed but landed awkwardly. The sudden movement alarmed Archie, who began barking ferociously again. Isabelle reached up to pull the window closed but, as she did, they heard the sound of the kitchen door bolts being drawn back. There was no time to get past, back out to the street, so they turned and ran for the outhouses, with Archie straining at his leash and snapping at Charlie's legs. He tried two doors that refused to give before a third opened. Pulling Isabelle inside, he slid the bolt across. They squeezed into the darkest corner.

Footsteps crunched on the packed snow. 'Good boy. They went that way, eh.' The voice was strong and clear. 'Who's there? I've got a cleaver and, if you think I won't use it, just give me the chance.'

He pressed against Isabelle, holding his breath. The door rattled but held. And again. A lantern shone at the window. Then the footsteps moved away. Another door rattled and another. Still, he hardly dared breathe. He could feel Isabelle's body, tense against him in the darkness. They stayed pressed against each other until Archie settled once again and the door of the house slammed shut.

Breathing out, he looked around. They were in Crompton's cloth store, surrounded by piles of cloth that was all waiting for the barges that would take it downriver to Hull. He shook his head at the audacity of the plan.

Turning back he glimpsed Isabelle's face in the moonlight. Her eyes were shining and fixed on his. He held her gaze. She smiled, grabbed his coat and pulled him down into the cloth. Her mouth pressed hungrily to his, sucking at his lips then exploring behind them with her tongue. He ran his fingers back through her hair and caressed the nape of her neck. Pulling away, he slid his tongue under her chin and down towards her cleavage, savouring the saltiness as he went. Under her skirts, he stroked the silky, warm skin of her thighs. She rolled him over and slid her hand into the front of his britches. At the touch of her cold, encircling fingers he let out a soft moan.

Bending to his ear, she whispered. 'That's the spirit, Charlie.'

18

Like much of the West Riding, the borough of Leeds was bound fast by snow. Few ventured out of doors unnecessarily. Fewer still travelled beyond the town's toll bars. Occasional mail coaches were getting through, with horses and riders utterly spent by their efforts, bringing with them a few hardy travellers. Otherwise, it was a rare person who journeyed in from the towns and villages around. Snow piled high on the roof tops, drifted against the buildings in the wide streets and made some of the narrow alleys virtually impassable. The impact was most noticeable on market day, when the resilient stallholders outnumbered their customers. News from the Cloth Halls was equally bleak with many clothiers and most of the merchants staying away.

Louis sat on a large trunk, shuffling cards – the table, covered in letters, was unavailable. Charlie poured over them.

'It's all here: sizes, colours, costs, delivery dates. They approach de la Croix…'

Isabelle looked up from playing with the kitten. 'Crompton's "van de Kruisen"?'

'I guess so – in Dutch for safety's sake. They ask him to act as an intermediary. Oxley brokers the deal – that's clear from his diary – at some risk to himself, apparently.'

'The man had some nerve.'

'Aye, that he did. Kerseys, so Nat Lee says, are mainly for military uniforms and we all know where the sales of cloth have been banned.'

Louis smiled ruefully. 'And where my countrymen also have an interest.'

Charlie nodded. 'So they get the cloth to Holland and then de la Croix does the rest. Within weeks it's clothing King George's enemies.'

'Oxley's illegal "enterprise",' Isabelle said, pensively.

'Many would call it treasonable. It would have been very lucrative but it needed to be.'

'So, you think someone discovers all this and bumps them off.'

'That sounds about it.'

'Why not expose them and let them hang?'

'I don't know. Anger blinds us to reason, I guess. If it was someone with a son fighting the colonists, I can well imagine them dispensing justice with their own hands.'

'Well there's a fair few of them to choose from.'

'I know,' he sighed, 'that's the problem.'

Isabelle snorted. 'So, after all our excitement, you end up in the same place as me.' He looked at her quizzically. 'I mean you've a nice theory but you're no nearer pinning it on anyone. Even if you guessed right, how are you going to induce them to own up?'

He pulled a face. 'Alright, don't rub it in, but there's something else here. There has to be.'

'Well, fascinating as all this speculation may be, I have work to do – the horses to feed for a start.' She rolled off the bed and made for the door. No smile. No goodbye.

He went over to the window and scraped the ice off the glass. Down below, Isabelle crossed the yard, picked up a spade and began clearing snow from in front of the stable.

He hadn't known what to expect after their adventures at the

Cromptons' house but certainly not this. She had greeted him as if nothing had happened. There was no hint of intimacy in her manner, no new warmth in her look. But neither did she seem at all embarrassed, as if their time of passion had been a foolish mistake. And when she had spoken of "our excitement" it was merely about nearly getting caught red-handed. Had she given herself up to the moment in the outhouse and then, unencumbered by any expectations, simply let it go?

In the yard, she propped the spade against the wall, eased the door open and stepped into the stable.

The window misted up and he turned away.

Louis was watching him from across the room.

**

Beth bent over a shovel as she cleared a path to her doorway one more time. A bit of snow wouldn't stop her customers wanting their ale and she was going to be ready for them. Putting her hands to her hips, she arched her back and looked to the sky.

'There's a thaw in the air, mark my words.'

Charlie, mug in hand, smiled affectionately. Nothing ever got the better of Beth Tinker. Alright, she sounded off at Sam and complained about her customers but she was indomitable. If the devil walked in and asked for a drink she would tell him to go back out and wipe his feet. He wished he had even an ounce of her spirit.

'I'd forgotten what that looks like.'

Sam flopped down next to him.

'What?'

'The smile. You've been a right miserable beggar for days. You're not the only one losing out in this weather.'

'I know Sam – it's not that.'

'Oh, I get it,' Sam nodded knowingly. 'I thought you hadn't been up to the White Swan for a while.'

'It's not that either. Well,' he grinned, sheepishly, 'not only that.

No, I just feel… I don't know, like I'm stuck in one of these damned snowdrifts. I can't see my way through it. And as soon as it all thaws, the Corporation will be meeting again and then my time's up.'

'It must be nice to be gentlemen of leisure,' interrupted Beth as she scattered fresh sawdust on the wet floor.

'Aye, well, someone has to keep you in work.'

'Cheeky beggar.' She flung a handful of sawdust in Charlie's direction. 'Go on, out with you, snow or no snow, and let my husband get on with *his* duties.' She scowled at Sam. The two men rose from the table.

'I suppose I'll just have to find somewhere else to do my thinking.' He reached for the door handle.

'Good luck with that, Charlie,' replied Sam, 'but, even if you can work it out, I still can't see how you'll get them to own up.'

He turned round slowly. 'You know, that's what Isabelle said – more or less. But what was the word she used?'

He hurried back across the taproom and up the stairs. Sam looked at Beth and shrugged. In his room, Charlie threw open his chest and rummaged through clothes and medical books until he found it – Oxley's diary. He sat on the bed, flicking through the pages.

'The inducement,' he read under his breath. They were greedy, yes, but this was dangerous stuff. It had to be something big. Or, knowing the sort of man Oxley was…

Beth was right: there was a thaw in the air. There would be more than a few wet floors by the time all the drifts had melted and flowed down the street. And then before long the banks would be overflowing again, filling the houses near the river with their icy waters and stinking mud. It was all part of life for those who couldn't afford to live any further away.

Sensing the imminent change, more people were out and about than Charlie had seen for days. Some looked around themselves with the naïve appearance of creatures emerging from hibernation.

And there was a freshness to people's greetings, as if, rather than a week, a whole season had passed since their last encounter. Some looked askance at him and others muttered amongst themselves. Although he responded with as cheery a 'Good morning' as he could muster, he felt weary of the increasing suspicion directed towards him. He sought sanctuary in St John's.

In the central aisle, his eyes drifted upwards to the angelic figures that supported the great roof beams. *It must be nice to imagine yourself surrounded by such beings,* he thought sourly, *guarding you and smoothing your way through life.* True, his childhood had felt like that but adulthood had brought only demons.

He wandered around, admiring the craftsmanship. He ran his hand over the ornately carved woodwork that filled the church. He thought of the other hands that had once laboured here with skill and devotion; hands that were now no more than a few disjointed bones under the earth.

At the wooden lectern, a large eagle stood ready to proclaim the message of the Great Bible. He heaved the book open at the marker and his eye was caught by the huge, ornamented letter, heralding the start of a chapter:

'Now faith is the substance of things hoped for, the evidence of things not seen.'

He didn't like the sound of that. There was still far too much evidence that he couldn't see. He read on.

The writer listed the men and women of faith in olden times: Abel, Enoch, Noah, and then Abraham and Sara, 'sojourning in the land of promise, as in a strange land'. His father had sojourned in this strange land with its grey skies and biting winds, its dull colours and coarse food. He had pitched his tent among this people, who only ever sang from their hearts, or laughed from their bellies, when they were full of wine or gin. And yet this had also become a land of promise. For a time. At least here his father had found his 'Sara'.

The only thing he knew about Abraham's wife was that she had laughed; he couldn't remember at what, but she had shared that gift with his mother. Above all, that was the enduring memory of her. One came to him now: being chased around the back yard by her, with his sister, Sophie, riding on her back, and all three of them whooping and shrieking. And through the study window, his father was watching them with a look of such contentment. Was that what had attracted his father to her: that childlike freedom; so alien to many of his mother's people and much of their Presbyterian religion? She could laugh at a squirrel scampering up a tree or at a fish leaping in a pond. She would point out birds or flowers but it wasn't just for him and Sophie to appreciate. They could hear the joy in her voice. She was constantly being surprised and delighted by things that others took for granted. For her, the whole of creation was a land of promise.

'These all died in faith, not having received the promises.'

Her eyes would never again take joy in the world or delight in the Creator. He gazed far off down the church. The old feelings welled up in his chest once more. He had been unprepared for them at the time and they had overwhelmed him again and again but he had learnt how to keep them at bay with the daily round and his busy mind. He took a deep breath and pushed them back down.

But then there was his father's death – where sadness wasn't the issue.

Clouds thickened outside and the light in the church paled. His mood darkened with it. His guard, weakened by thoughts of his mother, gave way.

There was a letter on the table. His father opened it. It was from Sophie with news of her life in London and the young gentleman who had begun paying his respects to her. Her words drew his father out of himself and they talked of hopes for her happiness. After a while, he became withdrawn again – his hands working on a new leather upper but his eyes vacant. However, as the day wore on, his father's mood lightened and he talked about life back in Italy. He had listened with fascination. It was longer than he could recall since his father had spoken like this. As a boy, he had squatted at his father's feet and been transported to the Umbrian village: to the festivals of the Madonna, as she was processed through the streets, surrounded by a carnival of music and dancing; to the night-time meals under the olive trees, with their strange foods, the flavours of which had been evoked on the tongue of his imagination by his father's words; or to the annual hunt for the wild boar, which had filled both father and son with exhilaration and fear, until the spears were driven into it and they had mourned for such a fine beast.

'I think I'll go home,' said his father, with just the hint of a smile.

In the evening he went out, leaving his father working on a pair of ladies' shoes, and feeling comfortable about doing so for the first time. One of their new neighbours had invited him to a dance. At the Newcastle Assembly Rooms he took to the floor several times with a young woman who had caught his eye. Whether it was her vivacity, the rhythms of the music, or the sheer physicality of the dances, as the evening wore on he could feel his cares ebbing away. He returned home more at ease with himself than he had been for months.

As he entered the pitch-black rooms, the stench of urine filled his lungs. The darkness pressed on his chest and his heart began to race. He called out. There was no reply. He groped around for his tinder box. In the first flicker from the lamp, he saw his father standing against the far wall, his head slumped forward. Could you fall asleep like that? On the floor around him, a pool glistened in the growing light. Tipped over in it was a small wooden stool. Then he saw that his father's feet were not standing in the puddle but suspended a few inches above it.

He ran forward, grabbed his father round the chest and tried to lift him up but the cord was tight around a wall hook. Bellowing, he reached for a knife. He hacked frantically at the cord. It snapped and he lowered the body to the floor. His father had plaited three bootlaces and knotted them together and the laces had cut deep into the folds of his neck. He dug at them with his fingers, trying to slip the knife underneath. He could see scratch marks and smears of blood on the skin where his father had clawed at the cord in an instinctive, desperate fight for breath, tearing his fingernails in the process. His knuckles had large grazes as well, where they had thrashed against the wall in his final, frantic moments.

He sat on the wet, stinking floor, cradling his father until first-light. Then he made a pile of the soiled clothing and the boots his father had been repairing, and set fire to it all. When customers arrived to reclaim their footwear, they greeted the news with horror. Some people backed away without a word. Others made futile attempts to offer words of consolation. One man demanded compensation. 'Go to hell,' he shouted back, 'and you can ask him for your money when you get there.'

'These all died in faith, not having received the promises.'

His father's Catholic faith had deserted him in his time of greatest need and the land of promise had become a barren wilderness. For the next few weeks, he had also wandered in that wilderness. Numbness stripped the world bare, only for the emptiness to crack apart and be drowned in rage. At what – his father; those who had dragged him down to despair; the injustices of life; God?

He tried to recall better times but his memory was now forever polluted. His father had robbed him of that as well.

He had hacked out a crude grave from the unholy ground beyond the churchyard wall, and along with his father's corpse he buried the turmoil of confused feelings. But they kept rising again. So standing on the bank of the Tyne and watching its never-ending flow, he had opted to outrun them.

Was that what had kept Abraham on the road for so long: not looking for a new future but fleeing from a past that haunted him? Yet, the past was always on your heels and if you stayed put too long it would steal a march on you.

He shut the thought out and made himself read on. The writer extolled the faith of some other Old Testament characters and among them he came across the pairing of Gideon and Barak. Barak he had never heard of but Gideon had been a childhood hero, routing a vast army with a few hundred men, simply by blowing trumpets, shouting and waving lamps.

He went in search of the story, eventually spotting Gideon's name and, just before it, that of Barak, coming at the start of a song celebrating another victory by the Hebrews. He wondered whether it had been accomplished in a similarly remarkable way but it turned out to be a far more predictable tale: the Canaanite army had been wiped out on the field of battle, with the exception of their captain, Sisera, who had fled and taken refuge in the tent of a man called Heber the Kenite. He read to the end of the story.

As he did, he felt the snow begin to melt.

He offered up a brief prayer of thanks and walked out into the warming world.

***

Set free from their wintry prison, the punters were glad of entertainment wherever they could find it. The Long Room at the White Swan was unusually full.

Isabelle held up the snuff box. All eyes were on her father, blindfolded on the stage.

'Might that be the possession of a gentleman?' he speculated. 'Something metallic, perhaps?'

It never did to go straight to the answer. Effort, or at least the appearance of it, was required. It also gave her time to explore a pocket or two – a convenient way to set up the next trick, when someone would discover that their watch had miraculously transported itself into a locked box that had been visible on stage all the time.

She withdrew her hand. Another snuff box. That wouldn't do.

'It feels like something for the senses.' There were encouraging noises from the audience. He was getting warm.

She slid her fingers out of another coat pocket. It was just some folded, crumpled papers – even less use. Then two words caught her eye.

They were 'Crompton' and 'kerseys'.

19

At the flick of the switch, the blades sliced into the woman's papery skin. She let out a sharp cry.

There was really no need for that, thought Henry Barnard as he removed the scarificator from her neck. She should count herself fortunate to live in such an enlightened age. This little brass box showed just how far the profession had advanced: twelve spring-loaded lancets piercing the skin to a precisely determined depth and just as quickly retracting again. It was far to be preferred to the normal lancet, administered by all too imperfect human hands. And as for the crude fleam, it was one thing to use it on brute beasts but that some were still bludgeoning it into their patients was barely to be credited.

Wiping the base of the scarificator with a cloth, he replaced it in its leather case.

'Now, Mrs Yeadon, we shall require twelve ounces today. So please breathe deeply and remain still.'

He reached for one of the four glass cups that were warming above his brass spirit lamp, and placed it over the shallow cuts. The woman winced at the touch of the hot glass but he held it firmly in place. As the glass began to cool, he watched the skin being drawn up inside it and the twelve tiny springs of blood merging into a single, steady stream. He tipped the filled cup into a pewter measuring bowl before reaching for another. Rinsing and reheating each cup in turn, the blood in the bowl slowly rose to the requisite line. He took a bandage and tied it carefully around the old lady's neck.

'That will do for now, madam, but a case of asthma requires us to repeat the treatment for at least a week. However, you will be out of bed within three or four days.'

At the front door, the maid held out his cloak and hat. He took them without acknowledgement.

'Stick?'

The maid blushed. 'Begging your pardon, sir.'

She was back in a moment. Standing in the open doorway, Barnard shook his head and snatched it from her.

He trod carefully up Kirkgate, scanning the ground for patches of ice amidst the slush and meltwater.

'Dammit man!' he cursed, as he collided with someone turning out of Vicar Lane.

'Doctor?'

'Mr Mayor, I do beg your pardon.'

Micklethwaite waved it away. 'Doubtless your mind is on other things – chills and chest complaints, twisted ankles and sprained wrists.'

Barnard scowled. 'And all manner of conditions that have remained safely housebound over this past week. I had hoped to complete some drawings of the seas of the moon but this thaw has put paid to that. If they beat on my door much more it will be needing new hinges.'

'Well, if you are that busy at least it would appear that the quacks are no longer having it all their own way.'

'Perhaps – for now at least.' Barnard pulled a face.

'Fear not, good doctor. Another week will see it done.'

'Really? I thought that maybe…'

'I know, I know.' Micklethwaite nodded, smiling thinly. 'Our priority has been to replace three, much-mourned members. And then there has been this.' He flicked at the remnants of the snow. 'However, all is now in place. The proposal will be coming to the next meeting – for an outright ban.'

'You won't regret it, sir.' Barnard reached for the mayor's hand but Micklethwaite pulled away. 'Our town will forever be in your debt. It will be a great day for us all. But my patients await.' He bowed low. 'I am, as always, your servant.'

Outside the White Swan, a small crowd clustered around a bill that was posted on the wall. A thin woman, holding a young boy's hand, tried to peer over the heads in front of her.

'Mrs Barnard?'

Emily Barnard turned at the sound of her husband's voice.

'Henry!' Her own voice quavered slightly. Isaac looked up at his father with wide, reverential eyes.

'What is this?' Barnard demanded.

'I fear it concerns the deaths of your patients.' Paling, Emily bit her lip.

Heads in the crowd turned to look. Others began to move aside. He stepped into the gap to read.

BELTESHAZZAR
Professor of Natural Experimental Philosophy
and other Occult Sciences,
will deliver an evening of Marvels
never before witnessed in this or any other town.
THE HAND OF TRUTH
which has amazed and enlightened both princes and paupers
will, this Saturday, for one night only,
be consulted about the MYSTERIOUS DEATHS
of THREE LEADING CITIZENS of this borough.
This singular event, which will be of UNIVERSAL INTEREST,
will take place at the Assembly Rooms, Kirkgate.

It is not to be repeated
as the great conjuror is soon to leave this town
to perform again in London by popular demand.

'What do you reckon, Doctor B?' called one man. 'Are you going along?'

Others grinned expectantly, nudging their neighbours, but they were to be disappointed. The doctor merely put his hands on his hips and laughed.

'Tripe!' he snorted. 'Utter tripe!'

***

The coffin sat perched on the side of the grave. Not one of the other mourners came forward to lend a hand. He looked around but in the darkness it was hard to catch anyone's eye.

'Please help me,' he mouthed but no sound came from his lips.

He gathered the ends of the ropes in his hands and pulled. To his surprise he found that the coffin moved and, slowly, he lowered it into the ground. As it came to rest, a muffled noise drifted up out of the grave. For a moment, he thought it was no more than the sound of the coffin hitting the earth but it came again and then again. Exhilaration and panic swept over him in turn.

He found his voice at last. 'My father! It's my father!'

People were stepping forward now. It was going to be alright. They would get him out.

But then, from nowhere, shovels appeared and, to his horror, the men started filling in the grave. The earth rattled on the wooden lid, drowning out the hammering coming from the coffin. He pulled at the men in desperation, trying to rip the shovels from their hands, beseeching them to stop.

'Can't you hear him? He's alive! You're burying him alive!'

Remorselessly they continued and, as the grave filled up, so the sound from within became fainter and fainter.

Then it was finished. The crowd had left and he was standing alone, silently weeping for the father entombed beneath his feet. He could still hear the knocking and with the knocking came his father's voice, calling to him from the darkness: 'Charlie. Charlie.'

And he knew that he would never escape it.

***

'Charlie!' It was Sam's voice; a fist rapping on the door.

He floated into consciousness. Relief washed over him, mingled with lingering pain. He chose relief and clung to it hard.

'Thanks, Sam,' he grunted back.

He levered himself onto the side of the bed, staring vacantly in the direction of the wash bowl. He had overslept but it had been a late night and it was going to be a long day. Whether it would all be worth it, time would tell. He stretched and willed his body into action.

Beth excelled herself at breakfast.

'I've done you a veal pie and got in some smoked herring. And there's a bit of bacon as well, love.'

In truth, he thought setting to, there was enough bacon to feed a battalion.

'Beth, you're a wonder. If only you weren't already spoken for, I'd be first in line – if you'd have me.'

'Don't be so daft,' she chided but her eyes were shining.

Sam appeared with a large mug.

'Here you are, Charlie, sup on that – first of a new barrel. The finest, clearest cider you'll taste in the whole county.'

He appreciated what the Tinkers were doing for him. They knew how much hung on this day. In their practical, unsentimental way, they were expressing their friendship and care. Not for the first time it struck him that, when he had arrived in Leeds looking for a place to pitch up, he couldn't have found anywhere better.

'I reckon this drizzle's set in for the day,' observed Sam, peering out of the window. 'Makes a change from snow, though.'

Charlie got up from the kitchen table. 'Well, I'll see you both later.'

Sam smiled. 'Aye, well, all the best, Charlie.'

Beth laid down the knife with which she was butchering a rabbit, wiped her hands on her apron, and came over to where Charlie was hovering by the door.

'You're a better man by far, Charlie Rossi, than any of them on that Corporation. So don't you dare forget it. Now get off out of here and don't come back till you've sorted this mess out.' She leant forward and kissed him.

He was glad that the door was close at hand.

On the tavern wall outside was one of the posted bills. He made his way up Briggate, passing others every hundred paces or so. Tom and Agnes had done a good job and yet more had been delivered by hand to various addresses around town. It was all they could do. Now he would just have to wait and see.

When he reached the White Swan, Louis was already in the Long Room dismantling his magical and scientific equipment, surrounded by an array of boxes. He greeted Charlie warmly.

'Good morning, *mon ami*. And how are you today?'

'Oh, you know – not a care in the world.' He laughed and headed off to the Broussards' room. On the stairs, he met Isabelle carrying a large crate.

She smiled sarcastically. 'I'm so glad you've decided to grace us with your presence.'

'Well, I didn't want to get under your feet.'

'Chance would have been a fine thing.'

'I know but then breakfast at the Tinkers' is not a meal to be rushed. It has to be savoured like a good wine – or a bad woman.' He winked but Isabelle only scowled in return.

'I don't suppose there is any chance that you might remember who we are doing all this for?'

'No ma'am, certainly not ma'am,' he replied with a mock salute.

Isabelle shook her head. 'Sometimes I don't know why I bother.'

He moved aside. In the close confines of the staircase, as she squeezed past he could feel the warmth of her body and her hips brushing across his britches. Taking a deep breath, he grinned to himself and carried on up the stairs.

It was late morning before the covered wagon drew up outside the Assembly Rooms. Charlie gave a low whistle. He had seen the building before but never with an eye to it playing host to his future. Over twenty arched windows towered over him in the two storeys of whitewashed frontage. Large as they were, they were dwarfed by a vast window set above the central doorway. While the panes on the ground floor illuminated the near-sacred activities of the White Cloth Hall, of which this formed the northern end, the windows on the floor above shed their light on the more worldly activities of the town's well-to-do.

It was Louis who had suggested the change to a much larger venue, brushing Charlie's protests aside:

'It's no trouble. In truth, the time has come for us to move on. It is a mistake to overstay one's welcome. This, then, shall be our Finale and I tell you, it will be one that people will not forget quickly!'

Patting Charlie on the shoulder, he added, 'For the sake of friendship.'

Having made enquiries, Louis had returned with the news that, due to the bad weather, the scheduled event for the evening had been cancelled.

'You see, fortune is already smiling on us.' Touched by the older man's support, Charlie had agreed.

From the back of the wagon, Louis passed the first boxes of equipment down to him and Isabelle, and they made their way into the building, climbing the grand staircase to the central window at the top. Up close, it seemed even more impressive.

'All this glass,' observed Isabelle, 'you know it's not here so that people can see out. It's so they can be seen – showing off in all their finery.'

He nodded. As usual, Isabelle cut through the social pretensions of the well-to-do but he couldn't help thinking that, were she to climb these stairs dressed for a ball, she would look pretty damned fine herself.

She led the way into the ballroom and looked up at the ceiling. 'Would you look at that!'

He followed her gaze to an array of bare-breasted creatures – half woman, half animal – that were looking down on them from the white, plastered ceiling.

'It's hardly respectable,' he intoned in a pious voice. 'One simply doesn't know where to look.'

Isabelle snorted and they held each other's gaze. She smiled softly for a moment but then Louis arrived carrying another load and they looked away.

Once everything had been brought up from the wagon, Charlie began rebuilding the stage at the far end of the ballroom. It was going to stand between a pair of doors, where two rooms offered respite to those who preferred their foursomes around a card table rather than on the dance floor.

By the middle of the afternoon most of the work was done and they sat down to discuss the evening's performance. He talked through his ideas once again and Louis made various suggestions: wouldn't it be better to arrange matters in this order; wouldn't it be better to phrase a question that way?

With everything agreed, Louis and Isabelle moved on to the rest of the show. He listened in for a while but restlessness got the better of him and he set off for his rooms in Vicar Lane.

As he opened the front door, he found a note on the floor. Once the snow had begun to melt, a steady trickle of communications had appeared under the door. Several of these had come from new clients, mostly people who had been recommended by existing patients. They were a welcome counterbalance to those from established customers dispensing with his services. Today's note was from a young lady from Hunslet who was worried about the effects of the change in weather on her nerves. He nodded with quiet satisfaction. His practice had life in it yet – unless the Corporation was about to snuff it out.

He walked back through the dark streets and the now steady rain. Ahead of him, a young couple and an elderly man turned in at the doorway of the Assembly Rooms. He cursed under his breath. Where was the queue?

He sprinted up the magnificent staircase. At the top, ignoring the main entrance to the ballroom, he darted left along the corridor until he came to a smaller door at one side of the stage. He pushed it ajar.

Inside it was mayhem. The lines of benches were hidden by those sprawling over them, milling around, shouting across the room to each other, or whistling and catcalling at the empty stage. Louis was making them wait.

Mary Crompton and Ann Thomson were sitting together over by the fireplace. A few rows in front was Elizabeth Oxley, her towering wig bobbing about as she acknowledged people. Sarah Armstrong was standing in her finery near the main door though there was no sign of Josiah – he had never really had any hopes of that. A group of weavers were laughing and jostling each other on the servants' benches. At the still centre of the storm, erect and impassive on the front row, sat Richard Micklethwaite.

A single trumpet note sounded. The room fell silent. Light and shadow danced across the walls. On the far side, the fire blazed in the grate. Above the marble mantelpiece, an enormous, ornately framed mirror played tricks of its own, multiplying the light from the dozen candle brackets.

The trumpet sounded again. As the note died away, the left-hand door opened and Isabelle stepped onto the stage to a chorus of whistles and lurid shouts. She bowed, and extended her arm towards the far door. From it swept forward Belteshazzar in all his glory: his jet-black robe flowed behind him and candlelight glistened off the golden thread running like liquid across the surface. In one hand, he grasped his staff. Winding its way up the length of the twisted wooden shaft was a carved snake, its gaping jaws pointing to the ceiling. Charlie nodded appreciatively: Louis was pulling out all the stops.

The magician raised his other hand, palm forward, in a sign of authority and greeting.

'Mesdames et Messieurs, in the name of the ancient magi and of all that was once occult but now enlightens, I bid you welcome.'

'About bloody time!' came a shout from the back.

'Time indeed! Since the dawn of time, man has dreamt of a wisdom, whose light would penetrate the veil separating our world from that which lies beyond. He has dared to believe in wonders that can transform our brief existence into an earthly paradise.'

'A night with Bella'll do that!' Isabelle stared stoney-faced at the heckler. Louis continued unruffled.

'Tonight, mysteries that our forebears longed to see will be disclosed; wonders that herald a world they could never imagine will unfold before your eyes. For our purpose this evening is not mere diversion. We are here in search of truth.'

'Nay, lad, we've come for a laugh.'

'And yet the truth is no laughing matter, Monsieur. Yes, some may call it a mere illusion, a conjuring trick of the senses, but if that were so, why are there those who fear it? Why do they slink away to hide in the shadows? Our Lord himself says that the truth will set us free. Well tonight, my friends, we cast off the chains of ignorance, for there shall be neither deception nor hiding place – only light.'

He touched the top of his staff and a bright white flame erupted from the jaws of the snake. The show had begun.

First came the electrical machine. Louis invited the front row to join hands and sent the blue fire down the chain of people to light a bowl of spirits at the end.

I must remember that one, thought Charlie.

While talking to an army officer, Louis used a magnetic loadstone to pick a knife out of the man's pocket, to the delight of the audience, and then re-enacted a recent sea engagement with two model ships – their canons ignited, Charlie guessed, using phosphorous.

He had seen much of this mixture of conjuring and natural philosophy before but he still couldn't be sure where one ended and the other began. For the audience, though, it was entertainment rather than enlightenment that was the order of the day. The air was thick with laughter, taunts and crude suggestions.

He smiled when the mechanical dog made an appearance; the tail now wagging dutifully in response to Louis' questions: 'Will this gentleman win the next lottery?' Two wags – no. Exaggerated groans of disappointment. 'Should this young lady marry her gentleman friend?' One wag – yes. Raucous cheers.

The performance drew towards its conclusion and Louis told his tale, unveiled the Hand of Truth and asked Isabelle to withdraw behind the screen. The air of excitement and expectancy in the room became almost tangible. As Charlie breathed it in, he could feel his mouth drying and his stomach knotting.

'Over the past weeks,' Louis continued, 'you have heard tell of the extraordinary powers of the Hand to reveal the thoughts of men. You may have even witnessed them for yourselves. Nevertheless, until now, audiences have possessed faith sufficient only to the production of mere trifles for their amusement. Tonight, however, we reach out into the darkness and pluck from it the burning torch of enlightenment.'

A woman called out, 'Oh God, not another bloody lecture!'

'My friends, we have witnessed in our streets a series of deaths. They have been, at the very least, surprising. Three leading citizens have died without warning. As you well know, rumour attributes their deaths to the treatments of Doctor Charles Rossi. I say "rumour", for thus far no evidence has been produced to support this claim.'

'Bastard quack!'

'What you think of his treatments is one thing, Madame. What concerns us here is what lies behind these untimely deaths. We shall ask the Hand of Truth to see into the miasma of human thoughts surrounding these events and unveil for us the truth.'

'I'd rather unveil Bella!' The heckler was cuffed about the head by the woman next to him.

Louis moved to the small table at the front of the stage, placed a pile of paper under the Hand, adjusted the quill slightly and stood back.

'For this task I require more from you than ever before. I require not only your faith but your cooperation. I ask that we open our minds so that the Hand may look within us all; so that it may see what we have seen but failed to notice; hear what we have heard but not understood; and bring to mind that which we have forgotten. Above all, it will expose what anyone has tried to hide.'

He took up his staff and pointed it towards the hand. 'In the name of truth, I address the Hand of Daniel, the Hand of Belteshazzar.'

There were a few sniggers but, by and large, Louis had them.

'Were the deaths of Mr Crompton, Mr Thomson and Mr Oxley occasioned by illness?'

After a few seconds the hand began to move and then, a moment later, it stopped. Louis approached the table, carefully withdrew the paper and held it up for the audience to see.

A shout went up. 'No!'

'Were these deaths due to any misapplied physic or treatment?'

'No!' The cry was even louder.

'Were they the result of misadventure?'

'No!' They were really enjoying this.

'What, then, was their cause?'

The Hand was still. The seconds went by. Louis asked the question again. Nothing happened. He frowned and opened his mouth to speak. The Hand started to move. The word was longer. Louis held it up for all to see.

'Murder!' The cry echoed off the plaster walls.

People leapt to their feet or on to benches, shouting and gesticulating. A fist was thrown. To Charlie it seemed that only one person was still calm: the mayor sat rigidly upright, his face a study in self-control.

Louis touched his staff. Flame and smoke burst from it once more. The hubbub began to subside.

'My friends, I beg of you. Please be seated. We have merely begun this journey of disclosure. We have so much further to go. We must clear our minds once more. Set aside prejudice or passion and open yourself to the power of the Hand.'

Louis turned back to the table. 'What was the instrument of death?'

The Hand was still for a while before it wrote.

'Hammer!'

Derisive laughter broke out.

'Wait!' Louis called. 'It is writing again. There is more.'

'Nail!'

'Hammer and nail, my friends, hammer and nail. That may seem strange to us but we have come thus far. Let us pursue this matter to its end.'

Louis stretched out his staff. 'In the name of truth I ask: who is responsible for these crimes?'

Silence descended upon the room.

The audience drew a collective breath as the hand began to write. It took well over a minute to deliver its answer. Louis picked up the paper and read it to himself.

'The Hand has brought to light much that was in darkness. However, its meaning in this matter remains hidden from me. Yet, it may be that others here are able to interpret this mystery more clearly than I. If so, I beseech them to speak out.'

He turned the paper toward the audience.

'The words of the Hand of Truth to us are these: Jael, the wife of Heber the Kenite.'

Catcalls filled the air. Projectiles swiftly followed. The audience had come prepared for disappointment. Louis had played them, building a wave of expectation, and had left them high and dry.

Charlie scanned the room but half the crowd were on their feet. There were simply too many people and precious seconds were passing. A movement to his right caught his eye. He looked towards the main doors and saw a face, as pale and grey as the winter sky. Their eyes met for an instant and in that look he saw both shock and desperation. Then the face turned away and the doors swung closed again. He paused for a moment, to master his feelings, before setting off in pursuit.

The rain beat down, masking the sound of his feet but he still moved cautiously, hugging the deeper shadows of the buildings. Tom Tinker came out of a ginnel and pointed silently towards the main street. He nodded his thanks. Reaching Briggate, he looked up and down the street. Dark alleys beckoned, taunting him to try his luck in their maze of passageways but he wasn't worried. He knew, now, where he was going.

As he crouched behind a low wall, the door of a nearby tavern flew open and a man was thrown out, landing in a heap amongst the detritus of the road. Struggling to his feet, the inebriate staggered away.

Surely it couldn't be much longer.

He sensed a presence behind him but not quickly enough. A hand closed over his mouth and a sharp point pricked the back of his neck. The image of a long nail flashed through his mind and he twisted away from the hand. As he did so, a woman's face appeared over his shoulder – Isabelle.

'Bloody hell!' he mouthed his reaction as she winked and squatted down beside him. His heart still racing, he turned back to the street.

Minutes passed. Isabelle looked at him. He shrugged. Still they waited.

He touched Isabelle's arm. In the alleyway opposite a shadow moved. A cloaked figure emerged and crossed the street. Opening the front door of the house, the silhouette disappeared inside. He hurdled the wall, ran forward up the steps and jammed his foot in the doorway. Forcing it open again, he stepped across the threshold and looked into the astonished face of Emily Barnard.

20

The wall clock echoed around the sparse parlour. Emily Barnard stared expressionless into the cold grate. From the threadbare sofa, Charlie was struck by how thin she looked; so much thinner than he remembered. Her mousey hair, tied back in a bun, framed skin that stretched pale and waxy across the protruding bones of her face. Her empty eyes, pooled in shadow, sank deep into her skull. She reminded him of a corpse he had seen once on a lecture table in Edinburgh. It had been waiting to be dissected. All that was missing were the bruise marks of the noose on her neck.

She shook her head. 'How?' The word was barely audible – a thought spoken only to herself.

'At the moment,' retorted Isabelle, 'the only question that matters is: why?'

Charlie flashed her a warning glance.

'I think I understand some of it,' he said slowly. 'If I do not go amiss, this tale begins with James Oxley.'

Emily flinched, closing her eyes.

'He was a hard and arrogant man,' he continued, 'ambitious and daring. His aim was to line his pockets while others were going to the wall. Doubtless he also thought that trading with the rebels would position him to reap yet more benefits once the war had ended and more merchants had gone under. But he needed to engage partners, men with good connections on the Continent, and the two he chose were Crompton and Thomson. But the risks seemed too great for them. Oxley's plan was both illegal and dangerous. If it was uncovered, then the law would exact a terrible price. But there was another possibility that they hadn't reckoned with: that someone with a dear one fighting in the army might learn the truth. What vengeance might they exact?' He paused. 'Who was it, Emily?'

She opened her eyes but she was frowning.

'A brother?' he pressed. 'A friend? A lover?'

The frown deepened. He'd got it wrong. She didn't know this. But now there was pain etched across her face as well. He had touched on something. What was it?

'It was none of them.' Isabelle's words broke into his thoughts. 'Oxley needed something to lure his colleagues in. Something they would find irresistible. And, as luck would have it, he had just such a prize.' Wide-eyed, Emily stared at her in bewildered agony. 'Before he went away, his brother Joseph had shared something with him, hadn't he? He'd entrusted him with a confidence.'

'But James betrayed him.' Charlie had got there at last. 'And he betrayed you as well.'

Emily's mouth dropped open.

'It must have been a nightmare,' he coaxed.

'It was.' The words were barely audible but now he knew there would be more. She gazed into the grate. They waited. The clock ticked on.

'Joseph and I were lovers.' Her voice was a little stronger. 'Just for a few months but I was already engaged to Henry. I was determined that it must end but I struggled to do so. Joseph made it no easier. He wept. He told me that he couldn't live without me. He begged me to marry him. But I couldn't break my pledge to Henry, not for all his faults. My father had arranged the match on his deathbed. Henry was his physician and he agreed to my father's proposal. I consented as well, out of love for my father – after all, I had no dowry, no prospects. And then, two days before the marriage, I had to tell Joseph that I was with child.' She smiled thinly. 'Isaac has been a source of great comfort to me. Yet it was not so for Joseph.' Her smile became rueful. 'Love is a strange thing. In the end, Joseph found that he *could* live without me. What he couldn't bear was to watch another man bring up his child. He took himself to London but when he returned he had not improved. We met one last time. He told me that he had taken a commission and that he had no hopes to see me or Isaac again. What he failed to say was that he had confided in James. He had asked him to provide for his son should ever the need arise – he always saw the good in his brother.' She laughed bitterly. 'He was the only one who did so.'

She fell silent, studying her hands.

'And so?' prompted Charlie at last.

'What?' she snapped. 'You want to hear it from me!' Then she shook her head. 'Why not?' She sounded so weary. 'After all, what is there left?'

Another pause. She was steeling herself.

'James came to see me after Joseph had gone. He would keep my secret, he told me, but in return for certain… favours. I hope it goes without saying that I rejected him out of hand. He gave me twenty-four hours to reconsider, after which he would write to Henry. I pleaded with him but to no avail: I had been his brother's whore and now I would be his – his "Fanny Hill" he called me. I wish I could say that my concern had been only for Isaac, though it's true, I feared greatly for his future once Henry knew the truth. Yet I feared for myself too: the disgrace; the destitution.' More bitter laughter. 'I was in deep and too afraid to stop going deeper. So it was agreed: on Saturday nights, when Henry was at Shadwell, I was to attend upon Oxley.'

Her whole body was taut. Charlie could see the sinews

protruding from her neck. Her shoulders were hunched; her hands twisting slowly round and round on themselves. Perched on the edge of the sofa, she looked to be on the edge of something much worse.

'It went on for weeks. Oh, he was careful not to repeat his brother's mistake and get me with child.' Her voice was full of disgust. 'I had never imagined such things...' A look of revulsion passed over her face. 'And then – was it only last month? – he told me that he had shared my secret with two colleagues and now they wanted to share me as well. I was beside myself. It was pointless pleading but I tried nonetheless: where would it end; was I to whore for the whole of Leeds? He just laughed. If it so pleased him, then yes. He was going away on business and if, on his return, his friends were not "satisfied" then it would be the worse for me.'

She fell silent again.

'And so you looked for a way out,' probed Charlie. 'And you found it, I believe, in the Scriptures.'

She shrugged. 'I was hardly eating or sleeping. I could barely live with myself. Yet I had no one to confide in. And as for prayer' – she snorted – 'what point is that when you have already damned yourself? But then, as I lay on my bed, I heard the words: "Thy word is a lamp unto my feet." You may think me already far gone in madness, yet the voice was as clear as yours. And so I turned to the Bible. Henry would "free" me from it but it is the only thing I still have of my father's. I opened it, having resolved to read until guidance came, and it was right before me on the page: the story of Jael taking her enemy into her tent, giving him something to drink and then, while he slept, driving a tent peg through his temple. Here was my path out of hell.'

'And into another one.' Emily acknowledged Isabelle's remark with a grim nod.

'I was due to meet Crompton that evening,' she continued, 'so I had only enough time to make my arrangements and none to concern myself with the outcome. Henry has a draught to aid sleep so I prepared a bottle of wine with some. Crompton had instructed me as to how and when I was to arrive and he took me straight to his room. When he saw that I had brought wine, how he made merry. He already thought me a whore and my readiness to play the part only encouraged him. It was small comfort that his needs were more conventional than Oxley's, as they came with a fair bit of pain. However, at least it meant that he dozed awhile afterwards. You might think it would be hard to kill a man in cold blood. I found that it was not so. In this case, it seemed harder – much harder – to let him live. After all, one blow was all that it took.'

'With what?' he asked.

'A meat skewer. It was to hand at home. Somehow it seemed fitting.'

'You must have sat a long while with him afterwards.'

'Until the blood was staunched but I was in no hurry. I had until first light.'

'And Thomson?'

Emily snorted in disgust. 'That was easier still. I didn't even have time to open the bottle. He was at me like a pig in a trough, burying himself under my gown. I only had to reach into my basket and drive the skewer straight down into his head. I couldn't even see him. But my God, the spasms. He ripped the cloth to shreds and nearly threw me over.'

A shudder passed through her body and she fell silent again.

'But you still had to see it through,' Isabelle encouraged her quietly.

'Oxley was away but as soon as he returned and found his two friends dead…' She took a deep breath. 'His sister had told me that he was arriving home on the day of the festival. My husband detests such things and I knew he would go to his mother's at Shadwell. Only this time he wanted me to go as well. I had no alternative but to take my chances and see Oxley in daylight. I found him at his mill. I offered myself to him there in his office but for once he showed no interest. Perhaps it was more about power than the act itself and a willing participant was less easy to humiliate. He pushed me away. He was on the stairs when I struck him. He fell and I hurried after him. I thought he might be dead already but then he groaned. So I dispatched him.' She paused and then looked up at Charlie. 'I'm sorry... I mean for all the trouble you've had.'

That surprised him more than anything else she had said. Unsure of how to respond, he held his peace and, in the silence, it dawned on him that he would need to make a decision. And she knew it too. Her cadaverous eyes were watching him – a mixture of utter resignation and lingering disbelief. She must have thought herself safe from the law even if madness beckoned; free from her tormentors while sharing a prison cell with demons.

One of the candles burnt out and the darkness in the room deepened further.

He spoke at last: 'I will have to go to the magistrate.'

'Of course.' Emily shrugged.

'Will you admit it then?'

'Perhaps.' There was the weariness again. 'Who knows.'

21

Charlie tossed and turned, and so did Emily's story in his mind. Should he hold his peace? After all, she had suffered enough. But he hardly knew her. And if he spared her then her husband would ruin him.

He got out of bed and picked up the book about Franklin's experiments, flicking through it.

Electrocuting turkeys – he shook his head – the man could keep an audience on the edge of their seats while taking them to the edge of enlightenment. He was deluding himself if he thought he could even get close to that.

He turned back to his favourite story – flying a kite in a storm. Was that what he had really been doing all these weeks? And now what? Keep the lightning bottled up or let it out? Electrocute another or let himself burn?

He dozed fitfully in the chair until first light, waking to the sounds of Sam and Beth, enjoying a Sunday morning lie-in. Their love-making only made him feel more isolated. They had each other. They belonged here. Certainly they had their worries for their son and the daily concerns that came with the tavern but they would live and die among these streets and these people. But he was no more than a sojourner in the land, a stranger to whom they had extended hospitality. And, however long he stayed here, that would never change.

But nor, he realised, was he hankering after Isabelle. He thought back to their parting the night before, with each absorbed in their own thoughts. In the moment of triumph, a gap had opened between them again. That which had brought them together was almost in the past.

He got up and wiped the cold moisture from the window.

The faint light of the morning star glinted over the roof of Sam's brew house. Like planets wandering the heavens, Isabelle had crossed his path for a time but the mechanical laws of this world would now carry them further and further apart – each on their own course.

Not wanting to face the Tinkers' questions, he left before breakfast and wandered upriver. Without any real intent, he found himself at the abbey at Kirkstall. It seemed an age since he had come here, seeking the acquittal of Jake and Abe. He wandered among the ruins for a while and then perched himself on a low wall not far from the river.

Would she confess? If not, he had little hard evidence to weigh in the balance against the Barnard family's reputation. It would seem like more fanciful and desperate ravings.

He watched the fiercely swollen water sweep everything before it: branches of every size; a group of ducks paddling vainly upstream; the bloated carcass of a sheep. Waters that promised freedom could also bring destruction.

He made his way slowly back to Leeds, wandering in along Boar Lane. At the turning for Oxley's mill, Nathan Lee was leaning against a wall, lighting his pipe.

'Mr Rossi,' Lee nodded.

Charlie was in no mood for pleasantries. 'I think you owe me an explanation.'

Lee frowned. 'What for?'

'This!' He touched the remains of the swelling on the back of his head.

'I don't know what you mean.' Lee drew on his pipe, nonchalantly.

Charlie held out some crumpled, folded papers. 'Oh, I think you do, Nat. You told me you didn't want any more bad news. And you knew there was some very bad stuff that could come out, didn't you. Making kerseys all day, everyday – you're not stupid. Did he pay extra for your silence?'

Lee cleared his throat and spat in the gutter. 'What, Oxley? Do me a favour. He were a stick man all the way – he didn't believe carrots existed. We would be out of work and out of our homes in a week if we breathed a word. For our boys in the army he said it were. But he didn't fool us – well not Rooky and me, anyhow. It were something fishy and the last thing we needed, once the bugger was dead, were for the whole thing to come crashing down around us. Or nosey sods like you digging up dirt. Anyway, how the hell did you get them back?'

'Just a quick movement of the hand – which reminds me.' He crunched a fist up into Lee's jaw, flooring him. The pipe, and a tooth, flew from his mouth into the dirt. *Not bad*, he thought, massaging his knuckles. Maybe Barnard was right and he had a future as a prize fighter after all.

As he passed Trinity Church, the sound of singing drifted out.

'… Forbid it, Lord, that I should boast save in the cross of Christ my God, all the vain things that charm me most, I sacrifice them to his blood…'

He paused and gazed across the road at the Barnards' home and, a few yards further on, at that of the Oxleys.

'… See from his head, his hands, his feet, sorrow and love flow mingled down; did e'er such love and sorrow meet…'

Such love and sorrow – all around. They had to go in the balance as well – and they weighed heavy.

Out of the Leopard tottered the woman he had first seen in Jake's cell and again at the pillory. Something had been nagging at the back of his mind since hearing Emily's story and now he knew what it was.

The woman crossed the road, steadied herself against a wall and then turned down an alley. He followed into the warren of passageways and yards that lay behind the church. Other women sat in doorways with their spindles, calling to each other or chiding their young children, who raced this way and that. Some tried to engage him in conversation but he pressed on – it was far too easy to lose someone in here. Coming round a corner, he was just in time to see the woman disappear through a door. The large first-floor windows proclaimed it the home of a weaver. He knocked, waited a few moments and, when no one answered, he followed inside.

The sound of the loom from the floor above was almost drowned out by the screaming. On a bed, in one corner of the room, wrapped in a thin blanket, lay a young baby. The woman was sitting in a rocker in front of a small range. She was looking not at the baby but out of a window, beneath which stood a spinning wheel, a pile of raw wool and a pair of combs.

He coughed. The woman didn't look round. He tried again, louder. She turned her head slowly towards him. Her brow furrowed as she tried to place him.

'Oh, you.'

'Pardon me for bothering you,' he began, though in truth she didn't look in the least bothered. It was he who was feeling uneasy. 'I'm sorry… your child?'

The woman turned back to the window.

He went over to the bed and picked up the baby. As his hands gripped the blanket, the body within was even smaller than it looked. The cloth stank of urine. He brought the child over to the woman, holding it just in front of her. Her response was to start rocking again and he had to pull the child away. Hesitantly, he began to cradle the little bundle in his arms and stroked the thin hair. Gradually the crying subsided. A moment later, the clatter of the loom also stopped.

'Joanna, is that you?' a voice called down. Then feet and legs and torso began to descend the narrow stairs. 'What the devil?' the man exclaimed as his head appeared.

'I was wanting to ask your wife something,' Charlie explained awkwardly. 'But… the baby was crying,' he added redundantly.

He held the child out and the man came forward and snatched it roughly from him. The weaver looked careworn. His eyes were dull; his lips pale and chapped.

'I'm sorry,' Charlie said again.

The man looked at him for a moment. 'I know you, don't I? You're that electrical man.'

'That's right.'

'Joanna said you were kind to her – when she were in the pillory.'

'I did what I could. It didn't count for much.'

'Kindness always counts.'

'I suppose so.' He shrugged. What was he doing here, intruding into these people's lives? He shouldn't have come.

'I'm John Bentham and this little scrap' – the man looked grimly at the bundle in his hands – 'is Matthew.'

'Charles Rossi.'

The man reached out with his spare hand and placed it on his wife's shoulder. 'She weren't always like this you know.'

'No, I'm sure.'

'It started when the bairn were born. She hears things, you see.'

There was an uneasy silence between them.

'They tell me to hurt him.' It was Joanna who spoke. 'The voices – they want me to kill him.' She fell silent again.

'That's why she drinks.' The man looked down at his son again and shook his head. 'I suppose you could say she does it for him. But he's barely feeding.' He looked up. 'Can you help her? Some say you can heal people. Please.'

The tone in his voice, the look in his eyes – it wasn't really hope, just the last shreds of desperation.

'I don't know… maybe… I'm not sure.' Charlie looked away. 'I ought to be going.'

The look passed from the man's face as quick as it had arisen.

'You came to ask her something?'

'Oh yes,' He squatted down in front of the woman. 'That gown you have, the other one, the one that's all ripped – how did you come by it?'

'What, you think I stole it?' Her face was an instant ball of anger. 'You think I'm too common for it? The pillory weren't enough, eh – you want me strung up, do you, Mister? Well you can just piss off out of here! Go on piss off!'

She picked a skillet off the grange and swung it at him.

'No, Joanna, listen!' Charlie grasped her wrists but spoke gently. 'Listen, please. I know you didn't steal it but maybe you found it somewhere. Was that it?'

She wrestled her hands free and glowered at him. 'Yes, I damn well found it! And what's it to you?'

'Can you tell me how?' he coaxed.

She carried on glaring at him. It was pointless. She was beyond sense. But then she relaxed back into the chair and closed her eyes.

'I'm down at the river one morning, washing Matthew's things, like. This woman comes along – I don't think she sees me as I'm sat by this bush – and quick as a flash she throws something in and then she's off again. So I'm wondering, you see, and I break off a branch and run after it – as it's still floating – and I fish it out again. And it's this gown – all ripped and torn, and there's blood on it but it's a good gown – too good to see go to waste.'

'And did you recognise her – the woman?'

'Oh, aye. It were the mad doctor's wife – Mrs Barnard.'

And the balance finally tipped.

A serpent coiled its way around the knocker. His hand hovered above it for a moment then he touched its head with the tip of his forefinger.

Was it wisdom or temptation?

He grasped the cold metal and rapped hard on the magistrate's door. The maid showed him through to the study where Ibbetson was relaxing; a glass of port in hand. A look of irritation passed briefly across the man's face but the dictates of hospitality won the day.

'Ah, Mr Rossi, to what do I owe the pleasure? Do take a seat. Would you care to join me?' He held up his drink.

'Thank you. That would be most welcome.' He felt that he could do with something just at that moment.

Ibbetson poured him a glass and passed it across. 'Now, what brings you to my door, today? Not another half-cocked theory, I trust?' He laughed.

Charlie smiled nervously. 'I hope not, sir.' He glanced at the little pile on his knees: the folded gown, Oxley's crumpled papers, de la Croix's letters. It still didn't seem to add up to much. 'You taught that lesson well enough the first time.'

'Indeed so,' nodded the magistrate.

'However…'

There was a knock. A lady's head appeared around the door. 'I'm sorry to trouble you Frederick but it's Ruth. She's asking for you.'

'Thank you, my dear. You will have to excuse me for a while, sir. Please continue to enjoy the port… or call again.'

Ibbetson left the room and his wife was about to close the door behind him when she recognised Charlie.

'It's Mr Rossi isn't it?'

He jumped to his feet. 'Madam.'

'Please forgive my intrusion but it's our daughter: she suffers with consumption.'

'I'm truly sorry to hear that.' He was – the coughing, the pain, the wasting, the very probable death. Now he could see the worry lines on her forehead and the deep-set concern in her eyes. 'How does she fare?'

'Weaker than she was, I fear, but the physician attends on her when he can.' His heart went out to her. 'And we still have hopes,' she added brightly.

'Yes, of course.' He didn't know what else to say.

'She has always been the apple of Frederick's eye and the affection between them only deepens as she approaches womanhood. I've known him adjourn a hearing because she had sent word that she wanted to speak with him. But then – what wouldn't one do for a child?'

'No... indeed.'

'Please forgive me. I ought to go.'

'Good day Mrs Ibbetson.' They exchanged bows.

He sat down with a sigh and looked again at the crumpled dress. Beside his hand was a dark stain.

Thomson's blood or Joanna's wine?

He picked at one of the loose threads on the edge of a ragged tear. Gazing vacantly across the room, he teased it out and let it fall to the floor.

What wouldn't one do for a child?

He pulled at another thread.

***

Henry Barnard arrived home from Shadwell a frustrated man. The weather had conspired to prevent any observations the previous night and his mother had seen fit to use luncheon to harangue him, yet again, on the inappropriateness of his chosen vocation: being at the beck and call of the lower sort was hardly befitting a man of his position; it would be little wonder if he were not carried off to an early grave; why not allow her to make use of his father's contacts in London? He had borne with it for as long as filial duty demanded and then had left the table to immerse himself in his books, in preparation for a forthcoming meteor shower. It was already getting dark by the time he rode back into Leeds.

Entering his study he lit one of the candles. As he did so, he felt the sharp prick of metal in the back of his neck.

'Do not turn round and do not call out.'

Barnard's body froze but his mind began to race.

'Put your hands together behind your head.'

The woman's voice was not one he recognised but it was laced with contempt, hatred even. She knew him.

'You will be sadly disappointed,' he said with a confidence he was not feeling, 'if you have come here in search of money or valuables. We live simply, despite the outward appearance of this house.'

'If I wanted your possessions I would be long gone.'

'Then if you mean me harm I should let you know that...'

'If I was going to kill you,' interrupted the woman, spitting out the words, 'you would already be dead.'

'What then do you want of me?'

The woman took a moment to reply. 'Let's say that I want your happiness.'

The cryptic remark emboldened him slightly. 'And how do you propose to take it from me?'

'By telling you a story.'

And so he stood there, watching the candle burn down, as the woman unfolded a saga of betrayal and deceit, of blackmail and sexual exploitation, and finally of murder. It was as preposterous as it was shocking. After all, this was his wife she was talking about.

'The fact that you have chosen to tell your tale to me and not to the magistrate betrays you,' he said disdainfully when she had finished. 'You can't prove a word of this.'

'But I don't need to.' She laughed coldly. 'The doubt will be quite enough. You're going to have to live with the possibility that I am telling the truth. And that is going to eat away inside you, day after day. Every time you see your wife you'll be wondering whether you know anything about her at all – her thoughts, her fears, her fantasies. When you sit at table with her you'll be thinking: could she be a murderer? When you lie with her in your bed, you'll be imagining what other men have done to her in theirs. And every time you look at Isaac you will notice all the little signs which whisper that he's another man's son.'

'But why are you doing this to me?'

He could hear her take a deep breath. 'Because when I was born you let my mother die, simply to prove a point.'

'What do you mean "a point"? To whom?'

'To my father.'

'What?' A distant memory stirred. 'Your father...? He started to turn around.

'Don't.' The blade pressed sharp against his neck once more. 'Why am I doing this?' The bitterness in her voice was clear now. 'Because you took away the only person who brought him joy. You broke him and he has *never* been the same man again. And because I never knew my mother and she never knew me. You robbed us of each other. So now, *Doctor* Barnard, it's your turn: Emily and Isaac may still live under your roof but they will never truly be yours again.'

She paused for a moment to let her words sink in.

'Believe me,' she continued slowly, 'I have dreamt of this moment for as long as I can remember and I want you to know this: it tastes good.'

'Is that it? Is that all this is about? Revenge?'

'God, you're more stupid than you are arrogant. Of course it's about revenge: revenge and justice. And on the subject of justice there's something else. You have made it your business to persecute Doctor Rossi.'

'What does that charlatan have to do with any of this?'

'What you think of him doesn't concern me. What you do about him does. Tomorrow morning you will go to the Corporation and withdraw your objection to him practising in this town.'

Now it was Barnard's turn to laugh. 'It's too late for that. The mayor is already persuaded to proscribe him.'

'Then you will persuade him to change his mind.'

'And why on earth would I do that? I, too, have waited for this moment and I am certainly not going to let it pass.'

'Oh, you will do it.' There was an unnerving confidence in her voice. 'Because if you don't then be sure of this: the whole of Leeds – the whole of this land – will soon know about the doctor's wife who killed three of his patients; that she did it with the help of his own medication; and that he tried to lay the blame on another. I don't think even you, in all your damned arrogance, would want to live through such a scandal. And you should also bear in mind that the self-same storm will break upon you should anything *ever* happen to Emily or Isaac – being thrown out of this house or disinherited. So, tell me: do we have an understanding?'

He weighed her words and felt a chasm opening up beneath him – a dark pit of uncertainty.

'Yes' – he was having to force the words out – 'I suppose that we do.'

He waited for the woman to acknowledge his defeat, to crow over it, but there was only silence. Very slowly, he turned his head. The room was empty. The tension flowed out of his body. He walked over to the heavy curtains and felt the chill of the evening breeze blowing through them.

***

Sam Tinker was incredulous. 'What do you mean you're leaving?'

'Just that.'

The two men were in the brew house at the back of the inn.

'Your ploy didn't work, then.'

'On the contrary, it worked perfectly,' replied Charlie with a smile.

'You mean you found out who it was! Go on then.'

Charlie shook his head. 'Sorry, that goes with me.'

'So, let's get this right,' Sam was getting aerated. 'You spend all this time getting to the bottom of these deaths, trying to clear your name – something that needs nothing short of a miracle by the way – and against all the odds you pull it off. And now you're just going to walk away from it all.'

'That's about the sum of it.'

'Well, why the hell would you do that?'

'It's complicated. That's all I can say.'

'Complicated my arse! You're going to let Barnard think he were right after all. And you're going to let those buggers on the Corporation think that all they have to do is wave a banning order at someone and people will run away. That's not "complicated" – that's plain cowardice!'

'And what the hell would you know?' snapped Charlie. 'You don't know the first thing about it.'

'No, I don't, because for some reason you want to keep your pretty little secrets to yourself.'

'Look, Sam,' he sighed, 'you have to live in this town when I'm gone. You've got to serve these people their ale, buy your goods in their shops, talk to them in the street. Knowing too much would make it all too... well, as I say, complicated.'

'Oh, bugger off.' Sam thrust an empty barrel aside as he stormed back to the inn.

Charlie left as well. He was doing the right thing, he felt sure of it. He couldn't see Emily hang after all that had been done to her. But Sam's jibe about running away had touched a nerve.

'Well I might as well make a start,' he said to himself.

A group of off-duty dragoons pushed past him as he turned into Vicar Lane, so he was right outside his door before he noticed that it was ajar. The lock was shattered; the frame splintered. It had been kicked in. He lit a lamp and made his way cautiously up the stairs. As he entered his lecture room the smell hit him. At the far end of the room, where his electrical machine should have been, the table was bare. As he moved behind it, a mass of shattered glass glistened at his feet – cylinders, Leyden jar, bent and twisted conducting rods – and rising from them was the reek of urine. His father's books lay on the floor, sodden – fit only to be burned.

For a moment he was back in another dark room – grief and rage mingling with the same stench.

It was sacrilege – a crime against knowledge and the beautiful machine and books that communicated it. He felt sick in the pit of his stomach – and dirty, as if someone had urinated on his whole life and was trampling over his father's memory. And it was the final nail in the coffin.

He looked down at the ruins of his life.

Setting the lamp on the table, he put his hands to his face. All the struggles and frustrations, all the hostility and abuse, all the risks and dangers – and now this. It swept over him like the Aire in flood. His stomach heaved in great, aching gulps and the tears flowed. And, for once in his life, he let them.

Then someone struck him from behind.

It was the shock rather than the force that felled him to his knees. Then a boot crashed between his legs and his groin exploded. He sprawled face down amidst fragments of wet glass. Some lodged in his cheek. As he gasped for breath, a body landed on his back, crushing all the air from his lungs. Then the leather belt from his machine was thrown round his neck.

A rough Irish brogue sounded in his ears. 'Thought I'd forgotten about you, did you? Oh, no my friend, Mr Rossi – Jimmy Doyle never forgets. And Jimmy Doyle always keeps his promises. You were the death of two of my mates and now I'll be the death of you. An eye for an eye, as the Good Book says. 'Tis only fair, now.'

Doyle ground his face into the floor as the other hand yanked on the belt and twisted it tight.

'Did my little surprise upset you? Never mind, you can't take it with you now, can you?'

Blood pounded in his ears. He reached behind and tried to

pull Doyle's hand away but the labourer's grip was too strong. He kicked up with his legs, striking Doyle weakly in the back and the Irishman laughed, mockingly. His chest was already bursting. Sweeping the floor with his hands, he found some broken glass. Jabbing frantically backwards, he struck home. Doyle cursed and he jabbed again. Doyle let go of the belt, grabbed his wrist with both hands and twisted it back until the shard slipped from his fingers. At the same time, air rushed into his lungs and, with a roar, he used his free hand to rip the belt from his neck.

The respite was short lived. Doyle's hands closed around his throat, yanking his head backwards; the grip crushing his windpipe.

'I think we'll be saying goodbye, now, Pimp.'

His strength ebbed away and the pain intensified until it burned in every part of him. He could sense the darkness getting closer. It would be a welcome relief.

He surrendered himself to it.

Then a woman screamed – a guttural yell of rage. Doyle cried out in pain and let go. The air surged violently back into his lungs as Doyle leapt off him. Rolling over, he saw Isabelle eyeing the Irishman across the table. A great gash in Doyle's sleeve, where blood was flowing, bore witness to her first attack. Jabbing and feinting with her dagger, she was trying to manoeuvre Doyle away from the door. He had drawn his own knife and was being careful to hold his position, lunging this way and that.

Getting to his knees, Charlie picked up one of the conducting rods with its now jagged end. Thus armed, he stood alongside Isabelle. As he did, Doyle tipped the table over and ran for the door. She hurdled the table and leapt down the stairs after him. Charlie hobbled after as best he could.

By the time he emerged into Vicar Lane, Isabelle had already raised the hue and cry, and people in the street, obliged as they were, had joined the pursuit. Doyle made for Kirkgate, where he cut down the side of the prison into an alleyway. More people joined the chase but the narrowness of the passage was hampering them. Charlie began to move more freely and he pushed past people towards Isabelle. He was worried that Doyle would disappear as he had before, going to ground in the maze of ginnels and yards but, apart from the odd twist and turn, he kept heading south.

As Charlie drew alongside Isabelle, she shouted: 'He's making for the bridge.'

Once over it, it would be easy enough for Doyle to escape into the fields beyond. And she was right. Reaching Briggate, Doyle turned left and began to cross the river.

Just then, a stagecoach appeared at the far end of the bridge. Charlie shouted as loudly as he could: 'Stop, felon!'

Seeing Doyle and the posse behind him, the driver pulled up the horses. The man alongside him brandished a coach gun towards Doyle, who stopped in his tracks. Charlie and Isabelle halted a few yards away from him and the rest of the crowd gathered behind them.

'Not so big and brave now, are you?' taunted Isabelle.

Doyle swung round and swept his knife out in front of him, daring his pursuers to approach. He glanced nervously over his shoulder at the men on the coach.

Isabelle circled slowly around their quarry. 'Come on, Doyle,' she said. 'Let's make an end of it.'

Others in the crowd followed her so that Doyle was being surrounded on three sides. The man growled. He spat; his eyes darting everywhere. Then, with a bellow of rage, he leapt onto the parapet and, without a moment's hesitation, plummeted into the swirling waters. Those on the bridge rushed to the edge. Peering into the darkness, Charlie thought he saw something break the surface – was it a head? – he couldn't be sure. Whatever it was, it was instantly swept away into the murky maelstrom.

'Well that's the end of the bugger,' growled a man alongside him.

'Aye, saved the hangman a job anyhow,' replied another.

The driver called to his horses, snapped his whip, and the coach moved slowly on into town. The crowd, with the entertainment over, began to follow suit. Charlie and Isabelle were soon alone, resting against the parapet, each one gazing down into the river.

'Thanks, Isabelle,' he said at last.

'Don't mention it,' she replied. 'I owed you.'

'Well, I'm glad we're all square.'

She looked at him and grinned. 'My God, Charlie, you look a mess. Here…' She reached up and pulled a small piece of glass out of his chin and then, taking her shawl she began to wipe the blood from his face. 'You should get Beth to look at those cuts.'

'I know. I'll do it when I get back.'

They stood looking at each other.

'I'm leaving in the morning.' He almost whispered the words.

'But why? You don't have to.'

'Yes I do. I found a woman who's got Emily's gown – the one she was wearing when she killed Thomson. She saw her trying to get rid of it in there.' He pointed to the river. 'I went to see the magistrate… but in the end I couldn't do it. I couldn't see her hang.'

Isabelle shook her head. 'You know, the trouble with you, Charlie, is you're too kind for your own good.'

'Maybe,' he shrugged. 'Not like you, I suppose!' he added with a smile.

'That's right. You've got to look after yourself and see to your own business, because you can be sure as hell that no one else will.'

'Perhaps. I don't know.'

The silence returned.

This time it was Isabelle who broke it. 'We're leaving tomorrow as well. I'd just come round to your rooms to say goodbye.'

'What about Barnard? What about your business with him?'

'All taken care of.'

'What?'

'I've paid him a visit and we're all square as well.'

'How?' There was concern in his voice. 'Isabelle, what have you done?'

'I simply took from him what he denied my father and me,' she replied nonchalantly. 'Now he'll never know if his wife was a murderer; if she loved another man; if she whored for his patients; or if his son was really his.'

'What? You went in there and told him everything?'

'That's right.'

'But what about Emily? What about Isaac? What's Barnard going to do to them now?'

'Nothing at all.'

'And how do you know that?'

'Because I told him, that if anything happens to them then the whole sordid story comes out.'

'But there'll be no one left here who knows.'

She laughed. 'Yes, but he doesn't realise that.'

'Damn it, Isabelle, that's a bloody big risk to take.'

'It'll be alright.'

'But we'll never know.'

'So what?' She glowered at him. 'Look, murderers just have to take their chances. Anyway, don't forget you were the one who was going to sing to the magistrate. You were going to have her dance. I'd call these much better odds.'

He bit his lip and took a deep breath. 'Well I hope you're right.'

'Anyway, you might like to know that I also told him to call off his witch hunt against you.'

'Thanks but there's not much point now.'

'Well, at least I damn well tried!'

She turned on her heels and set off into town. He followed a pace or two behind. Neither of them spoke. As he reached the King's Arms he put his hand on the door.

'Good night.'

But she was away up the street without a look behind.

22

He nursed a tankard in the corner of the taproom. Beth had patched up his face and he had patched up things with Sam. Even so, he sat brooding on the weird twists of fate that had become his life. He closed his eyes and tried to visualise his mother, sitting under a tree, blessing him with her smile.

'I think the expression is "a penny for your thoughts".'

It was Louis.

'Would I be intruding if I joined you?' Charlie gestured to him to sit down.

'Isabelle tells me you have had a most extraordinary twenty-four hours.'

'You could call it that.'

'Take it from an old man, *mon ami*, most of life is unremarkable and then, from time to time, everything happens at once. Good or bad, it doesn't matter, sometimes both in equal measure. And when those times come we may need a little help, just to tip things in our favour.'

Charlie nodded. He liked this man – his simple friendliness. He admired him too, for his skills, his patience, his down to earth wisdom.

'And she tells me that you are leaving tomorrow.'

He nodded again.

'What will you do?'

'I don't know, Louis – go to London, look for work. If I can restock the coffers then I'll get another machine and begin again. I may need to take a leaf out of your book, though, and change my name. How about…' he gave a flourish with his arm, '… the Great Rossini? I should even be able to manage a passable Italian accent.'

'I can see it now.' Louis smiled briefly. 'But, in truth Charlie, life in the city will be hard for you.'

'I know – but my sister's there.'

'Your parents too?'

'No, just Sophie. I haven't seen her in over two years. She's written a few times. I meant to reply but… well I'm always on the move. Anyway, I'm sure I can stay with her until I get back on my feet.'

Louis leaned forward. 'I have a different thought – a proposal, if you like.' Charlie frowned. 'I have an electrical machine of my own. You know far more of its possibilities than do I, who use it merely for entertainment…'

Waving his hand, Charlie interjected: 'No, Louis, I couldn't.'

'I think you misunderstand me.' Louis leaned forward. 'I am not offering you the machine. I am inviting you to join us, to come with us to London, to bring your gifts, your knowledge, into our show – at least for a while.'

He was dumbstruck. It was such a kind offer and he could learn so much from this man.

'But what about Isabelle?'

'Oh, you mustn't worry about her. She does like you.'

'I'm not so sure about that.'

'Charlie, compared to most of the men who try to cross her path, you're not on crutches. Yet.'

Charlie smiled. 'Aye, there is that.'

Louis chuckled. 'My daughter does have a wonderful gift for

teaching patience, doesn't she.' He reached forward and placed his hand on Charlie's. 'Sleep on it.'

As it was, he hardly slept at all. He sat up late with Sam, talking over the events of the evening, trying, above all, to lay Doyle's ghost to rest. Only when his friend resolutely refused 'just another ale' did he turn in. Then, rather than easing his passage into oblivion, the alcohol merely fuelled his churning thoughts. The lure of the new and unknown; the future that could still be shaped in his mind's eye; the irrepressible hope that next time things would be different; the nagging voice that said it wouldn't be – his imagination ran riot into the small hours.

He rose at the crack of dawn and packed his chest. Beth excelled herself with breakfast yet again – 'One for the road' – and then he set off with Sam for Vicar Lane. As they approached the still open doorway, low sunlight filled the bottom of the stairwell. It made him think of his mother.

'Come on, Sam. Let's get this done.'

He stepped into the bright beams.

Upstairs, they set about clearing away the remains of the previous night's havoc. Nothing was left undamaged except for the insulating stool but, sticky with urine, he just wanted rid of it all. Sam took pity on him and offered to take everything away on his cart. So, with the place looking and smelling tolerable, he set off for his final duty.

As he passed the market cross, his thoughts went again to Henry Barnard. What would the man do? Despite Isabelle's efforts, he found it hard to believe that the man would change his tune after all this time. Even if he did, how would the mayor respond? If it meant Micklethwaite losing face, there was no hope. Still, it hardly mattered now, except perhaps to some poor unfortunate who might follow in his wake.

He arrived at Red Hall to find Josiah Armstrong standing beside a horse and carriage.

'Ah, the troublesome Mr Rossi.' Despite his lack of height, Josiah still managed to look down on his tenant.

'And a very good morning to you, sir.'

'I am told that you are to be leaving us.'

How on earth? 'You are very well informed.'

'I make it my business to be. When my property is being used to send my competitors to an early grave, it pays to have good sources of information.' The sides of Josiah's lips curled slightly upwards.

'I suppose it does,' Charlie replied, with a reluctant nod.

'And my wife tells me that you solicited her attendance at a *performance*' – the word dripped with sarcasm – 'the other night. It appears that your investigations have led you to make some interesting conjectures.'

'Well...' He could feel himself colouring.

'You know full well what I think of you but you're a tenacious bugger, I'll give you that much. I won't ask whether it was all worth it because frankly I don't give a toss. But you did stick at it and I admire that.' Charlie shrugged. 'So what the hell are you doing now, running off with your tail between your legs? Barnard will have a field day. Cause of death? Quackery, plain and simple. We'll never hear the last of it. Still, I suppose you've got your reasons.'

Charlie said nothing.

The door opened and Sarah Armstrong emerged, dressed in a fine coat and bonnet. She walked towards the two men.

'Good morning Mr Rossi.' She dipped her head and smiled at him. 'It is *so* nice to see you again.'

She held her gloved hand out towards him. He was reaching for it when Josiah took it instead, helping her into the carriage before climbing up to sit alongside her.

'Goodbye, Mr Rossi.' Her eyes twinkled with amusement.

He bowed. Without a word, Josiah cracked the whip and the carriage moved away. Charlie watched it go, shaking his head.

'Now, Sam, you take care of that woman of yours. If you don't, you'll have me to answer to.'

'I know, Charlie. It's just as well you're off or I'd be getting worried.'

He grinned at his friend. 'It's been good, Sam.'

'Aye, I know, lad. Anyhow, I've had enough of all this excitement. Time to get down to a good bit of brewing or we'll be dry by Easter.'

'Now that *would* be a disaster.'

Beth appeared out of the kitchen, carrying a large package. She pushed it into his hands.

'Just a few things for the journey.'

'Thanks Beth – for everything. I honestly don't know what I'd have done without the two of you.'

'Our pleasure, love. And any time you're in these parts...'

'Of course... but I reckon I'd better leave it a while.'

'Well – as I say, Charlie – any time.'

Silence stretched between them.

'Oh, come here,' said Charlie and he gave Beth an enormous hug, followed by a slightly embarrassed Sam. 'And don't forget to keep those sparks flowing,' he added with a wink.

'Don't worry, we'll think of you every time,' laughed Sam, only to be tutted by Beth.

'Say goodbye to Jake and Lizzie for me. And thank Tom as well, will you?'

'Will do, Charlie,' said Sam. 'Now get off out of here or you'll miss your coach.'

In the market place, the 'coach' was already waiting. Louis was sitting up on the box and Isabelle was waiting at the back. She helped him to heft the chest onto the wagon and then they climbed up to join Louis. As the wagon moved away down the street, he looked back to see Beth and Sam standing in the doorway of the inn. He waved them farewell and turned to the road ahead.

They crossed the bridge over the river and moved slowly through the southern outskirts of the town. A small, open wagon turned out of a side lane and came towards them. He recognised the driver as one of the parish constables. The vehicles pulled up alongside each other.

'You're leaving town then?' asked the constable.

'That's right, off to London – streets paved with gold and all that.'

'Well, I hope you have better luck than this poor soul.' The constable gestured to the back of the wagon. 'Fished out of the river down near Fearn's Island – caught in the branches of a tree.'

'Doyle,' said Isabelle under her breath.

They jumped down and walked round to the back of the constable's wagon. Charlie lifted the edge of the tarpaulin. The boots were thin and small. They were those of a woman. With his heart pounding, he climbed onto the cart. Reaching for the far end of the sheet he pulled it back. The woman's face was white and swollen; plastered with hair and bits of weed. Her thick coat oozed grey water. It was Emily Barnard.

Isabelle let out a deep groan.

'She had stones in her pockets,' muttered the constable. 'Mind you, she wouldn't have needed them. Not the way the river is.'

Charlie climbed back down. The bile was rising in his throat. He shut his eyes.

And he was clawing at the cord around his father's neck, choking on the cloying smell, cradling him in the darkness – the anger surging up within him. He couldn't push it away any longer.

So he let it rise.

He swung round at Isabelle. 'You had to go and tell him didn't you? Did you think about her for one single minute? Did you think about that little boy?' The blood was pulsing, fiercely in his neck. 'No, you didn't – because all that mattered was having your precious revenge. Fine – so now there's one more child growing up without a mother. Well, I hope you're bloody satisfied!'

'Charlie, that's not fair.' It was Louis who spoke, his tones measured.

'Fair!' he bellowed. 'When was it ever fair?' He lashed out at the wheel of the wagon with his boot. His toe cracked and pain shot through his foot but he was still seething. He hobbled away from the coach, back towards town. Twenty yards along the road, Isabelle caught up with him. She reached out to place a hand on his arm but he thrust it away.

'Forget it,' he growled. 'I'll make my own way. It'll be best for us both.'

She walked alongside him for a while through the slush and the puddles.

'I'm sorry, Charlie. I really am.'

They carried on in silence.

'Are you going to be alright?'

'I don't know… maybe.'

Halfway across the bridge, he stopped and looked over the side. The waters flowed ever onwards towards the sea.

She waited beside him.

'You see it's… it's my father, he…' Charlie shook his head and sighed. 'Look, I'm sorry. I'm just going to need some time.'

She slipped her arm through his and, for once, her words came softly. 'Well, with our old nags, time's the one thing we've got plenty of.'